BROKEN SYMMETRIES

AGE OF ILLUMINATI

BROKEN SYMMETRIES
AGE OF ILLUMINATI

Copyright © 2015 H. A. Ormziar

All rights reserved. No part of this publication may be reproduced, stored, or transmitted in any form or by any means, electronic or mechanical, including photocopying, recording without the Author's prior permission, or under the terms agreed.

ISBN: 1517223881

ISBN-13: 978-1517223885

www.brokensymmetries.com

Disclaimer

This book is a work of fiction. Names, characters, places, organizations, and incidents are either products of the author's imagination or are used fictitiously. Any resemblance to actual events, organizations or persons, living or dead, is entirely coincidental.

The Abrahamic faith and the holy§cript in this book are a fictitious religion and text. Despite the similarities to the real Abrahamic faiths, the prophecies mentioned in this fiction are not meant to be an accurate reflection of the prophecies of any existing religions or texts.

Facts

Optogenetics is a real technology currently used to control animal brains for scientific research.

Conversion disorder is a psychiatric disorder; its symptoms can be relieved temporarily by faith healing.

3D bio-printing is a real technology; it can print living tissues and organs.

General purpose 3D printing technology is now available for the consumer use and it's expected to become one of the most revolutionary technologies of the 21st century.

Prologue

Physicists have recently proposed a theory which would answer questions that Einstein himself had tried to answer in his lifetime. The theory states that in an ideal universe for every particle there is a partner anti-particle with an opposite charge and direction to the particle, and both are necessary to achieve a state of symmetry in the universe. However, some string theory scientists have reached the conclusion that our current universe is a broken universe that separated during the big bang event from a much larger super-symmetric universe with eleven dimensions.

This has brought the notion of broken symmetries to the attention of many scientists; everything in our universe is almost symmetric but not perfectly so.

The famous physicist Richard Feynman addressed this issue in his lectures: "There is a gate in Japan, a gate in Neiko, which is sometimes called by the Japanese the most beautiful gate in all Japan; it was built in a time when there was great influence from Chinese art. This gate is very elaborate, with lots of gables and beautiful carving and lots of columns and dragon heads and princes carved into the pillars, and so on. But when one looks closely he sees that in the elaborate and complex design along one of the pillars, one of the small design elements is carved upside down; otherwise the thing is completely symmetrical. If one asks why this is, the story is that it was carved upside down so that the gods will not be jealous of the perfection of man. So they purposely put an error in there, so that the gods would not be jealous and get angry with human beings."

We could conclude from the broken symmetries theory that if God made the universe and living beings then he, similarly to the Japanese gate's artist, made them in a near symmetric shape. The right and left sides of our faces and bodies are created in almost a perfectly symmetric shape but not quite. For instance, we have two eyes on either side of a centrally placed nose and above a mouth, and all are almost symmetrical but not quite. The orbital system of planets, stars, and galaxies are almost perfectly symmetrical but not exactly, and everything that seems to be designed is symmetric to some extent; the intriguing puzzle is they are not made to be perfectly symmetrical!

Broken symmetries are evident in every dimension, space and time. If you toss a coin and you get the 'head' then you have broken the symmetry unless you toss it again to get the 'tail'. If you are happy one moment you have broken the symmetry unless you are sad the next moment…

The broken symmetry in space dimension tells us that life is unfair. There are rich and poor, healthy and diseased, weak and strong but these issues may be solved with a better justice system that humans are continuously striving to achieve. What is unfixable to restore is the broken symmetry in our time dimension, and we tend to dream that our unhappy past will be overridden by a happy future or that someday the oppressed will be relieved, children with cancer will be cured, and refugees will be sheltered. Unfortunately, because of death, the broken symmetry in our time dimension is unfixable, and what is gone is gone. The past and the future are hugely asymmetric, and the prime culprit for the growing asymmetry between the past and future is evolution which is fuelled by past sacrifices. The only salvation to return our universe to its super-symmetric state is to fix the past.

Chapter 1

Hast opened his eyes upon hearing a loud sound, and he became aware that a tremendous catastrophe like nothing he had seen before cast a dark shadow on earth. The sky was dark and the blood colored sun disk was visible behind the clouds. In the far distance huge buildings were falling apart, and the horizon of the city looked like a flat unrecognizable land covered with ruins of houses and debris. Hast quickly looked around seeing nothing but the unexplainable ruins. The house where he, his brother, and parents were living was now unrecognizable dust beneath him. He began to desperately check the area around his house for someone, first he shouted, "Sardar! ... Sardar! Where are you?" He heard no response then he shouted, "Mom ... Dad ... Where are you?" He heard nothing but silence.

As there was no response, a great fear came over him. This was a fear of great loss, a loss which meant he wouldn't ever see his beloved and caring people again. He then wandered away and to his relief, he finally saw a large group of faraway people marching in a long line and walking to somewhere!

Hast ran toward the crowd thinking that members of his family might have survived and were among the crowd. Once he closed in, he slowed down and looked at the faces of the people. They looked very frightened and their faces were like those of defendants waiting for a jury's decision.

"What is happening here?" he asked the crowd curiously.

"It is Judgment Day. Don't you know?" someone replied. At first Hast thought it was a joke, but he got the same response from everyone he asked. They all replied, "It's the Judgement Day!"

A look of shock appeared on Hast's face, not because he did not believe in the Judgment Day, in fact he was deeply faithful and always believed that a day would come when he would face his own creator, ∞Illuhim∞ - the omnipotent being in the universe best described in the Abrahamic religion. He was the one who had created everything, the earth, the heavens, the good, and the bad. The dream of any follower of Abrahamic faith was to come face to face to ∞Illuhim∞, not only because he promised eternal life for his followers, but because he was an idol who was the perfect being. Upon seeing him, eyes would be saturated with pleasure and one's body would be shaken upon meeting with him incapable of comprehending the view of his majesty since he was the ultimate being in the universe beyond human imagination.

All of Hast's doubts were swept away when he saw in the distance a shiny white cloud pondering upon a huge golden looking palace with a big central dome and many high branches. The palace resembled a fantasy to him. He also realized that the city he was living in was no longer recognizable. He no longer saw the ancient Citadel of Erbil which was previously situated on a hill at the center of the city and was visible from everywhere. 'Could we be in the heavens already?' he asked himself.

He began to walk with the crowd toward the golden palace, but along the way, he found some people crying. One of them, a young lady, was crying loudly and shedding lots of tears!

"Why are you crying my lady?" he asked.

"I'm afraid of hell," the young lady replied.

"∞Illuhim∞ is a loving God and will forgive all your sins," he said to the lady trying to comfort her.

"He will not forgive mine," she hesitantly replied.

"I'm sure he will. I am one of his devout followers and I have read a lot about him. There is no sin he won't forgive," Hast said to her with a smiling face.

"I did not believe in ∞Illuhim∞!" she replied in a frightened voice.

When Hast heard that, the smile faded away from his face. He could now no longer cheer her up because he knew that ∞Illuhim∞ tolerates all sins but one: the blasphemy, the sin of not believing in him or worshipping a false god. This was a sin that according to Abrahamic faith was central to all the other sins. It was the only sin that when one committed it would not be saved from the Lord's ultimate punishment, eternal burning and torture in hell forever and ever.

Suddenly! Hast remembered his atheist brother, Sardar. Sardar was two years younger than him and they were childhood companions. When younger, they played together, quarreled, competed and grew up together. They graduated from the same school until Sardar went on to study medicine and Hast went on to study theology.

When Hast had first awoke this morning, he was afraid that he might have lost his family, but now he was afraid about their afterlife fate, especially the fate of his atheist brother. Hast's parents were devout followers of Abrahamic faith. However, his younger brother was not! He and his brother used to engage in lengthy debates about God and the purpose of human existence. Hast was eager to bring faith to his younger brother, not only because he was afraid that his brother would go to hell, but mainly because he wanted to show God that he was one of his majesty's faithful ministers. Hast was desperate to convince his younger brother, but Sardar always asked for evidence.

"Can you show me a single, palpable piece of evidence about ∞Illuhim∞?" Sardar once asked Hast while looking at the sky and shouting in a mocking way. "∞Illuhim∞ where are you? Why are you hiding from us? If you want me to believe in you, show yourself!"

"You fool! Do not be disrespectful to ∞Illuhim∞," Hast angrily used to respond to him. "∞Illuhim∞ is not like humans.

He will not reveal himself to you from the outside. ∞Illuhim∞ reveals himself from the inside, and since our sensory organs are only useful to detect the materialistic world surrounding us, they cannot detect ∞Illuhim∞."

To which Sardar replied, "What should I do then? Why it is my fault if God does not reveal himself to me from the inside as you say?"

Hast always felt frustrated when his brother asked for the impossible in order to make him submit to ∞Illuhim∞. He was wishing for something, a supernatural miracle, to make Sardar realize his arrogance and regret his decision.

Now, Hast was convinced that he was experiencing Judgment Day, and remembering his brother and his debates with him, initially made him feel proud about winning the argument as finally the truth was revealing itself, but then shortly afterwards, he began to feel sorry for his brother and thought that his younger brother may be somewhere in the crowd crying like the young lady and awaiting his doomed fate.

It was impossible to find his brother among the huge crowd of people. They were everywhere! Some people were wandering around like drunkards while some were entering the long queue. Nevertheless, Hast decided to find his brother at any cost as he couldn't imagine the thought of him suffering in hell. This was a thought that had never occurred to him before or it did not seem to be so serious, just a harsh a warning to unbelievers, but now it was a reality!

He began to look around for Sardar. Shouting again, "Sardar! ... Sardar!" He kept circling back to his ruined house and looked everywhere he could. Finally, after several hours of waiting and looking, he found Sardar walking within a section of the queue. He was surprised by how quickly he was able to find his young brother among the huge crowd. "Sardar, are you OK?" he said while approaching Sardar.

Sardar turned to him with a pale and frightened face. "I don't know," he replied. "What do you think is happening? Is it post-earthquake chaos, or as people are saying, Judgment Day?"

"I'm also not sure, but based on what I see this is not an ordinary natural disaster. Look at the sun! I noticed it has moved to set in the east! This is one of the prophecies of Judgment Day," Hast said.

"I noticed that! Many other people noticed it too, but could this be some sort of a bizarre cosmologic disaster?" Sardar wondered.

"Brother, everything you see happening around us is described in the holy§cript. Any faithful follower knows and is confident about what is happening right now," he claimed.

They continued walking for a period of over three hours and were hungry and tired. It was getting darker, the sun was about to set in the east, and the only source of light was coming from the golden palace far ahead. Both brothers were waiting in the crowd and advancing slowly toward it, and once they were closed into one of its huge gates, they were shocked to see a huge figure, over nine feet tall which had white wings attached to his back and who looked similar to angels described in the holy§cripts of Abrahamic faith.

The angel figure was guarding the big gate, and another smaller looking angel was looking for people's names in his handheld notebook. Once their name was found, a person was handed either a red letter or a green letter. People who received the letter then could pass through the smaller doors that were installed all around the huge golden palace.

"Our turn is coming soon!" Sardar said in a frightened voice.

Hast sensed his brother's fear, "Don't worry, ∞Illuhim∞ is a loving god."

"It seems that I was wrong," Sardar said. "I still can't believe why I was so blinded by my arrogant mind." He turned to his brother with a sorrowful face, "It was all my fault and now I'm ready to face the consequences."

"Don't say that brother. I will be with you until the end," Hast sensed the deep regret in his brother's voice and he wished to have done more to introduce ∞Illuhim∞ to him before today because, according to the holy§cript, regret would not save anyone on Judgment Day. Still Hast was feeling there might be some hope because his brother was a good man. He had recently graduated from the college of medicine, and he was eager to help the elderly and the diseased and had already saved many lives.

"God will not forget your good work, brother," Hast said to Sardar trying to comfort him.

As both brothers came closer to the front of the queue, people behind them interrupted their talk and pushed them toward the two angels. Sardar, who was in the front, seemed to have collected his courage and walked toward the angelic guard. "Are you aliens who have invaded our earth?"

The angelic guard looked down toward Sardar. "I know who you are; you didn't believe in us, did you? And yes, we are the same aliens in your holy§cripts, human!"

Hast was irritated by his brother's rude question to the angel. It seemed to Hast that his brother was still in denial and looking for other explanations.

The angel looked in his notebook as if he was looking for Sardar's name. After a brief moment, the angelic guard signaled to the other angel who was standing by with the red and green letters. The smaller angel understood the signal and handed a red letter to Sardar, "Take it. This is your pass." Once Sardar took the letter, the angel followed with some instructions to him. "You can enter through any of the small doors after a symbol of a key appears on the letter. It has your identity, so you cannot use someone else's letter to enter. If the key symbol has appeared and you don't enter the palace in time, the key will disappear shortly and you will face your destined fate without any Judgment," the angel said.

"Does the color of the letter indicate anything?" Sardar asked cautiously.

"You will find out later! We won't tell you any more details," the angel replied curtly as if it wasn't interested in helping Sardar.

As the queue advanced and Hast's turn came, the angel looked at his name in the notebook to see the symbol which denoted Hast's destined fate, and then the smaller angel gave him a green letter with a smiley face and gave the same instructions to him.

Hast felt that the color might indeed indicate the determined fate, but he was afraid to ask the angel about it fearing to hear the news. Whatever the answer, even if it turned out good for him, it would not be for his beloved brother!

Moments passed and Hast was constantly looking for comforting words to say to his anxious brother. They waited in front of the small doors looking for the key symbol to appear in their letters before entering.

Sardar looked shocked and overwhelmed by the amount of inexplicable things that were happening. "Hast, I'm very scared," he said in a croaky voice. "I think my red letter means something bad will happen to me ... I hope it is not as bad as your holy§cript describes," he swallowed his sputum while trying to finish his sentence.

"Don't worry brother. We will enter the doors together and I will ask God to forgive us. I'm also not sure about my fate but ∞Illuhim∞ is very merciful," he said.

After around half an hour, a symbol of a key appeared on Sardar's red letter. "Hast, look at this!" he exclaimed pointing at his letter. "I think this is a signal for me to enter through one of the small doors."

Hast looked at his own letter, but he couldn't see any symbol yet on his green letter. "I think you should wait until the symbol appears on mine too so we can both enter together," he advised Sardar.

The idea sounded plausible to Sardar. He stayed still while carefully watching the symbol on his letter. "Hast look!" Sardar said showing his letter to Hast. "I think the symbol is gradually fading away on my letter. I need to enter soon; I don't want to face my fate without any Judgment."

Hast looked at his green letter, but no symbol had appeared on his letter. He thought the symbols could be like slots allocated to each person, and they might not appear in people's letters simultaneously.

"Hast, I think that even if your symbol appears, we might not be able to see each other on the other side of the palace when we enter."

"I think so too because God's judgment is private," Hast replied.

"Then, I'm going to enter before the symbol completely fades away," Sardar said. "Please, ask your God to forgive me when your judgment comes. Remember me!"

"I will never forget you, and I promise I will not go to heaven without you," Hast said.

Sardar emotionally burst into tears hugging his older brother. "Please don't do that," he said. "You should enjoy heaven. You deserve it. Don't worry about me. I was stubborn, and it is all my fault. Nobody should be blamed but me."

"Let's try to enter together," Hast said holding his younger brother's hand as they approached one of the small doors and tried to enter together. They both touched the door simultaneously; the door then magically pulled Sardar's hand and dragged him through. Sardar was swallowed into the palace.

"Sardar!" Hast shouted in frustration as he realized that he couldn't pass through the door to follow his younger brother. He became very concerned about what would happen to him inside the palace. 'I need to join him,' he said in his heart as he frequently gazed at his letter awaiting the appearance of the symbol. Many frightening images of his brother suffering in hell came to his mind making him more and more unsettled. He continued thinking about how his brother could defend his lack of faith when confronted by ∞Illuhim∞ himself. 'God, please forgive him,' he started to pray. 'God help us all…'

As time passed slowly, Hast feared that he would forget about his brother during his judgement because according to the holy§cript, God would take away emotions and mercy toward unbelievers so that believers who entered heaven wouldn't feel sorry for the unbelievers who were suffering and being tortured forever in hell.

After another half an hour the symbol finally appeared on Hast's green letter, and he quickly ran toward the door while reciting his brother's name so that he could keep his promise and try to defend him in front of God. Once he touched the door's handle, he felt a gentle force dragging him into the palace, and for a brief moment his vision became dark then he saw the light.

Hast found himself in a large hall with its walls covered in shiny, expensive looking marble which was covered with streaks of gold and silver. Far ahead, he saw an elevation on the floor where a nine foot archangel with a pair of asymmetrical red wings stood in front of a curtain. The curtain had a marvelous design and it seemed to be a barrier between Hast and between someone else behind it. Hast tried to look through the curtain by sharpening his eyes, he was eventually able to see a shaded figure sitting on a throne behind the curtain. 'Could it be ∞Illuhim∞ himself!' Hast thought.

"Welcome to the Lord's kingdom. Today there is no king but him," the archangel said. "You are one of the Lord's devout believers, and he will be glad to meet you face to face," said the angel who stood by the curtain. "Before the Lord reveals himself to you, he gives you two choices and you are free to choose either one. Would you choose to live with the Lord in the Garden of Eden forever, or would you choose to go back to oblivion?"

Although Hast had recited his younger brother's name before entering the palace, he momentarily forgot him when he was listening to the angel's question, but now he remembered his brother again and thought this could be the best chance to ask about his brother's fate before he forgot him possibly forever.

"What happened to my brother, Sardar?"

The angel seemed surprised by Hast's irrelevant question. "He is in his deserved place. You will forget about him once you choose to live with the Lord in heaven."

"Please, I need him to be with me in the heaven. I cannot enjoy heaven without him," Hast said.

"He cannot be with you," the archangel replied. "He did not believe, and according to the rules which you yourself have chosen to obey, your brother is now in his deserved place."

"Is he now being tortured and suffering?" Hast asked hesitantly. "He is a good person, and he didn't do anything bad."

"Because you are a believer, I'm obliged to answer you, but I don't recommend that you find out about the details of your brother's fate." The archangel continued, "During Judgment your brother himself admitted that he deserves to go to hell for eternity."

Hast knew he'd get such an answer but he still didn't want to give up and was determined to negotiate until he could save his brother or at least reduce his punishment. He looked toward the curtain, "Please God, could you not cover him with your mercy and save him after he spends time in hell for his sins?"

"God cannot break his rules. His punishment is eternal," the archangel interrupted. "You already knew the rules and believed in them, didn't you?"

"I know," Hast interjected, "but I also know that ∞Illuhim∞ is a loving God and can forgive any sin."

"Rules are rules," the archangel replied. "Your emotions are getting in your way and are preventing you from seeing the righteous Judgment, but this will all be over soon when you make the right choice and decide to live in the Garden of Eden with the Lord. Your brother will be unknown to you and you will be able to enjoy heaven forever without any memories of him."

Hast started to shed tears as he recalled his life with his brother. He remembered their childhood quarrels, happy moments and sad events as they all came back in a rapid but vivid flashback. He needed to do something to help his brother no matter what, and that moment he remembered his mother and father. "Where are my parents?"

"Your parents are in heaven already and they are waiting for you," the archangel replied. Hast knew his parents would be safe as they were faithful to ∞Illuhim∞. "Did they ask about Sardar?" Hast asked eagerly

"They did in the beginning," the angel replied, "but now they are living happily in the Garden of Eden and they have no emotions toward Sardar. In fact, they are disgusted by him and want him to suffer more. They are eager to see you, and you can follow them too if you choose heaven."

Hast found it puzzling that his parents had chosen to forget about their son! He wondered why they didn't insist on saving their son before they lost their emotions toward him! 'If they chose to forget him, why shouldn't I?' he thought in his heart. 'I have no option. I cannot save him … I wish my memories and emotions toward my brother were taken from me involuntarily. I cannot choose to ignore my brother voluntarily. In fact, it is not only my brother but so many other people I know who will face this doomed fate! And I still have a heart, so why am I in this situation?' Hast couldn't throw away all of his guilty and disturbing thoughts since they kept forcefully intruding into his mind.

"You are emotionally suffering right now," the archangel said reading Hast's expression, "but everything will go away once you choose to live in heaven and enter a persistent state of joy and euphoria."

A long pause followed…

"Time is running out," the archangel said. "Give us your choice. Heaven or oblivion?"

Hast thought deeply in his heart, 'It's only a moment, and the memory of my brother will be wiped out. I will not feel guilty about not keeping my promise to him. I have no choice about his fate, and I only have choice about mine. I tried my best to save him. I have advised him for years, but he chose hell! It is not my fault!' Hast kept reciting these thoughts in his mind which made him feel less guilty about the choice he would be making in seconds…

"I have made my choice," Hast finally declared.

"What is your choice?" the angel asked.

"I …," Hast said while looking at the shadowy figure behind the curtain. "I …," he continued to murmur. "… I DON'T BELIEVE IN YOU," he stated boldly facing the curtain. "YOU ARE NOT MY GOD!"

"What are you saying?!" the archangel asked while in shock. "You were already faithful before Judgment Day, so why have you changed your mind now?"

"I didn't change my mind nor my faith," Hast stated. "I'm still a devout follower of ∞Illuhim∞, the benevolent loving God, but the one behind this curtain is not ∞Illuhim∞."

"Then who do you think he is?" the archangel asked.

"He is the Antichrist," Hast replied. "∞Illuhim∞ doesn't reveal himself from the outside. He reveals himself from the inside. I felt much closer to God when I was praying in the holy☼house than now, and you can't be the god I believed in and waited for so long to meet!" Hast continued, "I know ∞Illuhim∞, and he is pure enlightenment. He is love and mercy, he doesn't hide himself behind curtains, and he is always close to us in our hearts."

"Then, I think you have chosen oblivion," the archangel said. "You will go back to oblivion now." He pointed a cane toward Hast's chest. "Unless you ask for forgiveness and bow to the Lord now."

"I will not bow to the Antichrist," Hast declared confidently.

He felt the archangel's cane pushing toward his chest then pain and darkness. He then suddenly felt like he was falling into a deep hole, but the impact with the floor made him jump from his bed and wake up in the middle of the night from a terrifying nightmare shouting!

"Are you OK?" said the woman sleeping next to him.

Hast realized that everything he had just seen was a nightmare! His wife Nergz was beside him with a sleepy look on her face and on her right side, his newly born baby was now starting to cry.

"You woke up the child!" Nergz said. "Did you have a nightmare?"

"I thought it was Doomsday. I didn't remember you, and I thought I was younger and living with my brother in my parents' house," he said. Hast stood up from the bed, and took his child on his lap kissing him on the forehead while trying to settle the crying baby who he had named after the person he most admired, Abraham.

"It would be a horrific day," Nergz said. "I wouldn't blame you for not remembering us."

"I did remember my brother, Sardar," Hast said. "That was probably because I thought he was going to hell and the reason why I was most concerned about him in the dream."

"This could be a sign from ∞Illuhim∞ to save your brother before this day comes."

"Doomsday is perhaps on its way," announced Hast as he walked back to his bed.

One week ago, he had read a news article where scientists were warning people that a deadly meteor was heading toward earth, and it was set to hit it by 2068. According to their calculations, if it hits the earth, all life forms would become extinct. This was because the meteor was the largest ever recorded, and hence the scientists were calling it the 'Doomsday Meteor'. Hast recalled that today's date was the 25th of March 2060 then he looked at his baby again. He thought that eight years was enough time for scientists to find a solution. 'I can't imagine my kid growing up just to face the horrors of that day,' he thought.

Chapter 2

Kogar Shervan was a well-known, self-made rich entrepreneur. At 30 years old, he had won the local election and became the governor of Shinar Land from the years 2051 to 2056, and under his rule, life and prosperity skyrocketed.

When he was 22, he graduated from the college of psychology, and his studies on this subject helped him to deeply understand some aspects of human behavior. He knew what made people afraid of new ideas and what made them resist and oppose them. He used to explain to his colleagues that some of the human brain regions evolved in controlling the language processing were particularly useful in transferring our identity and ideas to other people. He used to say that language was a cheap attempt by our brains to counteract entropy and achieve immortality. He argued that the information acquired in one's lifetime of experience can be retained forever through copying the thought contents in one's brain to other brains.

Kogar knew the best way to copy his own thoughts to other people and to spread the seeds of his identity was to use the social media effectively, so at the age of 23, he decided to do a TV show. He started presenting a show on the topics of science and society, and his TV show soon became a big hit for the local people because he was presenting and discussing novel scientific ideas which helped to solve simple problems in society in a very appealing way.

Kogar's ultimate dream was to become the governor of Shinar Land that is why in his show he used to indirectly criticize the current political system in order to attract the audience's attention. For instance, he used to say that the parliamentary voting system was an inefficient emulation of a human's central nervous system giving the impression to his audience that he knew a lot about the weakness of the country's political system.

"Democracy was invented by the Greeks when there was no social media," he used to say in his show. "Ancient people didn't have access to the tools and technologies we have today, so they invented a system where some people thought on behalf of other people to establish that country's policies. This was the best idea back then, but we can do much better today. Every political decision today is driven by polls and social media," he claimed. "Our politicians behave like they are independent and think for themselves, but in fact, they are all like me and you. They watch TV, surf the web to look at what's trending and what makes people happy or angry. We have to admit that today people are ruling themselves by themselves, and our politicians are nothing more than highly paid, useless statues. For example, take a look at our parliament. It has more than 200 members and we tend to think that 200 smart brains are thinking and looking for solutions to our life problems, but let me tell you, this is not true. Actually no more than two brains are actively working."

With this reference Kogar was talking about the two major political parties which had the most members in parliament, the conservatives and the liberals. "Nevertheless, we are still paying huge salaries to over 200 members. I have studied psychology and I know that the brain efforts don't add up if they are not independent, and this is hard to achieve with our current political system because all the parliament members belonging to a particular party are just following the decision of their head unanimously instead of thinking independently."

With his examples and his systematic expose of the corrupt political system, Kogar's popularity grew. People started to suggest to him that he should run in the next election. He continued criticizing the political system in his shows.

***

A few years later when Kogar was 26, he invested in a small but rising social website called 'zanzor.com', and initially the website was not very different than the other more popular and dominant social websites. It allowed its users to post, comment and follow each other until a small brain recording tool was introduced by Tek-Brain company. This tool, a sensor attached to the user's forehead, recorded brain signals and detected whether the person who was wearing it was happy or sad. Kogar saw potential in the device and immediately invested in Tek-Brain. He saw from this an opportunity to introduce something new on zanzor.com. The timing was ideal as at that moment another gaming company called Virtual-world™, had introduced a helmet which could take signals directly from the gamer's mind and use them to control the game flow. The company had already sold millions of the helmets and it had become a very popular gaming console among teenagers.

Kogar thought that if his Tek-Brain company produced a web application that could interface with Virtual-world's™ helmet, a million more users would then have the ability to register on his social website zanzor.com without purchasing their own sensors. People who were wearing the helmet could share their true emotions with others, and it didn't stop there since the brain recorder became increasingly more sensitive and could read a range of human emotions: sad, happy, eager, curious, love, or hate. This had made a big breach in people's private feelings because people usually tended to hide their true emotions. For instance, under the current social media's 'like' and 'dislike' system, a person could press 'like' when a friend posted something online even if he/she didn't really like the post. In zanzor.com you couldn't do that because the helmet recorded only true feelings. If a person logged on to the website, they couldn't enjoy using all its features without turning on the brain recording helmet, and if the user decided to click on a friend's post, the helmet recorded true feelings and shared it with the friend. This was a double-edged sword, and zanzor.com turned many friends into enemies and many enemies into friends. The honesty associated with the website was very addictive, and it became very popular among a specific sect of the population.

Soon young people started to use this feature for dating as the website provided a good measure of true feelings toward each other. The website became a hit and within a couple years, its user base jumped from one million to 100 million. Kogar himself claimed to have found his true love, who later became his wife, through the website he owned.

In 2051 the regional election for the post of governor was announced and Kogar was among the most prominent candidates. He used to tell people that they should trust him because honesty was his motto, and he claimed that if he wasn't honest, he wouldn't have invented a social website solely based on this trait. His star kept rising, but unfortunately tragedy struck. There was an assassination attempt on his life, and the bomb explosion, thought to have been plotted by his competitors, claimed Kogar's beloved wife. He survived but was in deep shock and mourning.

The election was postponed, many people got emotional against all the other competitors and pointed the blame toward them. After one month of the incident, Kogar appeared on TV and promised that he would stay faithful to his beloved wife's memory and would not marry again. His statement attracted the attention and emotion of many people, even those who didn't initially support him. It became clear that he would be the clear winner of the election and indeed he achieved 91% of all the votes and became the first governor to gain such massive support.

His legend didn't stop here, and during his five year rule, he achieved miracles for Shinar Land. He used science and technology to achieve many things that appeared to be impossible. Because of his social website, he gained a lot of experience analyzing the data collected online using artificial intelligence (AI), and so he was able to predict trends and changes. He could monitor graphs online to see the collective emotion of the people by what they posted on his webpage daily. He could also see how a specific decision made by him changed these trends. His aim was simple: maximize the happiness emotion.

During his role, he also invested heavily in 3D printing technologies as some Chinese companies had recently started to make and sell relatively cheap, large, general purpose 3D printing machines. The invention of these was labeled to be the humanity's crowning achievement in the 21st century. With them anything from a small cup to an entire building could be printed, and not only that. Items with dynamic parts, such as cars, generators, utilities could also be printed. It made the process of creation as simple as possible, and to produce anything, all that was needed was a design model inside the computer, the necessary elements for printing and then to hit the print button!

Kogar invested in many general purpose 3D printing machines and used them to build houses and provide shelter for the many homeless and refugees fleeing from war torn countries. With Kogar's investment in the technology, the 3D printing industry had a rapid boost in productivity.

The advantages of the large scale general purpose 3D printers were immense. They sped up construction time and reduced costs by a factor of ten. Despite the job losses due to the new technology, Kogar was still able to secure new jobs for workers.

During the last year of his rule, he tested another masterpiece of a recently invented new 3D printing technology. This one took advantage of the helmet which recorded and read brain signals and was able to transform imagination into reality. There were currently limitations, the primary one being the fact that the machine couldn't accurately detect the imagined shape in someone's mind, but the entire thing was an impressive leap in itself.

At this point it became clear to Kogar that in the near future he would be able to model reality using his imagination just like in science fiction. 'With this, I can achieve miracles,' he whispered in his mind, and then an unexpected thought came to him and he suddenly felt paralyzed! The disturbing thought was that he could sense the presence of a big conspiracy. 'I'm not the richest person around, nor the smartest, and not even the ruler of a big country. If I can change the trends with my decisions, then others are already capable of doing much more!'

He remembered that the USA had started using an artificial intelligence program called 'The Brain Storm' nearly 60 years ago to predict best outcomes for its political decisions! There was another hyped project trying to build a superhuman called '**The New ARK**' or TNARK project started 30 years ago in Europe. The Chinese entrepreneur, Lee Shark, the richest person on the planet who owned the biggest 3D company could already build entire cities in a short period of time. Many other rich and highly influential people had already started investing in God playing projects! And they were all ahead of him by miles.

He remembered all the conspiracy theories in his era which blamed the superpowers for wars and calamities. 'They could be all true!' he thought. 'If I can use my imagination to model reality and change trends, then other superpowers are already ahead of me by light years! I could be the last one who has entered this game,' Kogar thought. 'If someone is already playing God by controlling everything, I need to find that person!' he said to himself.

In the year 2055 at the age of 35, Kogar resigned from his position as governor. People were urging him to run for another round, as according to the polls, his popularity had increased even further and it was obvious that he could win another round easily, but he rejected them by saying that a change in power was needed and he wanted to give the chance for others to rule.

"My resignation from power will ensure that democracy will continue and power will be exchanged peacefully," he said in his last interview.

"What is your plan after you retire?" the interviewer asked.

"I will be hiding from the media and public and take some rest for a while," he answered. "Meanwhile, I will be funding revolutionary science projects. I will also use my money to encourage and fund education and health programs around the world."

Chapter 3

The next morning after his nightmare, Hast called his brother. "Sardar, you will not believe what I saw last night!" he said. "I just wanted to make sure you are OK because I had a bad dream about you."

"What did you see?" Sardar asked. "Dreams are normal things."

"I thought we were in the Judgment Day and you went to hell. It looked very real. I wanted to save you from the hell, but it would be much easier to save you now before that day comes."

"What is the big deal?! Of course you will have such nightmares," Sardar claimed. "You are always thinking about the apocalyptic fictional Doomsday."

Hast realized he couldn't convince him even a bit over the phone.

"I will pray for you until you will change your heart," he said ending the call.

After getting his degree in theology, Hast taught the subject to 10th graders, and his wife Nergz was a history teacher at the same school. Once she has given birth to their child, they were both given parental leave for six months. During this time Hast had created an online blog and had posted many articles about his views on theology and Abrahamic faith prophecies of the end-days.

Two days after his dream, he received a call from someone identifying himself as Agent Mark Robinson from Interpol. He had said he wanted to meet Hast to discuss an important topic. Hast agreed to meet Mark the following week in a local coffee shop in his hometown, the city of Erbil, where he and his family lived. He found it strange that someone from Interpol wanted to meet with him. He kept thinking whether posting controversial articles online had anything to do with the call he had received from Interpol.

***

Mark had worked for Interpol for five years and he was also a member of International Conspiracy Private Investigators, known as ICPI. His job was solving puzzling international cases and facilitating the work of Interpol through co-operation with local police in member countries.

One month ago Mark had received a call from Zaniar, a previous Interpol agent and a close friend of him, he told Mark that Kogar Shervan, the previous governor of Shinar Land, wanted to meet with him on a very important subject. When Mark finally met Kogar, he warned the Interpol agent that someone was trying to play the role of God and was planning to control everyone's mind. Kogar suspected that someone working for the highly hyped, futuristic TNARK project was already planning to control the world through controlling people's minds. When Mark asked him what made him so sure, Kogar told him that after he resigned from his position as governor, he made a deal with Virtual-world™, the pioneer gaming company, to produce a shared helmet that had better brain signal detectors and could be used by the clients of both companies, Tek-Brains and Virtual-world™. Kogar claimed to have found shocking evidence that Virtual-world™ and possibly TNARK were trying to control the minds of their users through their suspicious equipment.

Virtual-world™ was an offshoot of the bigger TNARK project, when a user put on the helmet he would enter into a huge online multiplayer universe that had over a million other users. The helmet acted as a brain signal detector, the gamer used his/her mind to send commands to control the online game without using any controllers. As a side project, the helmet also collected brain data from the users anonymously and provided this information to neuroscientists. The data would then be analyzed to understand how the human brain works, and this ultimately would help to advance the TNARK project.

During the meeting, Kogar showed Mark the newly designed helmets, the product of his deal with the Virtual-world™ company. There were 120 diodes emitting blue light all over the helmet. Kogar claimed that he didn't know the purpose of these small blue lights because for him these light emitters were separate and different from the normal 120 sensors that he used as brain signal recorders for his social website, zanzor.com. Kogar told Mark that brain sensors didn't need to emit any light to record brain signals, so someone working for TNARK or Virtual-world™ company must be up to something suspicious. Hence, Kogar urged Mark to investigate the matter further.

When Mark began his investigation, it turned out that the designers and engineers working for Virtual-world™ didn't want to share everything with him! The company's manager simply told Mark that the purpose of the blue lights on the outer surface of the helmet was just for aesthetics, mainly to make the helmet look more beautiful and technical! Mark didn't believe them. He urged Interpol to issue a 'Red light' and a formal letter to them so that the managers of TNARK and Virtual-world™ company would comply and reveal some of their classified documents to Mark. Meanwhile, he had also started to look online for topics related to mind control. Accidentally, he came across some articles and blogs written by a theologian named Hast about Abrahamic faith prophecies of the end-days and about mind control too!

Mark soon realized that there were a lot of similarities between what he was looking for and the prophecies of Abrahamic faith which claimed that the Antichrist would appear in the end-days trying to play God and control the minds of people. That moment, Mark decided to meet Hast in person and ask him more about the details of Abrahamic faith prophecies.

**

When Mark met Hast at a local coffee shop in Erbil City, he tried to explain the purpose of his meeting to Hast.

"Mr. Hast you may wonder why I wanted to meet you," he said.

"Please just call me Hast, and yes I'm very curious to find out why an Interpol agent wanted to meet with me," Hast said. "I don't recall doing anything outside of the law. Has someone I know done something bad?"

"No, not at all," Mark said. "Actually, I just wanted your expertise and advice in regard to something. I hope you don't mind helping me."

Hast thought there was a mistake. "I studied theology, so how can this expertise be useful to Interpol?" he wondered.

"I know," Mark said. "I have read your profile and checked your resume and records. You have an impressive knowledge about the history of religions, especially Abrahamic faiths. I have also read some of your online articles and blogs about the end-days and the rise of the Antichrist. I wanted to ask you more about that if you don't mind."

"Is this part of your mission or just a personal interest?"

"Well, maybe both," Mark said. "I think it could be related to something I'm working on."

"Is it crime related?" he asked. "Could you please tell me more?"

"In your articles you claim that the appearance of the Antichrist is near," Mark said. "Would you please tell me why you think that?"

"Well, because many of the prophecies have already come true," Hast said.

"How?" Mark asked.

"We have already seen the minor signs, and now I'm witnessing the emergence of some major signs too."

"What are the minor and the major signs?" Mark asked.

"The holy§cript describes some signs that will come true before the emergence of the Antichrist and Doomsday," Hast replied. "Minor signs include: wars, corruption, bankruptcy, earthquakes, drought, disobedience to parents, worshiping money, committing sins publicly, and the appearance of new diseases. All of these will increase before the end-days, and you know more than I do that these things are already happening and increasing. Don't you?"

"I see, but this could be due to the increase in population and more effective media coverage nowadays," Mark proposed.

"That is one of the explanations, but you can't deny the minor signs are increasing and there are major signs too which I think I have seen them emerging," Hast said.

"Like what?" Mark wondered.

"In the prophecies it says that before the end of days a talking Beast will come out. People will love to talk to it and believe in what the Beast says. Also the beast can do wonders and miracles," he claimed.

"And where is this Beast?" Mark asked.

"According to scripture the Beast is everywhere," Hast claimed. "It can travel at the speed of light to everywhere."

"And 'who' is that by your account?" Mark asked.

"It's the AI revolution," Hast answered. "Can't you see that chatting bots like Cortana-x and Siri-z are now in every mobile device and in every pocket. They do talk to people, answer their questions, customize what the users like to see in the social media and very soon they will do miracles. We will be increasingly reliant on them."

"This is an interesting analogy, but I'm not convinced to be honest," Mark said. "And do you think that AI is the Antichrist?"

"No, the Antichrist is a person with blood and flesh. The Beast which the holy§cript describes could be anything and that is why I suspect AI. I think the Beast is the false prophet who appears in the end-days too."

"And what does the false prophet do?" Mark wondered.

"The false prophet is the one who deceives and lures ordinary people to follow the Antichrist. The Antichrist is yet to reveal himself, but I am guessing he is almost here."

"OK, that will be helpful in order to identify him," Mark said. "So you think the Antichrist is someone who uses AI to his advantage to lure people?"

"I think so because that is in line with the holy§cript which says that the false prophet works under the Antichrist's command," he said.

"So it could be someone from the US government or Google headquarters for example?"

"It could be an organization in the beginning, but then someone would be controlling everything. I mean it should boil down to one single person who is evil and responsible for everything."

"You think it's a conspiracy like Illuminati?" Mark suggested.

"Actually, it's interesting you brought this up because Illuminati is a code name for the Antichrist," Hast claimed.

"Seriously?!" Mark wondered.

"Yes, the Illuminati word itself originally comes from Anti-Illuhim. However, because the word Anti-Illuhim was a very bold word and has caused a lot of irritation to Abrahamic faith followers, the word was changed to a more subtle one by putting the word 'Anti' as a suffix to form Illuhim-Anti, then gradually the word was merged to become Illuminati, which is more secretive but has the same intention," Hast said.

"So you think Illuminati is a code name for the Antichrist and both words are used interchangeably?" Mark asked.

"I do think so," Hast said.

"If the Antichrist has one power I should be aware of, what do you think it would be?" Mark asked.

"Mind control," Hast answered confidently.

"I think I should end the meeting here," he said. "Hast, you have indeed been very helpful."

"I don't quite understand your mission yet," Hast wondered aloud. "Are you looking for the Antichrist?"

"Kind of... honestly, I don't quite believe in the Antichrist, but maybe I'm looking for someone who is trying to play God."

"I'm interested in tracking that person too. We should combine our efforts," Hast said.

"I wouldn't recommend you to," Mark said. "My mission is risky and complex."

"I don't mind. I would like to save people from the Antichrist," Hast insisted. "Please understand that tracking that person is more important for me than for you," he claimed.

Mark saw determination in Hast's eyes, and although he wasn't very religious himself, he had a tendency to believe in the religious prophecies especially in his current case where he detected a pattern of similarity between Hast's warnings about the Antichrist and Kogar's warnings about the true intention of TNARK's project. He thought to himself that two minds reaching a similar conclusion independently shouldn't be taken lightly. Hence, he decided to share more information with Hast to see if he could be more helpful.

"OK, I agree but you need to promise me that anything that happens will remain confidential between us."

"I promise," Hast said with an eager voice.

"When you told me that the Antichrist's biggest power is mind control, I couldn't refuse your offer to help me because I think your theological knowledge might be useful in my case," Mark said.

"Well, I think too much about the Antichrist. I have read a lot about him, how he looks, how he behaves, and basically everything about him. I might even be able to recognize him if he walked down the street in front of us," Hast said jokingly.

Mark laughed. "I bet you could!" He continued, "I'm currently investigating a technology built by TNARK and is widely used by gamers. I fear it could be exploited by someone in the company to control the mind of its users!"

"Actually, that is what I think the Antichrist would do to control people's minds; use technology!" Hast said.

Mark thought for a bit about Hast's claim that he could identify the Antichrist if he met him. "If you don't mind, we can visit TNARK's headquarters in Cambridge, England together and meet some people over there," he said. "You might spot the Antichrist there!"

"I'm up for that," Hast said eagerly. "Let's do it!"

Chapter 4

Hast felt amazing after his first meeting with Mark. Next week he would be travelling to TNARK headquarters in Cambridge, in the UK. He couldn't be more excited, after all, his knowledge of theology finally proved to be useful.

He used to have lengthy discussions with his brother Sardar about theology during his time at college. Sardar used to mock him saying that all of what he studied was a myth and Hast used to engage him in lengthy arguments to prove that theology was no less important than any other scientific subject.

"You got theology wrong," Hast used to say to Sardar. "It's not like studying history or geography where you only describe an event or a place."

"I know, it describes fairy tales," Sardar interrupted in a sarcastic tone.

"No, it describes different sects of religious practices and their relation to each other," Hast said.

"But you take all your truth from one book, the holy§cript," Sardar said.

"No, the course I study involves many books written by historians and academics. They study the evolution of faith and religion just like biology is the study of the evolution of species."

Hast used to give his favorite example to illustrate his point. He said that a human's perception of ∞Illuhim∞ changed with time and ∞Illuhim∞ had revealed himself to humans gradually, and so far the God's revelation was in its fourth stage.

"The first stage was the Human-God stage. In the ancient times people used to worship their kings and rulers thinking that they were gods. After all, how can you unite cavemen under one constitution and one kingdom-ship if a god himself was not among them ruling by a fist of iron and fire. Nimrod, Pharaoh,

Cyrus and Zeus were examples of great kings who ruled over a large swath of land and declared themselves upon their fellow humans as gods. They were served and worshiped by their people.

"With time, great civilizations built up and humans became smarter, more united and more philosophical. The importance of living together in big societies comprised of multiple geographically separated cities and towns became clear and natural to humans without the need to be feared by a Human-God ruling them by an iron fist and urging them to unite by force.

"Here came the next stage, the God-Agent stage. In this stage people began to revolt against the Human-Gods, for example, Abraham revolted against Nimrod, the God of Babylon. Moses revolted against Pharaoh, the God of Egypt. Zoroaster revolted against Cyrus, the God of Persia and so on. Gradually people became more reluctant to pray and worship a person who looked like them, ate, slept, and died like a normal person.

"∞Illuhim∞ began to reveal himself to people as an omnipotent powerful being in the sky watching upon us. However, societies were still in need of a powerful respected king to rule over them and unite different cultures under one umbrella. Here, the kings and rulers declared themselves as God's-Agents, messengers of ∞Illuhim∞. Abraham, Zoroaster, and Buddha were prominent examples of God's-Agents.

"The third stage was the God-Agent-agent. In this stage, kings didn't declare themselves as direct messengers from God, though there were still some divinity about them. Their rule was respected among the people and people were still looking upon them as noble and transcendent human beings. King David, King Solomon, King Arthur, and many more were examples of this stage.

"The fourth stage, the one we are currently living in, is the Godless-Agent stage. People are now living in big countries with lots of cities and most of them follow the orders of their ruler, their elected president, or their king without looking at them as gods or god sent agents or even as a divine agent."

Sardar's reply after hearing Hast explaining the stages for him was, "So God is fading away from people's minds with each stage."

To which Hast replied, "Not at all. The majority of people still believe in a personal god. It is only our perception about who is that God is changing."

Then Sardar followed with his next question, "Why doesn't God reveal himself in his final form? Why does he need to go through different stages of revelation?!"

"That is an important point," was Hast's reply. "The answer is because our brain has not evolved enough to perceive God in its final form. I believe that ancient people who used to worship Nimrod, Cyrus and Pharaoh were not particularly wrong at their time because they couldn't have perceived a loving God like ∞Illuhim∞ as we do today. In other words, just like our biological brain evolves, our perception about ∞Illuhim∞ evolves too. He is gradually evolving from a human figure ruler with an iron fist to a loving power in the universe who guides us toward salvation."

"But many people today still perceive God as he was perceived by the ancient people!" was Sardar's usual complaint about religion.

In their recent discussions, Hast remembered his dream and his reply to him was, "You are right! I myself misunderstood God and I only realized my mistake recently when I dreamed about the Antichrist! I realized that my perception about God was not different from my perception about the Antichrist," Hast said. "I'm lucky because if that was not a dream I could have followed the Antichrist believing he was the true god! My understanding about God is still evolving, and it's like one of the things that I feel I have already understood, but then time passes and I reconsider and I realize I wasn't quite right."

Chapter 5

TNARK project was the most ambitious science project in the 21st century. It was started 30 years ago by a group of amateur researchers at Cambridge University where a famous genetic scientist, Catherin Smith, proposed a study detailing the possibility for genetic engineering to modify human genes in order to create a super organism. Essentially, this would entail combining the best genes from all the other species in the animal kingdom. Her lab was able to generate a hybrid human-crocodile skin, and the modified skin looked like human's skin but was as tough as the crocodile's and resistant to cuts and abrasions. Hence Prof. Smith concluded that as genetic engineering advances, they would be able to do the same for all other human body parts to create a biological super organism.

In her famous TED talk, she criticized the common view among some AI and computer scientists that saw the next stage of evolution as the end of carbon based organic life and the start of non-organic life such as highly intelligent robots. She said, "Human extinction is not an option because our genes are programmed to survive and they will fight until the very end. Even if we were optimists and believed that science could someday transfer human consciousness into a robot, there is no guarantee that rigid metallic bodies could survive the unseen threats posed by Nature any better. We need to adapt ourselves by continuously reproducing and mutating to produce different variations of a trait then the natural selection would pass the best traits to the next generation. Nature has done a great job so far; however, humans can make the process much faster through genetic engineering technology."

Someone from the conference asked Catherin whether a metallic robot could also adapt itself as it could be made to intelligently redesign and clone itself. Catherin was used to replying to this type of question, "Nothing can beat organic compounds in their ability to adapt fast and efficiently. All the diversity in organic materials comes from various combinations of only four elements: oxygen, hydrogen, carbon, and nitrogen. They make up nearly everything organic from oil to meat to the fruit you eat. Can you tell me any metallic material which produces compounds with such huge variabilities in their physical properties? Not only that, but these four elements are also among the most abundant elements in the universe. An organism either needs to be in the final stage of its evolution, which means that it can survive any imaginable catastrophe in our universe from the melting temperatures of hot suns to the crushing forces of black holes. In this case, this super organism is immune to extinction and doesn't need to change and upgrade itself farther. However, if the organism is not in its final form it will have to be able to clone and adapt itself when facing a new challenge. Imagine if such an organism was made from rare elements in the periodic table such as iron or uranium. How could it multiply and increase if it's made from scarce elements? It would definitely face extinction at some point and that is why I would not think that the next stage of our evolution is going to be non-organic."

Although Prof. Catherin Smith was labeled as the mother of TNARK project because of her influence and her detailed research on how to make hybrid organic tissues, she was not involved in the project by herself. TNARK project had started as an amateur idea in 2030 but had gradually grown to be a massive project with more than a thousand high profile scientists working on it. It drew the focus of many scientists after the famous astrophysicist Prof. Neil Baron threatened that life on earth would soon be over if science didn't do something about the huge meteor heading toward earth and due to hit in 2068.

TNARK stood for 'The New ARK', in homage to the ancient Noah's Ark which purportedly saved life on earth from a great flood and the initial TNARK proposal was to build a spaceship which could save all life forms on earth by selecting not only a pair of each species but the entire human population too. Due to the technical challenges facing the designers despite the huge advances in technology, social media mercilessly started to mock the idea by questioning the size of the spaceship. The jokes also served to hurt believers of Abrahamic faith who believed in the original Noah's Ark.

The obvious question was that even if the spaceship was successful, where would everyone go? The usual answer was Mars, Venus, or the moons of Jupiter. The Chinese billionaire and CEO of the largest 3D printing company, Lee Shark, made an intriguing proposal stating that if TNARK's spaceship was successful, he would offer many of his large and expensive 3D printing machines to print houses or even entire cities on those planets in a matter of a few months. Lee's idea was not fiction. In fact, 3D printing devices were already in work and were printing anything with unprecedented speed and negligible costs, however, the big problem was that all the planets in the solar system were inhabitable for human life. Life had evolved to survive the earth's gentle environment not the very hot Venus or the very cold Mars.

The famous astrophysicist, Neil Baron, thought that not only should we be able to adapt to our surrounding environment, but we should be also able to change the environment to suit us too. Although it sounded difficult, Neil was convinced that in order to maximize survivability we should find efficient ways to deflect meteors and even to change the weather on planets in our solar systems to make them habitable to suit our needs. One way to achieve this was to change their rotational speed around their axis. For instance, Venus, a very hot planet with a thick atmosphere, takes about 116 earth days to rotate around itself making it have very long days and very long nights. Its weather could become better if we could speed up its rotation around itself, and this could make the thick gas layer surrounding the planet disperse and make the planet colder. Also, we could make some very distant and cold planets hotter by stopping their rotations around themselves. This would make the sun facing surface hotter and hence suitable for life.

For a while, TNARK started a subproject called TNARK-planet lead by Neil to investigate the plausible ways of changing planetary rotations, and although he made detailed proposals for the project, due to the huge expenses, TNARK gave up on Neil's project and sought alternative ways to save life on earth from the Doomsday Meteor.

In time everyone came back to the original ideas proposed by Catherin which were to try to genetically engineer a super-organism which could survive harsh environments and adapt itself further when needed. To understand how scientists could achieve this, Catherin often used this example. "If all the species on earth were placed on another very hot planet, not all of them would suffer equally from the new environment. Some could endure the hot surface easily such as desert ants or the Pompeii worm. Likewise, if you put all of earth's species on a very cold planet, polar bears and penguins were likely to endure and survive longer. Similarly, if all the species were placed on a heavy plant with an extreme gravitational pull, birds and small animals would suffer though large muscular animals would cope better."

In short, it was clear that natural selection had already found the solutions on earth for such hostile environments. The only problem was not all species shared these traits, but if the virtues of all species were combined into one organism, the resulting super organism could survive any other planet in our solar system.

***

Initially, many of the proposals of the TNARK project were mere science fiction, but because of the real threat proposed by the Doomsday Meteor, the project attracted clever minds from all around the world. It became a lab for imagination where everyone proposed his cutting edge ideas for survival which were then reviewed by leading scientists in their field. In this way, many other side projects and amazing inventions came from TNARK. It became clear that TNARK-project was useful for scientific advancement even if it couldn't achieve its intended goal. The global support for the project grew day by day and it came from local and international governments. Huge international companies started to invest and fund different offshoots of the project.

Bernhard Johnson was TNARK's chairman in 2060. He was a well-known neurosurgeon and researcher, and during his period the project did complete genetic mapping for nearly all the animal and plant species on earth. It also ranked all the traits based on their survivability in various harsh environments. Now after 30 years from the project's start, its first super organism ideas had become almost a reality as scientists were starting to make animal hybrids from very different kinds of species. For instance, they were able to isolate the genes that made up the respiratory system of an aquatic animal and made a hybrid lung for an experimental monkey which was able to breath underwater. This was the crowning achievement of the project and was celebrated all around the globe. The super organism was no longer just a dream.

Some scientists began to think about post solar system survival and what could be the final form of evolution. The celebrated evolutionary biologist Prof. Schwartz suggested that humanity's final enemy in the universe were black holes. These were invisible dense stars with huge gravitational forces that could crush and swallow anything. No information, not even light, could pass through its gravitational field at the event horizon, the point of no return where space itself was reduced to nothingness. If an organism was able to survive the event horizon, then ta da! It would be the ultimate super organism with no further need to upgrade.

It was unthinkable to survive a black hole, but some physicists suggested that if two equally massed black holes met when their event horizons touched together, an organism might be able to pass through them as the gravitational force exerted would be equal on either side. A gazillion virtual particles would be generated in this narrow space between the two black holes which may even work as a fertile medium for an organism who needs to evolve further at the level of subatomic particles.

One last question remained majorly unsolved in TNARK project was how someone's consciousness could be transferred to a super organism. Among all the other scientific fields, neuroscience were still behind due to the complexity of a human's brain and the remaining riddle of consciousness. To solve the issues, Prof. Ericson Sanders, a leading neuroscientist at TNARK, asked companies to direct their funds toward this field so that it could catch up with the other fields.

The current proposal for transferring consciousness was to scan and record all the connections between all the neurons inside a human brain, and then by using a special 3D Bio-printer, print the brain tissue with all its neuronal connections again into the body of the super organism.

Chapter 6

Hast headed to the Erbil international airport to catch his plane to the UK to meet Mark and visit TNARK headquarters. Mark had told him that he had already made an appointment to meet Prof. Ericson Sanders, the leading neuroscientist at TNARK. Two days before the trip, Hast did some online search investigating about TNARK project and it became clear to him that looking for the Antichrist in TNARK would be like looking for a needle in a haystack. After all, the project had over a thousand scientists in addition to a huge number of funding organizations and affiliations. Nevertheless, Prof. Sanders seemed to be a good starting point for their investigation because his lab had close connections with the Virtual-world™.

Ericson's lab provided the commercial gaming company with the cutting edge brain reading techniques and the company used these in their gaming consoles. In return, the Virtual-world™ provided Ericson's lab with the data they collected from recording brain signals from gamers' brains through the game controlling helmet.

As Hast remembered what Mark has told him about the suspicious gaming helmet he began to ask himself 'How could a blue light emitter installed on a helmet be used for mind control?' He typed key words 'blue light brain control' into Google and to his surprise he found many web pages talking about scientific experiments controlling monkey's brain with a blue light! There was even a separate neuroscience field on it called optogenetics. Several YouTube videos showcased an optogenetics application where a controller was attached to a mouse's brain by a wire, and at its end a small diode was installed that emitted blue lights. These directed the mouse to the left or to the right. To Hast's shock many of the videos had been published back in 2010! 'Oh my God, this is real! If they could do that 50 years ago, what they can do now!'

He realized his findings might not be new to Mark and this might explain why the set of 120 unexplained blue light emitters on the helmet drew Interpol's attention to the matter. Hast kept thinking about his shocking finding before boarding the plane to London. 'The Antichrist is probably already here and plotting to diverge us from the true God ∞Illuhim∞ through mind control.' With this fear rising in him, he recited to himself, 'God help us all.'

Chapter 7

Hast arrived at London's Heathrow airport early in the morning. He was due to meet Mark and then they were to take a train together to a small town 10 miles north of Cambridge where TNARK headquarters resided. While there, they had a late morning appointment with Prof. Sanders at his office to take a tour of his lab.

"Hi Hast. I'm here," Mark called from in front of the arrivals exit. "Let's hurry up to catch a tube to Kings Cross station; otherwise, we will miss the next train to Cambridge."

"By the way, do you know about optogenetics?" Hast tried to start a conversation while rushing toward the exit.

"Yes, I have read about it," Mark answered.

"Do you think the blue light emitters were put in by an optogenetics expert?" Hast asked.

"That is quite possible. I guess Prof. Sanders should know about that and he might have had a hand in it, so we shouldn't immediately bring this topic up to him," Mark claimed. "I will try to ask him some random questions and let's see if he mentions it by himself."

"Oh, I see. You want to monitor his behavior," Hast said feeling that they might be close to finding the culprit.

"By the way, Ericson is Jewish. Do the prophecies say anything about the race of the Antichrist?" Mark asked.

"Well, the prophecies do say that the Antichrist will be a man who descends from the ancient Babylon, one of the first cradles of human civilization," Hast said. "But you know, ancient Babylon no longer exists, but now most people around the world in some way or another may have past descendants from ancient Babylon."

"So he could be any race?" Mark asked.

"Yes, indeed," Hast replied.

"That is not helpful in narrowing the suspect," Mark said frustratingly.

Before they caught the train to Cambridge, Hast saw a big poster hanging down from a building advertising the recent hit movie, *The Rise of the Antichrist*. Hast had watched the movie twice in the cinemas and nearly watched all the online trailers and interviews about the movie. He thought the movie was the first massively successful religious blockbuster movie in decades! Although followers of different sects of Abrahamic faiths didn't agree on some details presented in the movie, they all agreed that the basic plot was reasonably accurate.

"Have you watched *The Rise of the Antichrist* movie?" Hast asked.

"No," Mark replied.

"I think you should watch it, although I don't agree with their depiction of the Antichrist, but it was a good movie," he said.

"It was on my list to watch but now I have you," Mark said.

"Don't depend solely on me! You should watch it too," Hast said laughing. "It is quite informative about the Abrahamic views of the end-days."

Hast thought it was surprising how only recently the movie industry had started to appreciate the religious stories told in the holyScript. A few years ago the story of Adam and Eve was also made for the big screen and before that there were remakes of *The Exodus* and *Noah*. 'The industry is changing; they are finally seeing the beauty of Abrahamic faith and its meaningful tales,' Hast thought.

"By the way, on something more serious," Mark said suddenly interrupted Hast's thoughts. "Last night on the news,

Russia declared that they are missing one of their portable nuclear bags and the USA is now accusing Russia of selling the nuclear weapon on the black market to the terrorists. Have you read about it?"

"Oh. God that is scary," Hast said. "Do you think it's related to the Antichrist?"

"I don't know. I was asking you," Mark said. "Does the Antichrist want to destroy the world according to the prophecies?"

"Well, the Antichrist wants to control the world but…," Hast paused briefly then suddenly he remembered. "Oh my God, the second major prophecy. The third world war is near!"

"Are you saying the holy§cript predicts the third world war?" Mark asked.

"One of the major signs of the end-days is the increase in the number of wars, but the Antichrist will only appear after the final one, which is unfortunately according to the scripture the most horrific one."

"So you are saying that the Antichrist is not personally responsible for initiating the war?" Mark wondered.

"Well, the prophecy is unclear about that. It just says that the Antichrist appears right after the last major world war," Hast said.

Chapter 8

Ericson Sanders, the 71 year old leading neuroscientist, was waiting in his office for his visitors. He had accepted the meeting, despite his extremely busy schedule, because one of the visitors claimed to be from Interpol and in his emails he had stated he needed to meet him on a very important and urgent topic. Ericson had no way to reject the meeting; otherwise, Interpol might grow more suspicious. 'Do they know?' he asked himself. 'But why would they send an investigator from Interpol? And why are they asking for a tour around my lab?' He thought to himself, 'I need to look innocent and answer them with a straight face.' He kept looking at his watch and thinking, but at that moment, his secretary came and notified him about the arrival of the two visitors.

"Should I show them in?" the secretary asked.

"Yes, please," Ericson answered.

The secretary went outside and opened the door for the two visitors. "Please come in," she said.

Mark looked at her face when entering and wondered about her age. 'What a young lady serving such an old man! She looks like a 15-year old teenager!' he thought.

"Hello. Shall we go to the lab directly?" Ericson suggested as they entered his office. "There I have more space and we can tour around it while talking."

"Yes, please let's go," Mark said "Professor as you know, I'm working with Interpol and this is my colleague, Hast. You are probably wondering why we wanted to meet you."

"Yes, please tell me. Did I do something bad?" Ericson said laughingly while playing innocent.

Mark sensed that Ericson's laugh was fake and unnatural. "Actually we are investigating something unrelated to your lab, but I wanted to consult you because of your expertise in neuroscience."

"Sure, but you could have consulted me over the phone or by email. Why would you take all this trouble to come in person?" Ericson said.

"To be honest, we are investigating a homicide and we have already caught the criminal responsible for the murder," Mark said. "The problem is the criminal has had past psychiatric problems and now he blames his psychiatrist for his crime."

"Why he does that?" Ericson asked curiously.

"He claims his psychiatrist controlled his brain by giving him a pill and putting something like a helmet over his head." Mark continued, "We didn't believe him but he insists, and it's been a year since we captured him his story still has not changed. I'm now curious about this case so I've come here to consider your thoughts on this," he said before pausing briefly trying to answer Ericson's first question. "And the reason we came in person was to have a tour of your lab to see the cutting edge tools for reading and writing from and to the mind."

"Reading and writing from and to the mind!" Ericson laughed. "You are talking as if we are in a science fiction film. Such things are not so advanced yet, so I'm sure the criminal is lying."

"So you don't think his story is correct in any way?" Mark asked.

"If his story is correct, we should hire the psychiatrist immediately to work for TNARK," Ericson said chuckling.

"So you don't think any form of mind controlling is possible yet?" he asked again.

"Well, not to such an extent," Ericson said.

"Can you please tell us to what extent neuroscience is able to control someone's brain, so I can be more informative about the topic next time I encounter a similar homicide?" Mark asked realizing it was a silly line of questioning. 'I should have thought of some better lines before coming to this lab,' he thought to himself.

Ericson realized that the Interpol agent was making up questions on the fly and the purpose of this visit was not what he was claiming, nevertheless, he kept his cool. He coughed twice then started to explain, "As you know neurons in our brains are stimulated through involuntary and voluntary interactions with our environment. We can stimulate neurons externally by using a strong alternating magnetic wave called Transcranial Magnetic Stimulation (TMS) or through Induced Transcranial Direct Currents (ITDC)." At this pause, Ericson pointed toward some bulky coils over a bench. "However, these tools are by no way as sophisticated as the brain controlling conspiracy you were describing and they are only good for research purposes in our lab."

"Are there any pills to make humans more submissive?" Mark asked. "Or any other ways to induce brain stimulation with other more powerful tools?"

"No, not to my knowledge, if there are any, our lab should have it," Ericson said. "Some people claim the possibility of brain control through hypnosis, but that is controversial."

Hast and Mark looked at each other signaling their surprise at Ericson. They were thinking, 'Why doesn't he mention optogenetics? How can such a high profile neuroscientists not know about optogenetics?!'

Mark thought he had reached a dead end with Prof. Sanders as he seemingly was refusing to give them details on the more exciting and dangerous ways of brain control.

"What about optogenetics?" Mark asked abruptly to surprise the professor.

"Oh! You are right. I totally forgot about that," Ericson said. "Indeed, optogenetics is another way, but how are you aware of it, Mark?"

Mark did not sense any anxiety or confusion on Ericson's face when he asked him the surprise question, so he thought that either Ericson innocently forgot about optogenetics or he was a good liar. "Well Hast and I read about it briefly online before we came. Could you please tell us more about it?"

"Optogenetics is not my specialty," Ericson said, "but basically you induce brain stimulation through pulses of blue light."

"How can neurons be stimulated by a plain blue light?" Hast interjected.

"You cannot normally stimulate neurons with light, however, you can genetically alter them so that they can respond to it," Ericson said.

"And how can you alter them genetically? Through surgery?" he asked.

"No, much simpler," Ericson said. "You can infect neurons by injecting a specific virus which could alter the neurons' genetic composition and make them excitable to the blue light."

Mark knew that they shouldn't appear to Ericson as if they were interrogating him and suspecting him of wrongdoing, but the topic looked so dangerous so he was compelled to ask the next question, "Can you infect humans with this virus through other means, like putting the virus in food or the water supply or even making a bio-weapon from it?"

"No, currently the virus needs to be injected, but scientists could work to change the strain of the virus to make it airborne or waterborne," Ericson said. "But I don't understand why someone would do that because even if you could genetically alter the neurons in the brain, you can't stimulate them directly over the scalp. You would need to make a hole through the cranium and expose the brain tissue."

Hast and Mark thought this information, if true, was very important because it meant that the set of 120 blue light emitters on the outer surface of the helmet may not be intended for brain controlling purposes, however, Mark thought since Kogar was suspecting something unnatural so he needed to be sure.

"I have heard that your lab works closely with the commercial company Virtual-world™," Mark said. "Can you tell me the nature of your lab's cooperation with that company?"

"I don't know too much about that, but they have a lot of engineers who work on the ideas and brain reading technologies developed in our lab to make them suitable for their commercial use," Ericson answered.

"Just out of interest," Mark said, "what are the main goals of your lab?"

Ericson began to sweat when Mark asked this question abruptly, as if he was suspicious about the lab's main intention, nevertheless, he forced himself to stay cool and answer in a normal tone. "Oh, it's all on our website. I thought you had read it. Anyway, our main interest is to scan all the neural connections and their configuration in the human brain and then print them back using a specially designed 3D bio-printing technology developed specifically for printing organic substances," he said. "We are already successful doing this for an insect's brain, but unfortunately we are still far away from being able to scan all the neurons in a human brain."

With this last question answered, Mark and Hast thanked Prof. Sanders for his time and left the building which harbored Ericson's lab.

Chapter 9

After their meeting with Prof. Sanders, Mark and Hast were walking toward another office a few blocks away. The building was one of the branches of the famous gaming company Virtual-world™, and Mark had already made an appointment with the manager there. He had initially made a request to the manager to let him investigate his company's documents to see the detailed commentary behind the blue 120 light emitters and their intended function, but the manager refused to release the classified documents to Mark claiming that they were copyrighted and close source inventions belonging to the company. Mark had made an appeal to Interpol to issue a Red Alert which now forced the manager to comply and release the documents to him. Finally the manager agreed to reveal to him some of the classified documents which showed the process and design of their helmet along with the name of its contributors.

"Do you think Prof. Sanders is involved?" Hast asked Mark while walking along with him toward the Virtual-world™ building.

"It's hard to say. He answered everything in a normal tone, so either he is a good liar or he is telling us the truth," Mark said. "I think he genuinely forgot to tell us about the optogenetics; he didn't intend to hide it from us."

"I thought that too, also, he looks too old and weak to be the Antichrist," Hast said. "That is unless he genetically modifies himself!"

"I bet the real Antichrist would be able to do that," Mark said laughingly.

"Also, he wasn't blind in his left eye," Hast said.

"What! Is that one of his signs?" Mark asked in surprise.

"Yes, some Abrahamic faith sects believe that he is blind in his left eye according to their prophecies."

"Why only some?" Mark asked.

"Different sects of Abrahamic faith have slightly different prophecies about the Antichrist, and even those who believe the blind eye prophecy think it's just metaphorical and what it really means is that the Antichrist is blind to the truth."

"That makes more sense. If the Antichrist is so powerful, he should be able to fix his blindness or at least deceive people for not seeing it," Mark said.

"You are right, and that is why I criticized the recent movie *The Rise of the Antichrist* because its depiction of the Antichrist was very literal and simple minded," Hast said.

Hast and Mark finally arrived at the entrance of the Virtual-world™ building, and they were welcomed by someone waiting for them to direct them to the manager's office.

Meanwhile, Prof. Sanders was in deep thought in his office. 'I should be more careful in the future and I should be careful about what I say in my unencrypted phone and email communications.'

***

John Badu, the current head of Virtual-world™™, had already printed some documents containing classified information about the company's game console designs along with the names and addresses of the contributors. He also put the latest game console on his desk along with the controllers and the suspicious helmet with its 120 blue light emitters on the outer surface. He put it there in case the two visitors asked for it because he wanted to finish the meeting quickly as he had a busy schedule that day. He now heard a knock on his office door.

"Come in, please!" he shouted.

"Hi Mr. Badu," Mark said. "Oh, I see you have already put the products we've been querying on the desk!"

"Yes, I wanted to settle the dispute already," John said.

"Then you know why we are here," Mark said. "So to keep the meeting short, could you tell us who designed the 120 blue light emitters and the details of their function?" Mark asked.

"I know it's strange to say, but to be honest, we don't know the identity of the designer," John said.

"How is that possible?" Mark said.

John exhaled a sigh. "Part of our company's success is because we are using the recently advanced 3D printers which can print anything from your imagination to reality given the necessary materials. We usually invite clever minds to join our online service in which each person is able to give and share his own ideas and designs with us. They need to use our specific software for that purpose because we are then able to translate the ideas designed into reality directly with our 3D printer."

"Do they do that for free?" Mark asked.

"Not always," John said. "We filter out many of the designs and proposals, but the remaining ideas do make it to our final product and for that we transfer some money to their online bank account for their participation, however, many people do it for free. They just like to see their ideas come to reality through our company."

"But you have their profile information. Don't you?" Mark asked.

"Yes, I have printed it here for you on this document. The problem is that their details might not be authentic," John said. "From now on we will be asking for their authentic IDs, but even IDs can be faked."

Mark looked at the list of the names and their design ideas on the document, and he found the name 'Mr. *Young Nimrod*' opposite to the term 'blue light emitters' under the proposal column.

"Do you have more details about this developer?" Mark asked.

"Here are more details," John threw another document which seemed to have a computer generated drawing of the detailed circuitry for the 120 diodes. In the lower part, the details of its designer were listed:

Name: Mr. Young Nimrod
Age: 32
Profession: Inventor
Address: 44 Myfake Road, New Delhi, 212003, India
Email: my45632Account@mail.com

"This address is clearly false!" Mark said.

"I know and I realized that today. Unfortunately, he doesn't respond to our emails," John said. "As I said to date we haven't checked the authenticity of the profiles of our software users. We do have many users having similar accounts, and we plan to be stricter from now on."

"And did he give you his bank account?" Mark asked.

"No, unfortunately he is a free volunteer," John answered.

"And who is responsible for filtering the proposed ideas before publishing?" Mark asked.

"Me," John said, "and I don't understand the technical parts of the design, but I have read the short description and I thought it looked good to have some small blue light emitters on the outer surface of the helmet just for the aesthetics and to make it look more technical. As you know, we are competing with several other companies, and from my experience, customers tend to buy electronic stuff that looks more advanced. I thought a set of 120 blue emitters was a cool idea to make the helmet appear sleeker. Now, I really regret choosing that design for our final product because it has brought a lot of unnecessary suspicion toward me. You really need to believe me."

"Can I please take these documents with me?" Mark said referring to the design and the list of the names.

"Yes, of course," John replied.

Mark didn't sense any abnormal behavior from John to indicate that he was lying or hiding something, though it was hard for him to believe John's story that the main reason for making 120 brain reading sensors emit a blue light was just for aesthetics. This was especially true now that Mark knew that there was a real brain controlling technology which used blue lights in its design, so he decided to inform Interpol to put John and Prof. Sanders on their surveillance and monitor their communications.

Once Mark came out from Virtual-world™ he turned to Hast. "What do you think about John? Did he look to you like the Antichrist?" he said with a humorous voice.

Hast laughed. "He doesn't have the signs of Antichrist, but I didn't believe his story at all."

Chapter 10

Before heading back to the airport, Hast had a tour of Cambridge with Mark and visited some of its ancient landmarks. This was the first time he had visited the city that he had read about on many occasions. When he was training for his English proficiency exams, the name 'Cambridge' frequently popped up in his textbooks and papers, and even when he was researching topics on theology and the history of the Mideast, he frequently came across the name of the prestigious university. It was always in Hast's plans to visit the city someday and today was a great chance for him to kill two birds with one stone.

Hast and Mark were walking back along the King's Parade where the historical buildings of the university could be seen along both sides, the distinct medieval architecture was evident and it was beautifully preserved. On the right side there was the marvelous building of King's Chapel, with its splendid large stained glass windows and its perpendicular Gothic architecture.

After a half hour of strolling and exploring, they came across some nicely situated pubs and restaurants across the river. Some people were resting by the tables and on the chairs set outside. Mark was pointing to the buildings and bridges across the river describing their names and their historical importance to Hast.

"You seem to know a lot about Cambridge! Have you lived here?" Hast asked.

"No, but before working for Interpol, I studied politics at Oxford and I used to visit Cambridge frequently with my friends," Mark said. "Oxford is only a two hour drive from here."

Hast looked to the other side of the river and saw a small wooden bridge across it. Some people were punting beneath it and some were taking pictures on the bridge. "Is this another important landmark?" Hast asked.

"Yes, it's called the 'Mathematical Bridge'. It connects the old and the new site of Queens' College," Mark answered.

"And why is it called the Mathematical Bridge?" Hast asked.

"According to the legend, Sir Isaac Newton himself designed and built the bridge without nuts and bolts. Later, some scholars after him deconstructed the bridge to find out how Newton did it, but they couldn't put it back again without nuts and bolts!" Mark said.

"That is interesting!" Hast said. "I have read some articles about Newton, and he was a great theologian."

"Really?" Mark was surprised.

"Yes, I've read that he was deeply religious and he wrote about theology more than he wrote about physics."

"I didn't know that," Mark said. "My ex-partner did her thesis on Newton's life but she never told me about this side of Newton."

Hast tried to remember the article he read online about Newton and how he came across it. Suddenly he remembered that he had come across the article when he was looking for the prophecies and predictions about Judgement Day. "Oh God! I just remembered that Newton had predicted the date of the Judgement Day from his own calculations," Hast said.

"Interesting, do you remember his predicted date?" Mark asked.

"Not really, but I seem to recall it was two thousand something, but I can't remember exactly," he answered.

"Was it 2012? I remember reading that there was hype and even a blockbuster movie a few decades ago predicting that 2012 would be Doomsday," Mark suggested.

"No, I'm sure that 2012's prediction was not based on Newton's predictions. It was based on the Maya calendar's end date," Hast said.

"Ok, let me call my ex-partner. She lives in Cambridge and we are still good friends. She might know about Newton's predictions," Mark said. Mark took out his mobile, called a number then after few minutes, after talking over the phone, he turned back to Hast.

"We are in luck. She is now at Trinity College and is free to meet us," he said. "You can ask her any question about Newton's life and his prophecies. She's very knowledgeable."

"Is Trinity College far away from here?" he asked.

"No, we just passed it half an hour ago," Mark answered. They both began to walk back toward King's Parade in quick paces to meet with Mark's ex-partner, Kate Gould.

Chapter 11

Kate Gould was waiting in her accommodation room at Trinity College thinking about the call she had just received from her ex-partner. 'Mark said he was with a colleague and had some questions about Newton, but he was never interested enough to ask about Newton before, so why is he suddenly interested now?!' she wondered. 'He didn't tell me who his new colleague was. Could she be a co-worker or maybe his new partner, but why would he want me to meet her? Does he think I'm the jealous kind who cares about him?' she thought to herself as she couldn't believe that Mark was interested in Newton's life.

After a moment, her door buzzer rung and she thought this could be Mark and his colleague arriving. She walked down the stairs and opened the door, and when she saw Mark with another man, she felt a light relief.

"Hi Kate, good to see you. This is my colleague, Hast," Mark said starting the conversation.

Kate and Hast exchanged greetings as Mark introduced them to each other.

"How are you, Kate? It's been a long time since we last met," Mark said.

"I'm great. I'll soon be finishing my PhD and will be going to live with my partner," she said. "He is a very accomplished guy, and he's just bought a new house on the coast…"

"I'm very happy for you," Mark interrupted trying to change the topic. "You might be wondering why we wanted to meet with you."

Mark started to explain to her that his friend, Hast, was also exploring and researching some aspects of Newton's life and had some important unanswered questions. Then Hast asked her about Newton's religious life and his prediction for the date of Judgement Day.

"It's interesting that you ask about it, as this part of Newton's life is not very much explored," she said. "He was a very religious man and was deeply interested in the prophecies of Abrahamic faiths."

"I only know about Newton from physics lectures," Mark said.

"Actually, at his time there was no subject called physics. Newton was an alchemist." She continued, "He is well-known among the physicists because of his scientific works in PRINCIPA and OPTICKS, but other than that, he wrote many more books about theology and Abrahamic faith prophecies."

"It's amazing that he had this deeply religious side, yet we don't find the religious component in his scientific works!" Hast said.

"You are right. My partner also finds that part of my study interesting, and it appears that Newton had a double personality. His writings about science look very different to his writings about theology," she said.

"Like he was possessed by a spirit when writing about the prophecies?" Hast said curiously.

"I'm not sure. Scholars claim that his odd behavior was probably due to his work with chemicals like mercury and their poisonous effect on his brain."

"And what was his prediction about the Apocalypse date?" Hast asked.

"He predicted 2060 to be the end-day," she said.

"2060!" both Hast and Mark repeated loudly.

"You mean this year?" Hast asked fearfully.

Kate was surprised by their reaction. She thought, 'It's just a myth, so why do they look so serious and afraid!'

"Do you know the exact date?" Mark replied.

"Not really, but according to his predictions it's sometime within 2060, but he didn't specify an exact date," she answered.

Both Mark and Hast looked at each other communicating their surprise and wonder.

"Don't worry. It's just a myth, and I don't believe in Doomsday," she said.

"Are there any other specific prophecies by Newton about the Judgement Day?" Hast asked.

"Not that important. In my thesis I didn't explore this part of Newton's work but I can send you some references if you want," she said.

"That would be great," Hast said.

Mark turned to Hast. "Actually, we need to catch the next train to London; otherwise, we will be late to the airport."

Hast gave Kate his email so that she can send the references through, and then they both set out but first thanked Kate profusely for her help.

Hast was terrified to know that Newton's perdition was 2060, the current year! He had always suspected that Doomsday was near, thinking maybe in the next 10 year or so, but he never thought it could be this close! Now he started to think about his wife and his baby, 'I need to protect them. The Antichrist is already here and working behind the scenes. My recent dream, current events, and now Newton's prediction all are happening at the same time! It can't be just a mere coincidence.'

Chapter 12

Mark and Hast headed back to London after their long day of meetings and tour around TNARK's headquarters feeling exhausted. Overall, they felt their quest was not quite fruitful but they might have grabbed the tail of the issue, and they needed to act quickly and take Newton's prediction seriously. Mark tried to hide his cell phone screen from Hast on their way back while he emailed Kogar detailing his conclusions from his tour and telling him that someone called *Young Nimrod* was potentially responsible for the design of the blue light emitters. To his surprise, he received a reply back a few minutes later from Kogar:

Dear Mark,
Thanks for updating me about the investigation. I would like to find about the identity of the 'Mr. Young Nimrod' you mentioned in your email. Please update me with more information about him as soon as you can.
Best,

Hast began to think deeply about what they found in Cambridge and who Mr. *Young Nimrod* could be? 'Is this his real name or just a nickname?' he asked himself. 'I need to find his identity soon.'

"I think there is something wrong," Hast suddenly said.

"What do you think is wrong?" Mark asked.

"I think *Young Nimrod* is just a nickname," Hast said. "It doesn't look like an Indian name. Does it?"

"Of course the address was fake, so the guy could be anywhere on earth," Mark replied.

"Well, not only that. The last name 'Nimrod' has my attention," Hast said.

"Why?" Mark asked. "Is it because the name is mentioned in the holy§cript?"

"Exactly," Hast said, "you seem to recognize that name too."

"Yes, I have heard about it, and it's also the name of a ballistic missile."

"Well, that is because according to Abrahamic faith Nimrod was a great hunter," he said. "Have you heard the story of Abraham and Nimrod?"

"No, what is that all about?" Mark asked.

"Well, this is a long story, but the core of Abrahamic faith is based on this extraordinary historical encounter between Abraham and his nemesis, Nimrod, around 4000 years ago!" he claimed.

"Can you tell me more about it?" Mark said curiously.

***

Hast tried to make himself comfortable on the train chair as he prepared to tell the story he loved the most in the holy§cript to Mark. To him it was the immortal story between a powerful tyrant and a rebellious citizen, and it was the story that had repeated itself many times in history.

Hast's imagination brought him back to his childhood when his father took him to the Erbil museum at the top of Erbil Citadel in Kurdistan, the oldest continuously inhabited town in the world, and the location of the Hanging Gardens, one of the ancient world wonders which was built by the Akkadian king Nebuchadnezzar II for his wife Amytis, the daughter of the Median empire king Cyaxares.

The citadel rested over a mound that was 30 meters high from the ground previously surrounded by a river where the ancient people found an ingenious way to elevate the water to the town over the mound and also to water the garden of trees hanging over the castle. The feat of the technology used to elevate the water was admired by visiting Greeks who described the Ancient Wonder in their books. However, ever since the river drought, the actual location of the Hanging Gardens was confused with other locations in ancient Babylon until recent academics found evidence under the mound of the Citadel along with ancient paintings which were transferred to museums.

On the citadel, the younger Hast had seen a big tablet on the wall representing the glorious dispute between Nimrod and Abraham. Nimrod in the painting had a head of human, a body of a lion and wings of an eagle, a common depiction for ancient gods. In the picture, a group of people bowed to Nimrod, and among the group, a rebellious citizen who would later be known as Abraham, stands still, refusing to bow to the almighty creature.

Nimrod was one of the most known Human-Gods of the ancient world. He ruled the land of Babylon and the northern part of the ancient Mesopotamia. Nimrod was actually a nickname; it meant 'Immortal' in the language of the people who lived in this time. Even today, Kurds in this region put a similarly pronounced term 'Namrdu' after the names of their martyrs to describe them as immortals.

Anyway, Nimrod's real name was Zuhak but people called him Nimrod because his rule lasted 200 years according to the legends. This had re-enforced the belief that he was a god. Ancient people thought he was immortal and they used to make human sacrifices for him. Their anthem was 'no life without sacrifice' and their flag was two strips. The upper strip was colored red to denote 'sacrifice' and the lower strip was colored green to denote 'life'.

The reason why people volunteered to sacrifice for their Human-Gods was to keep the civilization from falling apart. Kings like Nimrod who declared himself a god needed devout followers to fight for him and to keep his empire expanding and sustainable. The ancient proverb says: 'Ask for more to get the least.' If you convince people to sacrifice for you in peace, they will definitely sacrifice for you in war. Human-Gods who ruled the ancient world knew this trick, and the unity of large empires and civilizations would not survive without devout followers ready to sacrifice for their king. Sacrifices and pure devotion to a higher power made the ancient empires work like a single unit where the king was the head and people were the body.

According to the legend, one day Nimrod met a winged person, and he thought it was an archangel from another star. The archangel called himself 'Son of the Morning', and he urged Nimrod to ask the people of his kingdom to gather and bow to him at least once every day saying to Nimrod that it was the time for him to transcend and follow the path of the other great gods on the other stars.

The next day, people were urged to gather in front of the gate of Babylon tower to pledge their allegiance to Nimrod and bow to him. People were facing their king who was sitting on highly placed, massively decorated, golden throne. The more inferior they felt toward Nimrod, the more superior and godly Nimrod felt of himself. His minister, Haran, stood before Nimrod, and he was the first to bow in front of him. The people in the first row began to bow for Nimrod after him then the next row and so on, showing their ultimate obedience.

Seeing the huge crowd bowing in front of him and showing their submission had a thrilling effect on Nimrod. He felt he was transcending, he opened both his arms and faced upward toward the sky feeling his ultimate power over the other earthly creatures, the humans. He was the immortal who controlled the life and death of humans. He controlled their feelings, their happiness, their sadness, and a single word from his majesty was enough to get anything done in his kingdom. Now it was the time for his kingdom to expand to heaven and for his body to transcend to its immortal god mode.

Nimrod closed his eyes waiting for the miracle to happen, the miracle promised to him by the archangel. Moments passed and nothing happened. He thought, 'Why am I still on earth? Why am I still on the same level as these low level mortals, the humans! Why am I not God yet?'

That moment when he was deep in his godly thoughts, Nimrod heard loud shouting coming from the crowd beneath him. Someone was using a disturbing phrase he was never used to hearing.

"YOU ARE NOT MY GOD…"

Nimrod opened his eyes to see what was happening, but again, he heard the same unsettling voice coming somewhere down from the bowing crowd.

"YOU ARE NOT MY GOD!" said the shouting voice.

Nimrod looked down into the crowd and saw someone standing among the bowing crowd. He gave an angry look to Haran who was still bowing before him, the bowing minister stood up quickly as he got the gist from his angry king. He looked down to the crowd, and to his shock, he saw a low level citizen standing and refusing to bow to Nimrod! This action was enough to justify being tortured and given a death penalty, but in this situation, the rebel needed to be humiliated among the people first! That is what Haran thought to himself.

Nimrod's pride and his sense of highness prevented him from directly confronting the low level citizen, so Haran himself shouted to Abraham, "Bow to your god now or you will face death."

Abraham's response to Haran was, "I only bow to the true god, ∞Illuhim∞. He is the one who controls life and death. Nimrod is just a man. Like us, he eats, sleeps, defecates, and one day he will die just like everyone," Abraham shouted loudly from below toward Nimrod to make sure everyone heard him defying Nimrod.

The gathered people were deeply moved by the extraordinary courage displayed by their fellow citizen. They felt a thrill pounding in their hearts for the first time as they witnessed the possibility of the impossible, the possibility of standing against Nimrod, the great God of Babylon. People looked up to Nimrod and all they saw was an angry Human-God clenching his teeth from rage! Then they looked to Abraham who was standing firm; they saw their next god, the god who was born among them and had the courage to express what was in their hearts without any fear. In their subconscious they learnt a vital lesson; a normal citizen can become a god too!

That moment Nimrod felt he was descending instead of transcending and killing and torturing Abraham wouldn't solve the problem. His status had already been shaken among the people; Nimrod felt the need to prove himself, so he stood up from his golden throne finally, and for the first time shouted directly to his people. "I'm your God, I'm Nimrod the Immortal, and I control your life and your death." He said to remind the people of his power and his dominion over them.

"Only ∞Illuhim∞ controls life and death," Abraham challenged Nimrod.

That moment Nimrod ordered his minister, Haran, to bring to him two prisoners. He ordered the execution of one of the prisoners and freed the other, and then he looked down to

Abraham and the crowds, proudly shouting, "Now tell me, was ∞Illuhim∞ controlling the life and death of these two prisoners or I?"

People turned to Abraham awaiting his response. Abraham thought for a moment then posed to Nimrod another challenge, "∞Illuhim∞ brings the sun from east, so if you have his power, bring it from the west."

The crowd of people turned to Nimrod awaiting his next move. They still believed in him so much they were actually expecting him to win the challenge, but all they saw was a furious Nimrod shouting at Abraham and threatening him with torture and death. Then moments passed and Nimrod challenged Abraham back, "If you are proclaiming the truth, ask your ∞Illuhim∞ to bring the sun from the west now."

Abraham closed his eyes and lifted his hand to the sky praying to ∞Illuhim∞ for a while, and then he looked back to Nimrod. "My Lord ∞Illuhim∞ has told me that he can bring the sun from the west now, but if he does, the world will be destroyed. ∞Illuhim∞ is a loving God and cares about his people, unlike you. He doesn't want to harm his creations, so he will only do that when the Judgment Day comes, and when that day comes, right and wrong will be revealed and you will be burnt in his hellfire forever."

Nimrod ordered his army to throw Abraham into a big fire to imitate the hellfire that Abraham threatened him with, but according to the legend, Abraham was later saved. The impact of his encounter with Nimrod was very big on the people of Babylon. People started to lose faith in Nimrod, and rebellious groups began to appear in the towns and villages holding a new flag that had the same two strips red and green but now with the symbol of a sun at its center. This was the sun that Nimrod had failed to control, and the new flag became the symbol of freedom. People who held this flag couldn't be controlled by Nimrod.

Nimrod eventually lost his power and he was ultimately defeated of his rule of 200 years by Kawa, a young blacksmith who led a rebellious group to Nimrod's final defeat. The day of his defeat was labeled as the new day for freedom and it is still celebrated in the region as the Feast of Newroz.

Abraham's ideological revolution demarked an end for the Human-God period. People from the surrounding empires started to revolt against their tyrants. Moses revolted against the Pharaoh, Zoroaster revolted against Cyrus, and Hercules against Zeus. The next stage of revelation began and people all around the world were united under the name of one God, ∞Illuhim∞.

****

Hast felt his story was making an impact on Mark, however, he still needed to make his point as to why he was telling this story and what its relevance was to their mission.

"Is it true that Abraham tried to sacrifice his son to ∞Illuhim∞?" Mark suddenly asked.

"People are always making this mistake because of their literal interpretation of the holy§cript," Hast said. "As you know ancient people used to make sacrifices for their Human-Gods. This was a very common practice around the world then. After all, look at the history of the Mayan empire, Egyptian empire, etc. They all made human sacrifices, and this was part of human culture at that time. People in certain regions still use sacrifice related terms in their language! For example, where I am from, we use the term 'Qurbant bim' which means 'I will be your sacrifice' to express gratitude or love toward someone," Hast said. "Regarding Abraham's intended sacrifice of his son, my guess is that when people began to worship ∞Illuhim∞ instead of Nimrod, they probably asked Abraham how they could make a sacrifice to ∞Illuhim∞ to express their gratitude toward him. It's true at that moment Abraham took his own son to be sacrificed, but then he sacrificed a goat instead and told people that ∞Illuhim∞ didn't need human sacrifices anymore. Animal sacrifices were sufficient for him."

"So does that mean ∞Illuhim∞ needs animal sacrifices?" Mark asked.

"No, not at all," Hast said. "People tend to understand things step-by-step and that is why ∞Illuhim∞ reveals the truth about himself slowly. All I'm saying is that if we don't take things literally, and if we understand the culture back then, it will become clear for us that Abraham didn't sacrifice his beloved son. Instead, he freed us from human sacrifices and introduced animal sacrifices. It's now our responsibility to take Abraham's revolution further and free animals too from unnecessary sacrifices."

Mark found Hast's claims about the god who reveals himself in steps intriguing. "I have recently read a psychology book, and it claims that our brains are prediction tools. We tend to understand and see things that we can predict. If our brains cannot predict or comprehend something, it fails to see it even if it was all around us," Mark said. "So do you think that we are unable to see ∞Illuhim∞ or comprehend his actions because our brain fails to predict it?"

"Yes, that is what I meant," Hast said. "I don't think ancient people who worshiped Human-Gods were wrong at their time because that is probably what ∞Illuhim∞ wanted them to do. God reveals himself to us from inside ourselves, and as time passes, our perception and understanding of him improves. First we thought God was a powerful king who needed human sacrifices, but then our perception of God advanced. We began to think that God was a powerful being in the sky, and he only needed animal sacrifice. Now our understanding has changed further and we started to think that God as an omnipotent spiritual entity that is everywhere and doesn't need any sacrifices, and some Abrahamic sects even believe that God himself made a sacrifice for us not the other way around."

"I love the symmetry in your description," Mark said smiling.

At that moment the train arrived at Heathrow Airport, and they left the train and checked in for their flight tickets. Mark was set to go back to Interpol headquarters in Lyon, and Hast was returning to Erbil.

"I think I understood your point from the story," Mark said before departing from Hast. "You think Mr. *Young Nimrod* is someone who admires Nimrod and tries to imitate him."

"That is what I think," Hast said. "In fact many theology scholars believe that Nimrod himself was the first Antichrist."

"I get your point even clearer now. You think Mr. *Young Nimrod* could be the last Antichrist then?" Mark said.

"That is what I fear," Hast answered.

"Let's keep each other informed. I will try to look up this name in our database at Interpol headquarters."

Then they both shook hands and went their separate ways.

Chapter 13

It was midnight when Hast arrived home. En route, he couldn't stop thinking about the *Young Nimrod*. 'What a dangerous time we are in,' he kept thinking to himself. His wife, Nergz, was holding the baby in her arms as he arrived. He took the baby from her and held him in his lap kissing the baby's forehead.

Hast had first met Nergz at college when he was studying theology eight years ago and she was studying history. They met for the first time in the library when they were both looking for a book titled *The Prophecies of Abrahamic Faith*, and since they bumped into each other while looking for the same book, they began to talk about it and soon realized there were so many similarities between them. It was as if they shared the same mind. Later on, Hast found that Nergz had the same views as him in regard to the end-days. Like Hast, she thought the Judgment Day was close and all the minor signs had already come true. The two like-minded people soon decided to develop their relationship to marriage.

After his arrival from the long journey, Hast knew that Nergz was eager to hear his news, so he first took a quick shower then came back to the bed holding the baby, the little Abraham, in his lap and kissing the baby's forehead again. "I'm sorry my little angel. You are growing up in a very hard time," he said in sorrow.

"What is happening? Is Doomsday close?" Nergz asked Hast.

Hast always felt that Nergz had a strong intuition about things, and when she felt something was going to happen she was always right. It was as if her brain had developed a sixth sense to predict danger. 'If she thinks the Antichrist is close, then the end-days are close,' Hast thought.

"A portable nuclear bag is missing and someone calling himself *Nimrod* is already working behind the scenes," he said.

"Is he planning to ignite the third world war?" Nergz asked.

"Yes, I think so. The political tension between all the major powers is at its peak. Russia and USA are blaming each other over the missing nuclear bomb. All the European countries are now in conflict with Russia, and the current economic breakdown is threatening their union. North Korea already claims to possess nuclear power and is threatening the USA with it if dares to attack. The Mideast is in total chaos, and the polarizations between the West and East is like never before. It will only take a small step to ignite the next world war," Hast said.

"The Antichrist thrives on chaos," Nergz said. "The survival instinct will urge people to seek safety, and they will be vulnerable to anyone providing them with hope. The Antichrist will be the only one who can provide them with this hope but it will be a false hope."

"His power is mind control," Hast said. "So he takes advantage of anything. Technology is now so powerful that scientists are able to control the brain directly and there are several ways to do so. I think the Antichrist is already using some of these techniques."

"Do you think the Antichrist is a scientist working for TNARK?" she asked.

"I think so; I wonder what you think?" Hast asked trying to get his wife's opinion.

"I tend to think that the Antichrist is a famous person who has a lot of followers," Nergz said. "He might use scientists to achieve his goals though."

"A famous person! You mean like a singer, movie star or even a religious preacher?" Hast asked.

"Or a corrupt politician who tells a lot of lies and is able to convince a lot of people," Nergz replied.

"I would guess he is a charismatic person, smart with mind controlling abilities and people tend to follow him," he suggested.

"According to the prophecies, he can also heal people from diseases," Nergz reminded Hast.

"Like a doctor or a scientist?" Hast queried.

"Or like a faith-healer," Nergz suggested.

Hast suddenly felt he caught the tail of an important clue after hearing the word 'faith-healer'.

"You are right! How did I forget that!" Hast said. "Faith-healers are the best candidates for becoming the Antichrist, since many of them are charismatic religious preachers with lots of devout followers."

"And the scientist who is helping him could be the false prophet," she suggested. "However, a faith-healer can only be the Antichrist if he declares himself to be God. Are there any faith-healers demanding their followers to worship them instead of ∞Illuhim∞?"

Hast found her suggestion really good, so he opened his laptop and entered 'faith-healers' into the search engine. He found a Wiki page detailing the meaning of the faith-healing and countless many other pages, however, what caught his attention was an article by BBC News on their news page. This piece was published one week ago and it was about a faith-healer in India who was able to heal any cancer within a short period without any complications!

Although by 2060 scientists had found radical treatments for many cancers with 80% survival rate, patients still had to undergo a tedious protocol of chemotherapy for years and still suffered from its side effects before they could be cured completely. The BBC article claimed that the faith-healer's healing rate was 100% and without any side effects. This was something beyond conventional medical science at the time! Hast began to read in more detail about the faith-healer. His name was 'Padsha Mali' and he was 55 years old from a small town near New Delhi. When Hast entered the faith-healer's name into the search engine, he found many results about him. Seemingly, he was already famous and there was even a Wiki a page about him.

"Wow, this guy is really famous and can heal cancer," Hast said to Nergz showing her the articles and pages he found about Padsha Mali.

"Look at his Facebook, Twitter, and Zanzor pages! He has more than one million followers already! I have never seen such popularity for a faith-healer," Hast said admiringly while peeking through the posts. "Oh, my God! He is even blind in his left eye!" he said while browsing through his images.

"What does he mainly preach about in his social media pages?" Nergz asked.

Hast begun to read through some of his page posts and the videos made about him "He seems like a devout follower of Abrahamic faith. In most of his posts he asks people to return to their true God, ∞Illuhim∞!"

"We don't know what is in his heart," Nergz said. "He may be trying to gain people's affection by healing their loved ones and preaching for Abrahamic faith. He might show his true face once many people fall under his spell," Nergz said.

"You are right. After all, his main power is mind control," Hast continued. "But how come I haven't heard about him before?"

"Maybe he became famous recently, or maybe he just recently got his cancer healing powers," Nergz suggested.

Hast looked at the news articles from the BBC and the information on the faith-healer's Wiki page. They stated that Padsha Mali had realized his cancer healing powers just a few months ago!

"Wow! According to these articles, the news about this guy only got viral recently!" Hast said.

"This means his followers and his fame will increase even more in the upcoming months," she said.

Then out of interest, Hast put the combination of words 'Padsha Mali, the Antichrist' into the search engine, and to his surprise, he found several posts from writers and bloggers claiming that Padsha Mali could be the Antichrist!

"Wow! There are other people like us who suspect him of potentially being the Antichrist," Hast said.

"This looks clear cut," Nergz said. "I suspect something is tricky going on!"

Hast always hated the literal interpretations of the holy§cript and its prophecies, but this time the signs of the Antichrist were so evident in Padsha Mali and everything matched so well with literal interpretations of the holy§cript. Hast hated to admit this but how could the signs of the Antichrist be so simply evident and yet people were being deceived and were following him!

"Everyone following Abrahamic faith will be able to tell he is the Antichrist if he ever declares himself as a god," Hast said. "I wonder how can he deceive us?!"

"Isn't his power in mind control?" Nergz reminded Hast.

***

The next day, Hast dialed Mark's number to tell him what he had found, and after four beeps a voice answered.

"Hello."

"Hi Mark, I think I know who Mr. *Young Nimrod* might be," Hast claimed. "He is a famous faith-healer living in a small town near New Delhi, and his name is Padsha Mali."

"How can you be so sure?" Mark asked.

"His physical features match exactly with the prophecies. We need to go there and make sure that he truly has these extraordinary healing powers," Hast said. "If he is truly healing cancer, then I suspect he is the guy we are looking for!"

Chapter 14

Bakir was a 28 year old man who worked as an accountant for a small private company, and his life had changed one year ago when his 61 year old mother was diagnosed with stage four inflammatory breast cancer with wide spread metastasis to her lungs. The condition has made her breathing eventually more and more difficult, and it was as if she was gradually drowning, even a slight exertion made her suffer from breathlessness. She endured all her chemotherapy sessions, but unfortunately there was no response. Her cancer was out of control, but Bakir didn't give up and took her to many doctors, but they all told him that her cancer was unfortunately among the most aggressive breast cancers and the survival rate was very low. At her stage of the disease, it was not curable and all they could do for her was to give her pain killers to alleviate her pain and suffering. She would also need to be admitted to the hospital to administer oxygen everytime when she had attacks of breathlessness. Bakir had to move to live with his old, diseased mother to take care of her; after all, he was her only son.

    This was now Bakir's new life. He took his mother at least twice a week to the hospital because she was having sudden attacks of shortness of breath due to the accumulation of a fluid around her lungs (pleural effusion). The accumulated fluid in her chest made her feeling choked unless the fluid was drained out by a doctor, the process called thoracentesis, however, the relief only lasted for a few days and the problem returned.

    The frequency of her breathless attacks increased with time, and her son started to skip work because of her. As a result the company he was working for fired him because his numerous absences.

Bakir's mother realized that her son no longer went to work and she saw the distress on his face grow by the day.

"Why are you not going to the work?" his mother said to Bakir.

"Don't worry mother. I'm on a paid leave for three months, and I can be with you now all the time," he said smiling to her trying to hide the facts. He thought telling her the truth would only make her sad and worsen her condition.

The mother felt she was a burden on her son and she wished to die, but because of her religious beliefs she couldn't commit suicide. "I wish I could die soon so that you can enjoy the rest of your holidays," she said.

"Don't say that, mother!" he said. "I can't enjoy the holiday without you."

The next night at 3:00 a.m., Bakir's mother had another acute attack of breathlessness, so he took her to the emergency ward again, but this time a young junior doctor seemed to be in charge. He looked like he had recently graduated from the college of medicine and appeared inexperienced. When the junior doctor examined Bakir's mother, he was hesitant to act. He made some calls and consultations before he came back to Bakir and his breathless mother.

"I'm sorry for this, but I haven't done thoracentesis alone before, so to be safe, I have called a senior doctor to come and assist. He will be here shortly," the junior doctor said.

Moments passed, and Bakir felt his mother was deteriorating so he urged the junior doctor to do something. The junior doctor put on a pair of gloves and took some antiseptics with a large bore needle and a catheter and tried to empty the fluid in her lung alone. He demarcated the site of the needle insertion, before he advanced his hand began to shake. 'I can do it. I have done everything correctly according to the textbook,' he recited to himself to increase his confidence but then his courage left him.

"I can't do it alone!" the junior doctor said. "There is a risk I might induce a pneumothorax, which is dangerous and could take her life, so I think it's better to wait until the senior doctor arrives," he said.

When Bakir's mother heard the words 'pneumothorax take life,' she looked at her son's face who looked very tired, pale, and lifeless at the same time! 'My son needs to enjoy his holidays. I'm burden on everyone,' she thought before looking at the other patients around her. 'They deserve more attention than me. I'm of no use. I'm just a burden and pain to others. The pneumothorax could take my life and I would not remain a burden,' she said to herself. She hinted at the junior doctor trying to tell him her thoughts, but her voice didn't come out. 'I need that pneumothorax. Please give it to me, as it's the best cure, not only for me but for everyone.' At that moment she thought of an idea. She could commit suicide without doing it by herself, and this way she was not violating the commands of the holy§cript! She began exacerbating her symptoms hoping the junior doctor would try and give her the cure she wanted. She started to pretend she was choking and gasping to death. The junior doctor realized the need to act immediately, so he collected all his courage and inserted the needle straight forward into the patient's lung with the hope he had done it correctly. A moment later a sigh of relief came to him as he saw the watery fluid was coming through the needle to the catheter powering it into the collecting bladder. Her vital signs and the oxygen concentration started to come back to normal ranges again.

"That is great. I have done it successfully," the junior doctor said smiling.

"Thanks a lot doctor," Bakir said with relief as he watched his mother starting to breathe again at a normal pace.

Bakir's mother shed a tear of sorrow as she thought, 'I haven't got the cure I needed today.'

***

A few weeks later, Bakir saw the news article on the BBC about a faith-healer called Padsha Mali who could cure cancer effortlessly and he was only 200 miles away from Bakir's town. Without a second thought, he took his mother to the faith-healer in the next day. When Bakir arrived, he saw a huge crowd of people from all races queueing before the faith-healer's house. Because his mother seemed so unwell, the guards who were registering people's names and arranging the queue gave Bakir's mother a quick pass; otherwise, Bakir could have waited days for his mother's turn to come!

During the meeting, the faith-healer told Bakir's mother to lie down on the ground. He then put his hands into a bucket of water while reciting words from the holy§cript before scrubbing his wet hands on her face. Once finished he looked toward Bakir. "It is not me who is healing her, it's ∞Illuhim∞, and you should be thankful to him not to me," he said.

A few days later, the miracle happened. Bakir's mother walked up the stairs without feeling breathless, and she started to get better day-by-day. One month later, her x-ray results showed shrinking tumors in her chest. The doctor who was following her case was speechless after examining her medical tests. No chemotherapy he had used before could do such amazing work without hurting the patient! It became clear to Bakir that his normal life was now back, thanks to ∞Illuhim∞ and Padsha Mali's blessed hands.

***

The following week after the good news about his mother's shrinking tumors, Bakir went to a fast food restaurant to have a quick sandwich during his lunch break. He heard two voices behind him talking about the rising faith-healer, Padsha Mali.

"Did you hear about Padsha Mali?" one guy said.

"Yes, I've heard about him, and what is wrong with the social media these days? I keep seeing posts and videos about him and many of the posts are sponsored!" the second guy wondered.

"That is because he looks exactly like the Antichrist! He is blind in his left eye and has a reddish face and frowned eyebrows!" the first guy replied.

"But he doesn't claim to be God," the second guy said. "He himself is a devout preacher of Abrahamic faith."

"I guess he is trying to control our emotions through curing diseases and preaching for Abrahamic faith. I saw a viral post yesterday, and someone had taken a close shot of Padsha Mali's face. The wrinkles on his forehead show the figure of triple 6s in Hebrew!"

"Wow!" the second guy responded.

Bakir bit his lips from rage while listening to them as he really wanted to punch them in the face as hard as he could.

"I really pity those who follow this faith-healer," the voice behind him continued. "They have to be very ignorant of Abrahamic faith to not know the signs of the Antichrist!"

That was the straw which broke the camel's back. Bakir stood up and turned to the two guys grabbing their table. He lifted it and turned it upside down so that everything was thrown on the floor. Angrily he shouted, "If you suffered from cancer you would understand the truth better."

Other people in the restaurant grabbed Bakir from behind and tried to calm him down.

Chapter 15

Sardar, Hast's brother, who had recently started practicing medicine, didn't believe that prayers had any effect. He believed that most faith-healers were either deceiving people or ignorant about what they were dealing with. Most of the patients identified as being 'possessed' by these faith-healers do not have a real physical disease. According to Sardar and many other doctors, these patients are usually suffering from psychological problems known as conversion and dissociative disorders. The afflicted patients usually had emotional problems which they usually do not want to declare or which reside in their subconscious. Their brains would then present the emotional problem in a form of a physical disability which could then be treated by controlling or coping with the original emotional problem residing in their subconscious.

The problem is those patients are seeking emotional care by their relatives or close friends and this is how the supposed faith-healers take advantage. They label the patients as having a possessed spirit and this makes others pity the patient and not hold them responsible for their behaviors. This is exactly what a patient with a conversion disorder wants and finds it comforting. Sardar usually tried to explain this point to his brother to demonstrate for him why a conversion disorder is sometimes responsive to faith-healing giving a fake impression that there is something supernatural about faith-healing.

Sardar remembered his first time in the Emergency ward when he was having his first night shift. On that evening, a 17 year old boy who was presumably unconscious and brought to the ER by his parents. Sardar immediately checked the boy's pulse rate and all the other vital signs they were all normal, then he sent out for blood and sugar tests and they all returned normal. Sardar asked the mother whether the boy had experienced any emotional problems recently. The mother said that yesterday his son had a major argument with his father. To Sardar, this looked like a typical case of a conversion disorder. Here he had a young patient with a healthy medical history and normal medical tests which ruled out any physical disease.

However, the boy's father denied that his son's problem was emotional and due to the argument they had, so he started to accuse Sardar of misdiagnosis. Sardar tried to explain to the father that he didn't blame his son's condition on him.

"Your son has a conversion disorder. I can refer him to a psychiatrist so that he can be treated properly," Sardar said to the father.

"Are you saying my son is crazy?" the father asked in an angry voice.

Sardar realized that he was talking to a very ignorant man so he gave up the case but warned the father that if didn't take his son to a psychiatrist to receive proper treatment and advice, his son's unconscious episodes would be repeated every time he encountered emotional distress.

What made Sardar's frustration even more was when he realized that the father had taken his son to a faith-healer instead of a psychiatrist. He figured this out a couple of weeks later when his brother, Hast, brought him a recorded video of a local faith-healer called Mam Jameel who was residing in a nearby town to Erbil. In the videos Mam Jameel was showcasing the treatment of some patients he claimed they were 'possessed', and to Sardar's surprise, one of the patients was the same the 17 year old boy. Again, the boy seemed to lie unconscious in front of the faith-healer. In the video, the faith-healer was reciting some words with smoke all around him and the boy's body began to shake. After a few minutes, he woke up, fully conscious again. His father profusely thanked the faith-healer for saving his son from the bad spirit.

Sardar heard the father saying in the video that he had taken his son to so many doctors and none of them were able to diagnose what was wrong with his son. "I believe this was a bad spirit who possessed my son's body and now God has shown us this miracle through your blessed hands," the father said in the video.

Sardar facepalmed himself while watching the video thinking 'if conversion disorder still has such a big impact on re-enforcing superstition in the twenty first century, then how big was its effect in the ancient times?' Nevertheless, Sardar himself was baffled by how responsive patients with conversion disorder were to the suggestions of a faith-healer. In the video, there was another young girl who was mute but started to talk immediately after the faith-healer recited his magic words over her, and there was another man claiming recent deafness but who started to hear again after the faith-healing. For Sardar, conversion disorder looked like a functional brain disorder which was hard wired specifically to be cured by faith-healing!

He thought that in the ancient times humans lived in small communities and societies; their size could have ranged from hundreds to thousands. If there was a conflict or a war among them, then bigger communities with larger sizes had better chances of winning and survival. However, larger communities would not have been possible if they hadn't had a strong leader. A strong leader would not have been possible if people hadn't seen their leaders as gods. People would not have seen their leaders as gods if they hadn't possessed faith-healing powers, and hence, conversion disorders helped to create the illusion of some having supernatural or godly powers!

So in short, the genes that produced this weird disorder re-enforced superstition among people and the latter had a greater survival value at least in the ancient times; this was Sardar's thoughts about this psychological disorder which was commonly depicted as exorcism. So for Sardar, the whole situation was like a conspiracy imposed upon them by Mother Nature.

On the contrary, Hast thought conversion disorder was a sign that Mother Nature herself wanted us to adopt religion and believe in God! "There are countless ways for Mother Nature to evolve something that promoted unity among humans, so why would she choose superstition to do that?" he asked.

"Maybe, that was the easiest," Sardar answered.

"No, I think Nature wants us to believe in something higher than ourselves, and superstition was the first step for us to realize that there was something supernatural about the universe. This is how ∞Illuhim∞ has revealed himself to us," Hast said.

***

Sardar hated conversion disorder a lot, not only because it was the main tool in the hands of faith-healers, but he also thought that the disorder was no longer useful for human survival. He remembered one of his night shifts alone in the emergency ward. It was on a night he was exhausted after treating more than ten serious cases. His last case was a young 19 year old girl. She was brought to the ER by her friend, and she was unconscious. Sardar checked her vital signs and they were all normal. There was no serious neurological signs like pupil dilatation or an increase in her reflexes. Her friend said that the young girl had caught her boyfriend cheating on her today and she felt upset. She arrived at the friend's house in tears and moments later fell unconscious. To Sardar, this was a typical case of conversion disorder again, an emotional problem presenting itself as a functional neurological problem. He thought about sending her for an MRI scan to be extra sure and exclude any possibility of a real neurological problem, but after hearing the story from her friend, he became certain that this case was just another conversion disorder and sending for an MRI was not necessary, but he decided to keep her under observation for a while. After all, a doctor's job was to filter out serious diseases from non-serious ones and send only the needy patients for further expensive medical investigations; otherwise, the MRI queue would pile up unnecessarily.

To his horror, one hour later, the young unconscious girl started vomiting and showing signs of a serious underlying neurological problem. When Sardar finally sent her for a brain scan, it turned out that she had a ruptured brain aneurysm, a life threatening condition. Unfortunately, she didn't survive the resuscitation. The hospital's administration didn't blame Sardar for mismanagement because the disease was known to be hard to diagnose and manage and its mortality rate was high, but Sardar's feeling of guilt was immense for not taking her case seriously from the beginning. 'If there were no conversion disorders, I would have taken the girl's unconsciousness more seriously from the start,' he thought. It became clear to him that conversion disorder was now doing more harm than good. 'Stupid, blind Nature has invented a disorder without realizing its harmful long term consequences.' From that moment on, he hated both conversion disorders and faith-healing holding them responsible for spreading superstition and deception.

***

Like everyone else, Sardar recently came across the news about the rising faith-healer in New Delhi who could heal patients with end stage cancer within a short period of time without any complications just by reciting the holyScript and using some sort of a holy water. Sardar couldn't believe that initially, but as he looked online further it became clear to him that many of the patients the celebrated faith-healer had treated were verified cancer cases. 'How could this be possible!' he thought to himself, 'There must be something tricky going on.'

Chapter 16

A week after reading the BBC article, Hast made his next lengthy flight from Erbil international Airport and met Mark again but this time in New Delhi, India, one of the greenest capitals in the world. Upon their arrival at Padsha Mali's location in a small town south of the city, they saw a long line of people in front of a building which looked like a recently built holy☼house. Guards and many staff members were standing around its doors taking names and regulating the meetings with the world renowned faith-healer, Padsha Mali.

In the queue people from all races and backgrounds, rich people, poor people, and even some high profile people all could be seen as they spoke different languages and wore different clothes. The locals in this small town started getting upset from the sudden surge of people from around the world coming to their town. Hotels were filled so some patients were sleeping on the pavements near Padsha Mali's holy☼house or staying in the queue for days. Mark pretended to have cancer so that he and Hast could meet with the faith-healer in person. After registering his name in the queue and waiting for two days, their turn had finally come. Mark went on to lay down and let the faith-healer scrub his face with his wet hands and read passages from the holy§cript. When he finished, both Hast and Mark came out of the building and Mark showed Hast a small tube with some water inside it.

"What is that?" Hast asked.

"I stole it from the small bucket that Padsha Mali immersed his hands," Mark said.

"So sneaky! I didn't see you do that," Hast said.

"That is what I'm trained to do," Mark said.

"So do you think there is something in the water that cures cancer?" Hast asked.

"I don't know but I have a friend who is a genius biochemist. Her lab works on finding better cures for cancer so she might find something in this water," Mark said.

Before coming to New Delhi, Mark remembered Dr. Aabha, a previous friend of his at Oxford University. She was a clever biochemist working on finding new treatments for cancer. Fortunately, Mark realized that she had travelled back to New Delhi and he thought this would be a good opportunity to visit her and ask her opinion on the faith-healer's abilities. 'She most have heard about Padsha Mali and must be frustrated that a faith-healer was doing a better job than her right now,' Mark thought to himself.

Hast and Mark took a train to New Delhi to meet with Dr. Aabha and test the water sample in her lab.

"What do you think about Padsha?" Mark asked Hast while on their way to New Delhi.

"Well, I don't like the literal interpretations of the holy§cript, but this man looks exactly like the Antichrist of my nightmares," Hast said. "However, since he doesn't claim that he is God I still can't say he is the Antichrist."

"Do you think he is planning to have more followers before declaring himself as God?" Mark said.

"That is what I fear," Hast replied.

"If he looks so obviously like the Antichrist of your prophecies, how do you think he could deceive people into worshiping him?" Mark asked.

"That is what I ask myself too, as no one following Abrahamic faith will fall for this fraud if he declares himself as a god," Hast said.

"But if he is the *Young Nimrod*, then maybe he is trying to use optogenetics to control people's minds," Mark guessed.

"That is what I fear," Hast said.

***

After a half hour they arrived at Dr. Aabha's lab, and after the initial greetings, she took the water sample from Mark eagerly and asked them to wear a special lab coat if they wanted to come to the lab and take a look while she tested the water.

"It will take only a couple hours," she said.

"That is quick! I thought it would take days," Mark said.

"We are in 2060 not 2050 anymore. Things are much faster," Dr. Aabha replied.

"Then, I think we will wait outside till you finish," Mark said as he felt too lazy to change his clothes and wear all the gloves, head covers, and plastic coats.

A few minutes later, Mark received a phone call. He apologized to Hast and went to an isolated corridor and talked for around 10 minutes with someone called Agent Roger from Interpol. The agent informed Mark that Prof. Sanders seemed to have changed his communication habits suddenly after their last meeting with him, and it appeared as though he was hiding something! Mark asked the agent to monitor Ericson Sanders and his secretary more closely. After the phone call, he came back to Hast.

The laboratory building had a nice cafeteria near the reception so Hast and Mark decided to have a drink while waiting for the results. After waiting for two hours Dr. Aabha came out from the lab very excited as if she had discovered something very important!

"You can't believe what I found in the water!" she said. "A genetically modified virus that selectively attacks cancer cells." Dr. Aabha showed them an image of two slides showing two clusters of cells. One cluster was composed of normal cells and the other cluster was cancerous cells. When a drop of the water which contained the genetically modified virus was added, the virus attacked and destroyed the cancerous cells while leaving the normal cells unharmed.

Dr. Aabha herself was working to develop a type of immunotherapy against cancerous cells by artificially selecting the T-cells outside the human body. She was trying to induce random mutations in these immunity cells then selecting those which were attracted selectively to the cancer cells but not the normal cells. Her latest results were quite good, but it was in no way as good as this virus which seemed to have been genetically engineered to perfection to attack the cancerous cells only.

"I have read most of the recently published scientific papers and have never found anyone talking about this virus." She added, "This is something completely new and revolutionary, so how come a faith-healer has had access to such technology?"

"Maybe he is a scientist," Hast said.

"From our investigations, we couldn't find any information that Padsha Mali had received any higher education. He was pretty much a normal faith-healer and only recently obtained this cancer healing ability," Mark said.

"Then maybe another scientist is helping him," Hast suggested.

After a period of discussion with Dr. Aabha about why a scientist would hide such an impressive invention and only reveal it through faith healing, Hast was pretty much sure about an answer he believed in; Mark didn't want to reveal more information in front of Dr. Aabha. They thanked her for her help and then went out for a walk to discuss the implications of their findings.

"Why did you think a scientist is helping Padsha Mali?" Mark asked Hast as they came out from Aabha's lab.

"Well, I've thought that the false prophet is an AI-robot who works under the Antichrist's command to lure people toward the deception, but now I think the false prophet could be a scientist who is helping Padsha Mali, the Antichrist, to lure people into loving him and believing in him through cancer healing," Hast claimed.

"So in this case *Young Nimrod* could be the scientist who is helping Padsha Mali," Mark suggested.

"That is what I think," Hast said.

Mark recalled the recent call from Interpol moments ago which found evidence that Prof. Sanders was hiding something. 'Could he be the scientist Hast is talking about?' he said to himself. Mark was impressed that Hast's prediction about the faith-healer had come true; this was not the first time for Mark to find that his investigations converged with the prophecies of Abrahamic faith!

"By the way, you said Abraham told Nimrod that ∞Illuhim∞ will bring the sun from the west in the end days. Is that another sign of the Judgment Day according to the holy§cript?" Mark asked.

"You are right, and I have been avoiding this point so far," Hast replied, "but indeed, according to the prophecies the Antichrist uncovers himself after the sun rises from the west!"

"Could this be metaphorical?" Mark suggested.

"That is what I have always thought, but I'm no longer sure," Hast said.

"You said a world war would happen, and we already know a nuclear bag is missing," Mark said. "Could a world war

95

involving nuclear strikes cause a major change in the earth's rotation?"

"We could ask this to an astrophysicist," Hast suggested.

When Hast mentioned the word astrophysicist, the only name that came to their minds at that moment was Prof. Neil Baron and his TNARK-planet project which was about changing the planetary rotations in the solar system making them habitable for human life!

Prof. Neil Baron, a famous astrophysicist who was working at TNARK too, has spent many years on a project which aimed to control the speed and the direction of massive planets using human-made, powerful thrusting engines. Although the project was mainly theoretical, Neil's lab had made many models of the powerful thrusts which operated by nuclear power. It was one million times more powerful than the ordinary thrusting engines used to push airplanes and space rockets. Installing those powerful thrusts on a planet could change the direction and the spin of a planet to make it more similar to earth. However, many scientists opposed Neil's projects and had convinced the public that finding a suitable planet to live on would be much cheaper and more convenient than changing the dynamics of a non-suitable planet to make it more suitable, so Neil's project was stopped a long time ago.

"Do you think Neil is involved in this conspiracy?" Hast asked.

"Neil Baron seems very benign," Mark said, "but *Young Nimrod* could be among TNARK and might have access to the documents and proposals in Neil's lab."

"Or may be *Young Nimrod* himself encouraged Neil Baron to work on such a project so that he could take advantage of his ideas for his evil purposes," Hast suggested.

"I wonder if it's practical to apply Neil Baron's models to change the earth's rotation," Mark said.

"Maybe we need to ask professor Neil Baron himself," Hast suggested.

"Perhaps after I make sure that he himself has not been involved in this conspiracy."

Mark took out his cellphone and asked someone from Interpol to provide him with the names of all those involved with Neil's project.

"I'm going to Cambridge again," Mark said. "We can go together if you want. This time I'm going there with a private jet."

"A private jet! How did you get that?" Hast asked.

"I have asked the head of Interpol to provide me with a private jet because my mission requires me to travel a lot between the different parts of the world," he said.

"Wow, it looks so easy to request a jet from Interpol!" Hast said.

"It wasn't that easy. They only agreed after I successfully convinced them that my mission was linked with the missing nuclear bag and my investigations could possibly lead to uncovering its location and the suspect," he said.

Chapter 17

Howard 'Nerd' was a nickname given to Howard Nick who was a final year physics student at MIT, the Massachusetts Institute of Technology. He was very obsessed with quantum mechanics and its implications and during this year, he had presented a self-made theory of everything that he called 'The Mind Quanta-Soup'. His theory was based on the Copenhagen interpretation of quantum mechanics which in turn was based on the weird observations of particle physics: small particles behave differently depending on whether there is an observer measuring their position and speed or not!

The implications of the Copenhagen interpretation, if true, were profound. According to it, if in one reality a tree falls from a mountain but no one was there to see the tree falling or to detect the effect of its fall, then this would be the equivalent to a reality where the tree didn't fall at all. The theory mandates that for an event to happen there should be an observer measuring it, otherwise, it would be equivalent to a non-happening event.

Howard Nerd took this notion further with his theory proposing that if in a reality where everyone believed to have seen a tree falling from a mountain then this would be the equivalent to a reality where the tree was actually falling. For Howard there was no absolute truth, only a relative truth which was determined by the degree of belief in the observer's eyes in a closed system.

The quantum phenomenon was a well-accepted theory in physics but its presence and effects were only detectable in a small scale, hence, it was only applicable for the small world: atoms and subatomic particles, but the larger world was usually deterministic and followed the Newtonian's rules of motion, and the uncertainty due to the quantum effect being so small it was better to be ignored than to be considered in real life.

Through 'The Mind Quanta-Soup' Howard tried to extend the Copenhagen interpretation of quantum mechanics to the large world too. His thesis didn't get a good review and was largely considered as wishy-washy, voodoo science. His paper was rejected by many scientific journals and his articles on the online forums were usually labeled as 'crackpot' or were debunked. Nevertheless, Howard still insisted that the quantum effect was detectable on the large scale too and everything surrounding us followed its rules.

***

Howard considered that reality was nothing more than a shared dream among people. According to his theory, the reality follows the rules set by its perceivers. The reality wouldn't exist if everybody gave up detecting it through the five sensory organs or through the measuring tools invented by science, and hence, the rules of physics could be changed if someone were able to convince all the minds in the world to detect and perceive things differently.

"The wall in front of us will disappear if everyone believes strongly that it doesn't exist," Howard said to his friend.

"That is nonsense! Last night I was trying to test your theory. I stood in front of a wall and tried to convince myself that it didn't exist," his friend said. "Guess what? I couldn't pass through it."

"There may have been someone else around you observing the wall too and believing that wall did exist," Howard claimed. "You need to convince everyone around you so that the wall disappears."

"I swear I was alone. I was sure nobody was around me at that moment," his friend replied.

"That is because the earth is not a closed system. Maybe an alien on another planet was observing you through his telescope and believed that the wall did exist," Howard suggested.

"Oh, gosh your theory is really untestable," his friend said in frustration.

"No, my theory is proof that aliens do exist and they imagine and share the same reality as we do," Howard said. "If we want to change the rules of physics, we need to convince everybody in this universe to perceive it according to our new rules. Reality can take the shape of our minds just like soups take the shape of its container."

"Can we perceive our world independently and not share our imagination with others?" his friend asked.

"We always do that when we dream alone," Howard said.

Howard also believed that sincere wishes and prayers could work according to his theory, but they needed a strong wish or belief and many prayers to have an effect. He said to his friend, "If you wish or pray for something to happen, it will happen provided that there are no others wishing something opposite to yours." He continued claiming, "If everyone in this world united and wished for something to come true, it would come true no matter how impossible."

To which his friend replied, "If everyone wishes for something to happen, many will most likely work hard to make it happen. This is not magic, or science, just common sense!"

***

Howard had recently witnessed an increase in online posts filled with articles about the signs of Judgment Day, the

Antichrist and ∞Illuhim∞. Many of those posts he was seeing in his social media pages were sponsored! For Howard, it seemed that rich religious people were trying hard to convince the public to have their beliefs. This would have an effect on reality itself according to Howard! He himself believed that the Doomsday would happen, and it would happen similarly to how it was described in the holy§cript because so many minds in the past and in the present had tried to imagine its events and had actively sacrificed for it through the many wars that had taken many lives. So Howard thought Nature would try to model itself according to people's wishes and prayers, otherwise, it would mean a huge waste of the people's wishes, aspirations and sacrifices. 'The symmetry would be hugely broken unless Nature changes itself to fulfill everyone's wishes,' he thought.

One of the examples Howard always used to demonstrate this concept to his friends was that of the ancient civilizations who ruled the ancient world for a very long time like: Sumer, Egypt, Babel, Ashur, Medes and Persia. They all depicted their gods as human-animal hybrids. Famous examples included Shedu and Sphinx. These godly creatures had the head of a human, the body of a lion, and the wing of an eagle. Because people believed in such creatures strongly, worshipped them and even sacrificed for them for a long time, it would be a huge waste of energy if they have done that for nothing. The Mind Quanta-Soup theory demanded Nature to model herself to fulfill their wishes and their beliefs.

According to Howard, Nature was not able to fulfill the wishes of the ancient people immediately because doing that was very time and energy demanding, but she has modified herself slowly through centuries of scientific advances and achievements. Now a project like TNARK was actively trying to take the best genes from all the species in the animal kingdom and combine them together to build a super organism, and who knows, the resulting super organism could look like something similar to Shedu or Sphinx!

Howard had a popular blog which recently reached over a million subscribers after one of his previous posts went viral. One year before Padsha Mali appeared, Howard predicted that someone who looks like the Abrahamic faith Antichrist would appear at some point. His point was that because so many people in the past and present thought about the Antichrist, the prophecy should come true to restore the symmetry between reality and the collective imagination of the masses.

When Padsha Mali appeared and his news became viral, some of Howard's followers remembered this article and re-shared his prediction on other social media which made Howard's page popular with lots of new subscribers. This encouraged him to post even crazier predictions. For Howard, the question was no longer whether ∞Illuhim∞ exists or not. It was whether ∞Illuhim∞ does already exist or would come into existence! He made the following nerdy post in his online blog:

I believe God is either:
∞*Illuhim*∞
or
Illuhim∞

Chapter 18

After their visit to New Delhi, the private jet took Hast and Mark directly to TNARK headquarters again. Just before take-off, Hast called Nergz to tell her that he would be staying abroad for a bit longer.

"I'm sorry for leaving you so long, honey," Hast said.

"Are you still looking for the Beast?" Nergz asked.

Hast peeked at Mark at that moment and saw he was still busy speaking with someone else on his cellphone. This call had already lasted over an hour.

"Yes, I can't tell you the details because of the non-disclosure agreement I made with the Interpol agent, but I hope you understand that I'm trying to save people," Hast said with a lowered voice.

"I understand," she said.

"I love you honey. Please take care while I'm away," Hast said.

"I love you too and don't worry about us," she said.

Hast finished his call then turned to Mark who also seemed to have finished his lengthy call.

"Guess who funded Neil Baron's project?" Mark said to Hast.

"Who?"

"Mr. *Young Nimrod* again," Mark said. "Interpol has investigated the names of all of those involved in his project."

"Did they find more information about him?" Hast asked.

"Not really. Again a fake address and ID, and he did fund the project through non-trackable sources," Mark said.

"If he was trying to hide his identity to Neil Baron too, does that mean Neil is not involved with his evil plans?" Hast suggested.

"I think so, but it's obvious that *Young Nimrod* wanted to take advantage of Neil's ideas for his own plan," Mark suggested as he was impressed again to find that tracing the predictions of the prophecies has led to uncovering another link!

When Hast and Mark arrived at Prof. Neil Baron's office, Mark revealed the reason of their meeting to him as he had decided to be more direct with Neil about his questions. "We are curious to know whether it's possible to make the sun rise from the west by changing earth's rotation using your ideas," Mark asked.

"Theoretically, everything is possible," Neil said. "But why would someone want to do that?!"

"Let's assume someone is trying to achieve this by using your model," Mark said. "How could he achieve it and what would he need to do?"

Neil began to explain his model to Mark and Hast. "In our model, we suggested using powerful thrusts that were designed in our lab. These could be installed on both sides of the planet to generate a torque force which would change the rotational speed or the direction of the planet. The thrusting engine in our model uses nuclear power to generate a huge amount of ions that come out from the back of the engine at light speed and this would generate an immense force in the opposite direction according to Newton's third law. Generally, our model is around a million times more powerful than the traditional thrusting engines used in NASA's rocket engines," he said.

"And does someone need to stop the earth's rotation first to change the direction of the sun rising?" Mark asked.

"You could use the torque force to turn the earth upside down instead; this would produce the illusion of the sun rising from the west," Neil suggested.

"Does that require less energy and is it more practical?" Mark asked.

"Don't underestimate the power needed. This solution would still require an immense amount of energy," Neil said. "Though you could turn the earth's axis less than 180 degrees and still produce the wanted illusion in some countries because the earth's axis itself is tilted."

"How damaging would this be for the life on earth?" Mark asked.

"It depends on whether you want to make this change slowly or rapidly," Neil said.

"What if someone wanted to make the sun rise from the west within 24 hours," Hast interrupted.

Mark understood Hast's intention; he asked this question because the prophecies indicated that people would suddenly realize the change in the sun's direction so this meant the change would need to happen quickly.

"That is impossible," Neil said. "The amount of power required to achieve that would be too immense."

"How is that impossible?" Mark asked.

"First you can't practically fix such powerful thrusts to the earth's surface. If the ground beneath it was not very hard and solid, the thrust would expel like a projectile. You may be able to fix it if you tilted the thrust's front slightly down, but you'd lose a lot of energy. You would also need to make the surface area of the engine's front very wide, otherwise, it would penetrate the ground beneath it. You could perhaps attach its front end to the base of a mountain and that way you could make sure that when the powerful thrust pushed the mountain forward it would drag with it the ground below and the force could change the earth's axis, however, there is no guarantee that even a mountain wouldn't fall apart under such power!"

"Let's say someone was able to do that. What about its effect on life on earth?" Hast repeated Mark's question.

"I don't know how life would adapt itself to the new changes in the environment for the long term," Neil said, "but for the short term, lots of earthquakes and tsunamis might happen."

"Do you have any knowledge if someone is already trying to implement or build the thrusts you designed?" Mark asked.

"No, not to my knowledge. Our project has stopped, however, we are currently using public funds to continue its sister project," Neil said.

"And what is that?" Mark asked.

"We are trying to modify our designed thrusts to make them work as deflectors to change the direction of the Doomsday Meteor."

"How long will it take for the Doomsday Meteor to reach us?" Hast asked.

"According to our estimations it will be hitting us in 2068 so in less than a decade!" Neil said.

Hast thought that although the danger of the Doomsday Meteor was still far away, there was a much more immediate danger if Newton's prediction about the date of the Judgement Day was true!

That moment Neil looked at his watch. "By the way, I need to go soon, so do you have any other questions?"

"Just out of curiosity, do you think aliens exist?" Hast asked.

"Of course, I believe advanced life is all over our galaxy," Neil said.

"And why do you think they haven't visited us so far?" Hast asked.

"I get this question a lot! Personally, I think it is because we are living in unlucky spot. We live on the outer edge of the Milky Way galaxy, a very empty spot, and our nearest neighbor star is four light years away!" Neil said. "Imagine if there is an advanced life somewhere and capable of interstellar travel. Why would they choose to visit an empty spot instead of the center of the galaxy which is full of stars, planets, and energy?"

Prof. Neil Baron stood up preparing himself to go. Hast and Mark thanked him for his precious time.

"I didn't understand your last question," Mark said to Hast when they left Neil's office. "Was it relevant to our quest?"

"No, it was just a curiosity," Hast said. "I'm curious to know whether Doomsday globally affects everywhere in the universe or it's only specific to earth."

Mark looked at his cellphone which beeped twice indicating that he had received a new message. Looking at it, he realized it was from Kogar.

Dear Mark,
Have you reached any new clues about the identity of Young Nimrod? Please keep me updated. Thanks
Regards,

Mark turned to Hast before writing his response. "So far, you think *Young Nimrod* is the false prophet who is helping the Antichrist, Padsha Mali?" he asked Hast.

"Yes, that is my thinking," Hast confirmed.

"Do you think the word 'Young' in *Young Nimrod* refers to the false prophet's age or to the period?" Mark asked the question remembering the age of his prime suspect, Prof. Sanders who was 71 years old.

"I think the word 'Young' means 'New' here. I guess *Mr. Young Nimrod* greatly admires the ancient Nimrod and that is why he chose this codename for himself," Hast said.

"Do the prophecies say anything about his age?" Mark asked.

"Unfortunately not," Hast said.

"Does the prophecy say that the false prophet is helped by anyone else or is working alone?" Mark asked again as he was thinking about Ericson's young secretary.

"The false prophet and the Antichrist could be helped by anyone else, but they are all innocent and deceived people who need our help. No one is to be blamed except the Antichrist himself," Hast said.

Mark turned to his cellphone again while trying to send a reply to Kogar. Hast was eager to have a peek at Mark's cellphone to see what he was busy about writing but he was too shy to do so.

Dear Kogar,
You were right about suspecting someone from TNARK, as we've already found some suspicious activities there. We are still investigating. I'll update you once I have more information.
Regards, Mark.

***

On their way back, Hast and Mark engaged in a lengthy discussion about the prophecies of the end-days and the Antichrist's goals.

"I wonder if the Antichrist was mentioned in other faiths?" Mark asked trying to take advantage from the theologian's knowledge.

"Well, similar characters to the Antichrist are mentioned in many other non-Abrahamic faiths such as Ahriman in the Zoroastrian religion which is equivalent to the Antichrist," Hast said.

"Does it have the same signs?" Mark asked.

"No, theirs is somewhat different. The Antichrist in Abrahamic faith is just a bad human being, but Ahriman in Zoroastrianism is a mischievous deity," Hast answered.

"Is it like the polar opposite to ∞Illuhim∞?" Mark asked.

"Yes, that is how they view it," Hast asked.

"Can you tell me more about their prophecies?" he asked.

"In my theology courses, I didn't read about them a lot but I know their basic ideology," Hast said. "Zoroastrianism is one of the oldest monotheistic religions which has had influence over other monotheistic faiths including Abrahamic religions, however, Zoroastrianism itself couldn't preserve its strict form of monotheism and it became gradually dualistic in nature."

"How old is Zoroastrianism?"

"Scholars believe Zoroastrianism was started by Zoroaster, a prophet who lived during the Medo-Persian Empire around 1000 BC. He rejected the worship of the many gods in Hindu and Greek religion and identified one god who he thought was worthy to be worshiped, Ohrmazd, the God of Light and Wisdom," Hast said.

"Is Ohrmazd the same as ∞Illuhim∞?" Mark asked.

"Yes, I think so. Zoroastrians name their god differently due to the language differences, but their concept of Ohrmazd is very similar to the Abrahamic concept of ∞Illuhim∞," Hast answered.

"Why did it become a dualistic faith then?" Mark asked as he began to show interest.

"Well, the core Zoroastrian religion defined Ohrmazd as an all loving, benevolent god who wouldn't create bad things and everything he did create was good and perfect in nature," Hast said. "As you see, the problem with their assumption was that they couldn't explain the origin of evil and the bad things that were happening in the world."

"Why they didn't blame the evil on human's actions and their free will then?" he asked.

"Because Zoroastrians believe that evil can't come from good, and since they defined their god as all loving and all good, hence, they couldn't explain why their god would create evil."

"So they blamed the bad things on a separate god, the God of Evil," Mark tried to explain.

"That is what they did," Hast confirmed Mark's conclusion. "They resorted to the concept of a triune God where they defined 'Zurvan' as the Lord of Time and the progenitor of the twin gods: Ohrmazd, God of Wisdom, and Ahriman, the God of Evil. Zurvan himself is agnostic, meaning he doesn't care about good and evil. Ohrmazd, God of Light and Wisdom, created us and the universe. On the contrary Ahriman, God of Darkness and Destruction, tries to destroy what Ohrmazd has created, so in other words, Ohrmazd is matter and Ahriman is anti-matter. Ohrmazd derives his power from: Humata, Hukhta, Huvarshta, which translates to the 'three good': Good Thoughts, Good Words, and Good Deeds. While Ahriman derives his power from the 'three evil': Evil Thoughts, Evil Words and Evil Deeds. According to Zoroastrianism, Ohrmazd won the war and the matter became dominant over anti-matter, and that is the reason why our universe mostly consists of matter rather than anti-matter according to them. Since Ohrmazd derives his power from the 'three good', he needs humans to do the 'three good' continuously, so that he can progress the world into perfection and ultimately defeat Ahriman forever."

"And what do they think will happen in the end-days? Will they think Ahriman will rise again?" Mark asked.

"Yes, that is their prophecy," Hast said. "They think in the end-days, humans will do less good and since Ohrmazd derives his power from our good acts, he will no longer be able to throw over Ahriman. The anti-matter will increase in our universe and Ahriman will rise again but he will be defeated again in the great final war that will happen in the heavens between the good and evil."

Mark remembered a scientific documentary he saw recently on HDTV about the world-renowned physicist, Richard Feynman, explaining anti-matter, "I heard anti-matter is just normal matter but it's gone back in time!" he said to Hast.

"That is interesting," Hast said. "Do you mean that matter itself will become anti-matter if it goes back in time?"

"Yes, according to Feynman, a positron which is a well-known anti-matter particle is just being an electron that has gone back in time. That is why it has an opposite charge to the electron and why some scientists call it anti-electron," Mark explained.

"I see," Hast said, "but what if an electron collides with a positron? Would they annihilate each other?"

"Yes, according the documentary matter and anti-matter can't mix in the same place," Mark followed.

"I think this concept goes in line with the Zoroastrian's belief that Ahriman is the god of anti-matter and he can't exist in the this world without destroying it, and that is why Ohrmazd's plan is to eliminate every source of anti-matter to help this universe reach its perfection," Hast claimed. "It's like two different pyramids. One has 'three good' at its base leading to the truth, ∞Illuhim∞. While the other pyramid base has 'three evil' leading to deception, or a fake reality ruled by Illuminati or Ahriman."

Mark tried to conclude, "So in Zoroastrianism they have two separate pyramids each ruled by a deity with polar opposites, but in Abrahamic faith they don't explicitly separate the two pyramids and there is only one deity, ∞Illuhim∞."

"Yes, ∞Illuhim∞ is the ultimate ruler of both realities. The truth pyramid which leads us to heaven and everything good we envision for ourselves while the deception pyramid leads to hell and everything bad we envision for ourselves. Also, conceptually the god of Abrahamic faith is infinite. Even his name is an infinite set of letters, and nobody can spell or pronounce it. We are only able to see and pronounce a small portion of his name, Illuhim."

Although Hast was a faithful follower of the Abrahamic faith, he never devalued the concepts and beliefs of other religions. He always thought that all faiths boiled down to the same core concepts and tenets in their purity and their ultimate goal was human salvation. Unfortunately, greed and evil always tried to hijack faith, and feed upon it and use it for its own deeds.

Chapter 19

Deep underground at an unseen site, an elevator had just reached the ground. Media Rozhgar pushed the button to open the elevator door, and the AI-robot installed inside had recognized her immediately enabling the red light to become green and the door to open. Leaving the elevator, Media walked along a long corridor which ended at a spacious hall full of computers, cameras and TV screens. At the center of it, sat the man of her dreams wearing a helmet and specially designed eyeglasses through which he was connected to the entire world: internet, news agencies and television programs, etc.

When he was underground, he preferred to be called *Young Nimrod* and he behaved as if he was in charge of and responsible for everything happening in the world.

When Media Rozhgar entered the hall, she saw that he looked exhausted. She thought his fatigue was from his viewing of all the horrible things happening in the world through his visual eyeglasses! 'I need to stop him; otherwise, he will get seizures again.' She called him but there was no response, so she looked at his hands and they were shaking. She immediately realized it was the seizures again, so she took the helmet and his eyeglasses off. His eyes were rolled upward and his teeth were clenched so Media quickly looked around and found a needle syringe on the table along with an ampule of diazepam, a seizure suppressant. To her it looked like he was expecting to have seizures again, so she grabbed his hand strongly and injected him with the ampule. His seizures gradually started to fade away, and he became sleepy, he looked into the eyes of his faithful lover. "I love you Media. Thanks for everything you have done for me," he said.

"I love you too, so please don't harm yourself again," she said with eyes full of tears while she hugged her lover.

"I saw a lot of pain in the world today" he slurred. "Many children have died today in the world from hunger and from cancer. There was a video of a mother being hit by a car in front of her young daughter, and another video…"

"Please, stop!" Media urged him while hugging him. "You are not responsible for any of this, so don't blame yourself."

"They are all gone! They are all gone," he kept repeating with tearful sorrowful eyes. "I need to do something."

"Let it go. Let it go please," Media said while putting *Young Nimrod*'s head on her lap.

"I want to marry you," he said repeatedly as he gradually went into a deep sleep.

Media Rozhgar was deeply in love with *Young Nimrod* to the extent she was ready to sacrifice herself for him. She was attracted to people who had a strong sense of responsibility, and when she first saw him, she saw an aura of energy around him. It was so powerful she could have felt it from a distance, and at that moment, she decided to be with him even though he had betrayed her once, but she couldn't imagine being with anyone else. 'This man wants to change the world to be a better place. No one else can do this, so I need to help him until the end,' she told herself. She had met many people who said they wanted to change the world, but when *Young Nimrod* said it, it was like no one else. He meant something totally different, and he didn't only mean to change the future to be better. He meant to change everything: the past, the present, and the future. 'No one feels as responsible as he does. He is the only one who could hold himself responsible for everything just like God himself,' she thought.

***

Young Nimrod woke up the next morning in the bedroom of his underground operation. He looked at the table beside him and saw a toasted cheese sandwich, milk, and water there. 'She's saved me again,' he thought to himself. He looked forward and saw the beautiful young lady coming forward to tell him something.

"Last night, you said you loved me," she said.

He immediately realized that his frequent declarations of love for Media made her think that he wanted to progress their relationship to marriage, but because of his seizures last night, he couldn't remember whether he said anything more than that. "Of course, I love you more than anything, but you know we can't marry publicly. Don't you?"

"I understand. Don't worry, I was just teasing you!" Media gave him a kiss and walked back to the door. "Are you coming outside today?"

He looked at his watch then replied, "I will stay here for a bit longer. I need to finish something."

"OK, but please don't harm yourself again. I won't be here to save you so be careful with your experiments," she said then she walked toward the elevator and disappeared.

Young Nimrod thought about her and wished he could do something to pay her back for her loyalty. 'She is the most trusted person to me,' he thought to himself. 'I can't trust anyone but her, and she helps me even though she doesn't understand the details of my plan. She trusts my intentions, and she is everything to me. I need her to stay on my side until the end.'

After he ate his food, he went back to the hall of his main operations. He looked at the blue progress bars on the huge screen in front of him, and one of the progress indicators in front of him pointed to 99%. 'The thrust engines are about to finish soon in Siberia.' He remembered back to a few years ago when a company he owned went through all the hassle to convince China and Russia to provide some of their bordering towns and cities with very cheap electricity using his newly invented revolutionary electrical generators. However, since the installments were huge, they agreed to place them in Siberia in an empty, unpopulated spot exactly where *Young Nimrod* wanted! His company dealt with everything, and within a couple months he would be providing them with unlimited cheap energy, but with one twist, the electricity generation was not the true purpose of the project at all.

Another message appeared on one of the screens informing that the setup of the portable nuclear bag was complete and it was in a secure position in its final destination. Now it was ready to blow at a push of button controlled by *Young Nimrod*! It looked like everything was about to finish soon. 'The world will soon see my master plan,' he thought. He looked at another screen and saw a recent viral video of Padsha Mali pop up. In the video, the faith-healer was talking about the end-days and urging people to follow Abrahamic faith before the Judgment Day came. He was not a good preacher and had a croaky voice, but his healing power had made him a celebrity and made his videos and preaching go viral. Nevertheless, his physical features made people fear him at the same time because of his extreme resemblance to the Antichrist!

Young Nimrod remembered the hassle he went through to find Padsha Mali after one of the labs sponsored by him were on the verge of finding a revolutionary cure for cancer, *Young Nimrod* immediately put a hold over the invention rights. He then changed the direction of the lab's work to something else while he transferred the cure into the hands of a faith-healer to use it as a weapon, not an ordinary one, but a weapon that could change minds and challenge beliefs! Then he remembered his efforts to find the suitable faith-healer for that purpose. When he had examined the list of all the famous faith-healers around the world, he found several having a blind eye, but among them someone looked exactly like what he wanted! 'Padsha Mali was my choice. There was no one better than him at representing the Antichrist!'

Next *Young Nimrod* sponsored and promoted all the videos and articles about him, so that the whole world knew about him. On the other hand, *Young Nimrod* needed to sponsor and promote all the videos and articles that showed him as the potential Antichrist. 'I need people to know about the signs of the end-days and to believe that the apocalypse is near,' he thought to himself. 'I live in a lucky time where 95% of people are connected to the internet. I can make any idea go viral through sponsoring it with money.'

He then looked at another progress bar indicator which showed that 85% of the people online were currently estimated to know or at least heard about Padsha Mali and the signs of the end-days. 'I need to increase this rate further; after all, the success of my plan depends entirely on it.' He then assigned another 100 million dollars to promote Padsha Mali's videos on various social media.

Then he walked toward a detailed schematic he had recently finished and to his masterpiece weapon, the death ray! This weapon was first suggested by the genius Nicola Tesla, and it shot a narrow but a powerful thunder-like ray to its victims burning them or even evaporating them immediately! Although the weapon was invented a long time ago, it was not adopted by the military. The world powers at the time didn't find it effective and practical in real wars because the weapon needed much time for charging and powering before it could be used again for a subsequent shot, hence, soldiers could only shoot at one person at a time. Nevertheless, *Young Nimrod* thought it could be used to produce great fear and horror in the enemy's eye if it was used properly.

The final thing that *Young Nimrod* needed for finalizing his plan was the powerful AI-hacker robot. It was currently under further development by a genius programmer hired by him, and the program once finished would be able to hack into any website, TV and media.

Then he looked at his helmet and the visual glasses at the center of his operation hall and asked himself, 'How many people are suffering today?' He held the eyeglasses out to have a peek at the day's most tragic trends online but then he remembered Media's words. 'Wait, I shouldn't do that. I can't save them by looking at their misery. I need to stay healthy and live so that I can execute my master plan perfectly. After all, in a couple of months the world will see the light!'

Chapter 20

Mark was sitting in his small office at the ICPI department near the Interpol headquarters in Lyon, France. He was looking at his computer reading of the information he had received from the surveillance and monitoring of his suspects. The data he was looking at indicated that Prof. Sanders, among all the other suspects, was clearly hiding something. It was evident from the drastic changes in his behavior after Mark and Hast's meeting with him, and he was now being very careful with his communications and phone calls by using encrypted messages, but whenever he needed to make an unencrypted call, he used code words in his language!

Mark also found within the data that the name *Young Nimrod* was repeatedly used as a funder or a contributor in many important labs around the world and not only in TNARK, however, each time the user had provided a false identification, image and address. It was very hard to track *Young Nimrod*'s true identity through the information Mark had. 'This suspect is very careful,' Mark thought to himself. 'I hope that Ericson Sanders who is acting suspiciously is the person I'm looking for.'

At that moment, Agent Roger entered Mark's office. "I've found something interesting when I hacked into the email account of Ericson's young secretary. Roger put an email print in front of Mark. "Look, Ericson's secretary sent this to her sister:"

I think the cops are following me, and I'm so scared! What should I do now?

Mark read the email. "It's obvious that Ericson's secretary is hiding something from the police," he said. "How would she know it was the police and why should she be scared of them?"

"Exactly, that is what I thought," Roger said.

"Did you get her sister's response?" Mark asked.

"Unfortunately not, but we retrieved another email she sent to her sister after her first one," Roger said referring to another email.

Please don't respond. I'm so stupid! I forgot my emails are not secure. I will meet you soon and we'll talk together privately!

"My guess is that Prof. Sanders told his secretary to be careful with her communications, and once she found out that one of our cops was following her, she might have panicked and sent those emails to her sister," Roger said.

"But why would she send emails to her sister and not to her boss, Prof. Sanders?" Mark asked.

"Probably, she had already told her boss since she would see him daily in his office, and I would guess Ericson might also know that we are following them," Roger said.

Mark examined both emails carefully thinking, 'Now, I know for sure that Prof. Sanders and his secretary are hiding something relevant to my quest. His lab has close links to Virtualworld™ who designed the suspicious gaming helmet. He is also a well-respected scientist with lots of links within TNARK and other labs around the world. If he is the one who is helping the faith-healer then I'm sure he is *Young Nimrod*,' he thought to himself. "I need to know if Ericson has any links with the faith-healer," Mark said.

"Padsha Mali?" Roger wondered.

"Yes," Mark said. "From my investigations, I noticed many of the faith-healer's online videos have been sponsored, and I would like know who is sponsoring them. He is also getting his healing power from a special water, and I don't know where he is getting it from nor what supply he is holding, but I'm hoping that sooner or later the faith-healer will need more help from *Young Nimrod.*"

"I can easily track the accounts that sponsor Padsha Mali's videos," Roger said.

"I'm sure if you track them you will reach fake accounts and IDs, but it may be worthwhile monitoring Ericson and his secretary carefully as we might catch the tail sooner," Mark said.

"Ericson knows that we are monitoring him so he is very careful," Roger said.

"That is actually good for us. I'm sure he and his secretary are confused by now and sooner or later they will make a mistake and give us the evidence we need," Mark suggested.

Chapter 21

Going back to his childhood when *Young Nimrod* was eight years old, he was the smartest student at his elementary school. Every day he came back home to tell his mother glorious stories about how good he was in class and how he alone had answered all the questions asked by teacher. Teachers sent praising and complimentary letters to his parents describing him as an exceptionally polite and clever student. He was number one in every subject, and his scores were always top, but he was envied by his peers.

His father was a retired engineer and his mother was a nurse. He had a three year old sister who he always took care of. The day when *Young Nimrod* had turned eight, she began to pronounce his name correctly. A feeling of thrill, love, and passion came to *Young Nimrod*, and that was the best birthday gift anyone so far had given to him! He held his little sister in his lap and kissed her on the cheek. He was very happy that finally she could pronounce his name correctly.

From that day on, *Young Nimrod* started to teach her spelling and the names of everything around her. He urged her to pronounce the difficult words correctly. Her pronunciations were funny and cute at the same time, and they made *Young Nimrod* and his parents laugh out loud every time she spoke. The family bond between brother and sister grew daily. Their parents were happy to have such a strong united family, and his mother was particularly relieved to think that when one day she and her husband left this life, her older son would take care of his sister.

"It's only two years before your sister goes to school like you," the mother said to *Young Nimrod*. "She will grow up beautiful and smart just like you and she needs you to protect her."

"I promise you mother that I will protect her with my life," *Young Nimrod* said confidently.

As a retired engineer, *Young Nimrod's* father liked to do everything by himself. He had the habit of not asking for help from anyone, and this trait extended to his beliefs. He himself didn't believe in Abrahamic religions, and he always pitied people for praying to ∞Illuhim∞ to fulfil their wishes instead of doing things themselves. He wanted his kids to grow up following his path. "They need to depend fully on themselves and never ask for help especially from a mythical being," he used to say. "This world is a jungle. There is no big universal 'daddy' as they want us to believe. No one cares about us but ourselves."

One day, *Young Nimrod's* father decided to take his son to a museum where there was an ancient painting on the wall depicting the immortal dispute between the two ancient world titans, Nimrod and Abraham. Nimrod was depicted in the painting in his god form and his followers were bowing to him in the painting.

"Who is that creature?" *Young Nimrod* asked his father referring to Nimrod's character in the painting.

"He is God, a real god who lived among his people, not hiding in the sky," his father answered.

Young Nimrod was very smart, and he was quick to understand what his farther was referring to.

"Have you heard about the Seven Wonders of the Ancient World?" father asked.

"Yes, they are amazing structures and buildings. We still wonder how ancient people were able to achieve them without any technology!" *Young Nimrod* answered.

"Listen boy," said the father to the son. "These people made wonders when they ruled the earth. They transcended us from lower beings living in the jungle into humans living in sprawling wondrous civilized empires that have ruled the entire ancient world as a single unity, a single super organism where kings like Nimrod, Zeus, Pharaoh, and Cyrus were the minds and their followers were the muscles. They all shared the same dream and aspired to transcend further to something even more than a human, a god."

"And why didn't they transcend into gods?" *Young Nimrod* asked.

"Because of this man." The father pointed to Abraham in the painting who was standing alone among the bowing crowd refusing to submit to Nimrod. "He took the power of God from the humans and gave it to a mythical being of his imagination he called ∞Illuhim∞." The father continued, "Imagine if Nimrod or Pharaoh who built the great pyramids and the Tower of Babel had the knowledge and the technology we have today? They would have taken us to the center of the galaxy by now!"

***

Later that day when *Young Nimrod* returned home, he couldn't sleep but kept thinking about the possibility of becoming a god, someone who could do anything, and was unlimited by the rules of Nature. Inspired by his thoughts, he took out a pen and a paper and started to draw Nimrod's figure in his mind depicting him as an omnipotent force in the universe. As he drew one stroke after another, he thought about how to depict him as being omnipotent. He ended with an image that looked to him like his finest artistic creation so far. He decided that in the morning he would put the drawing in a frame and fix it to his wall to be an inspiration for him.

Since he had spent the entire night drawing, he felt very tired and fell asleep beside his painting. The next morning when he awoke but before his eyes were completely open, he remembered the figure he had drawn the previous evening. He lifted his head, and to his shock, he saw that his little sister had scribbled all over his masterpiece! All of the sudden his eyes filled with anger and his teeth strongly clenched. He took the paper forcefully from his sister shouting at her, "Why have you done that! Why!"

The little sister looked terrified as she had never seen her brother so angry!

"I hate you!" he said to her.

His little sister's eyes filled with tears, and she started to cry and scream from fear and sorrow. That moment *Young Nimrod* was very angry to see that his masterpiece was now destroyed. His rage made him say to his sister, "I wish you didn't exist."

By that time his mother had heard her child's screams, and she hurried into the room to hold the crying toddler on her lap to comfort her. "You shouldn't do that to your little sister," she said. "You promised me to protect her and not to harm her."

"She destroyed my work," *Young Nimrod* said defensively.

"She is just a little girl," his mother replied.

Young Nimrod realized he had overreacted over the sketch, but looking at the clock he realized that he was late for school so he hurried to quickly get dressed. His mother put a sandwich in his backpack before he left for school. That day he was generally inattentive to his lessons. All he was thinking about was his aggressive response toward his little sister. 'If I want to become God, I should become a loving god not an aggressive one,' he thought. 'How can I be so upset over such a minor thing!'

Young Nimrod thought he owed his sister an apology, 'When I go back home, I will hold her and show that I love her. She will have only me to protect her when our parents die.'

That same day, in the last class, the teacher finished the subject early before the bell rang. She decided to spend the remaining time asking the students about their hobbies and what they wanted to become in the future until the class was over. This is what she usually did in other classes when they were about to end and she was feeling too lazy to start a new topic. So she sat on the desk and held the attendance notebook looking for a student's name.

"Let's see, Adam, what do you want to become in the future?" the teacher asked the first student on the list.

"I want to become a lawyer," Adam replied.

Then she turned to Helen and asked her the same question and she replied that she wished to become a doctor. The teacher continued to ask the students in the class one by one in the order of the alphabetical appearance of their last names. After asking around twenty students, most of the answers were: doctor, nurse, teacher, and engineer. Then she peeked at the clock and saw it was only couple minutes to ring, so she followed the same routine to ask the remaining students in the list. "Sarah, what would like to become?"

"I want to become an engineer," Sarah Sarkawt replied.

Finally, the teacher turned to *Young Nimrod* and asked him the same question: "What would you like to become, smart boy?"

"I want to become a god," *Young Nimrod* replied.

"A guard?!" she wondered if she heard the word correctly.

"No, a god," he repeated more firmly.

The teacher failed to grasp the word again as it was very alien to what her brain expected to hear for a career, so she repeated for the third time, "I'm sorry. I don't understand what you said. Can you please repeat?"

"I mean I want to become like ∞Illuhim∞," he clarified.

"Oh! I see...," the teacher responded with a smile although a bit irritated with his proposition. "∞Illuhim∞ is the only god, and no one can become like him," she said.

"Why? What if I worked very hard?" *Young Nimrod* asked.

At that moment the bell started to ring and the students stood preparing their bags to leave the classroom.

"I know you are the smartest student in the class, but ∞Illuhim∞ was the smartest in the entire universe," she said while turning away from *Young Nimrod* toward the classroom exit door.

***

Later that day, a group of three boys from his class who had the reputation for being bullies stopped him on his way back home. They started to beat him until he bled from his nose.

"How dare you compare yourself with ∞Illuhim∞?" one boy said.

"If you are God then why can't you defend yourself?" another boy asked aggressively while punching him in the face. "Say I'm the slave of ∞Illuhim∞, or we will kill you now."

"Say it now," the other boy repeated while he kept kicking *Young Nimrod* as he fell onto the ground.

"I'm slave of ∞Illuhim∞," *Young Nimrod* said then followed with a lower voice, "not."

"What did you say?!" one boy said angrily when he heard him and began to kick him again. "Say it again loud and clear."

"I'm the slave of ∞Illuhim∞," he said again a bit louder than the first time while he kept repeating: *not, not, not ...* in his mind.

The bullies left *Young Nimrod* on the ground. "∞Illuhim∞ will give you cancer if you repeat your blaspheme again!" one of them shouted while they were about to walk away from him.

Young Nimrod tried to stand up again. His clothes were torn and dusty and his nose was still bleeding. This was the unluckiest day for him: first his masterpiece sketch were destroyed, second, he made his little sister upset and now he was bullied and humiliated. 'Maybe this is a curse and warning from ∞Illuhim∞ to me,' he thought to himself as tears started to fall from his eyes mixing with the bleeding from his nose. He walked slowly and regretfully toward the home that day wishing that he could forget about everything by tomorrow. When he got back home his mother saw him in his terrible condition and she quickly hugged him.

"Tell me who did that to you?" the mother asked furiously.

"Nobody, I fell on the ground," he replied.

His mother felt he was hiding something, but she was in a hurry. Her young daughter had developed a high fever and dizziness a few hours ago, and as a nurse the mother had tried to reduce the fever by giving her daughter some antipyretics and cold pack applications, but the fever hadn't subsided, so she decided to take her daughter to the hospital.

"Your father is on his way driving back home to take your sister to the hospital," she said.

"Why, what is wrong with my sister?" he asked.

"Your little sister has a high fever. Go check on her while I grab and collect some things before we set off for the hospital," his mother said.

Young Nimrod remembered that he owed an apology to his little sister, so he quickly went to her room to check on her. To his shock, he found her lying on the bed looking dizzy and tired.

Her breathing was fast and her forehead felt very hot to him. At that moment his sister opened her eyes slowly to look at her brother. She tried hard to say the words, "Sorry brother for touching your stuff." She was barely able to say it in her primitive voice, but the message was clear to *Young Nimrod*; she was still concerned about him even when she was in this terrible situation. A large tear rolled down his cheeks while he tried to reply to his beloved little sister, but then his most terrific nightmare started at that moment!

Her little sister's body began to shake involuntarily up and down, and her eyes rolled upwards and her mouth started frothing. *Young Nimrod* stood there terrified! He screamed loud for help. The remaining god-pride inside him shrunk into a freaked desperate chicken. The mother quickly got there to see that her daughter was having tonic-clonic seizures, so she immediately put her onto her left side and asked *Young Nimrod* to call for an ambulance.

That moment, his father arrived home and came to the room, but luckily the seizure had subsided quickly. He suggested taking their daughter to the hospital using their own car because waiting for the ambulance might take longer, so the mother took the ill child onto her lap and they quickly got in the car with *Young Nimrod* on the back seat.

The father quickly drove to the nearby hospital. Fifteen minutes later, they took the child directly to the Emergency ward's pediatric section. There doctors and nurses were able to put in a cannula after many trials into her little invisible veins, and they also put oxygen tubes into her nose. After taking the initial life saving measures, her blood was taken for medical tests and a CT-scan was taken of her brain. The little child was admitted to the pediatric ward, but only the mother was allowed to stay with the child. Both the father and *Young Nimrod* waited outside wishing for reassuring news soon which sadly did not happen.

Young Nimrod's little sister stayed for the next few weeks in the intensive care unit, and with every passing day her condition deteriorated. *Young Nimrod* needed to skip school frequently, and even when he attended some of the classes, his mind was inattentive. All he thought about was an apology he owed to his sister. He was waiting for the day to see her wake up again from her coma, speak and point to the things in the room again and call out their names with her funny and cute accent.

Unfortunately, weeks later the horrible news came. The neurologist who was in charge came to tell the parents that their child would never be able to return to her normal state. Her brain cortex was badly damaged and she would no longer remember anything. Her body was totally paralyzed and she wouldn't be able to even chew food by herself because her mouth muscles were paralyzed too. All they could do from now on was to feed her through a tube inserted from her little nose directly to her stomach. Her brain stem was still intact which meant her breathing and heartbeat would continue, but in reality, she was in a persistent vegetative state, a situation between life and death, and nobody could do anything for her at this stage. All what could be done was to take care of what have remained of her, to feed her and clean after her until the day came when a cure was found or she finally rested in peace. That was the doctor's conclusion.

Young Nimrod was looking and listening to the horrible news from behind the doors, and although he couldn't hear everything the doctor said to his parent, he knew from their emotions and responses that nothing looked good. 'How can I apologize to my sister?' he thought. 'She will never hear me or remember me again.'

Since the mother was a nurse herself, later that day the hospital staff decided to discharge the disabled child to clear the intensive care unit bed for other needy and newly admitted children. They instructed the parent on how to take care of her and how to feed her through the naso-gastric tube. They also needed to administer the dissolved anti-seizure medications through the tube to prevent future seizures and to turn their daughter from side to side several times in a day to prevent her from developing bedsores.

The parents realized the new conditions they had to face. There was no cure for their child's condition and nothing yet discovered to bring back their beloved daughter, but they decided to stay patient and to do whatever they could to take care of their disabled child until one day a cure was found.

That night they all came back to their house tired and depressed. *Young Nimrod* remembered his final words to his sister wishing that she didn't exist; he couldn't stop crying from the guilt as he secretly hid under his blanket. When midnight came, he realized his parents had fallen asleep. He got up from bed and went close to his comatose sister. As he switched on the small light bulb beside her, he was shocked to see his sister lying on the bed like a lifeless body, and he almost didn't recognize her. Before, she was so beautiful with full cheeks but now she was emaciated, just skin and bone. Her eyes were sunken and dry, the orbits swollen because of edema, and there were multiple lesions and previous sites of bleeding on her tongue and nose because of the tube insertion and frequent tongue biting due to the multiple seizures. With each breath *Young Nimrod* could hear a high pitch but faint sound as if she was still suffering in pain and asking for help. Her weak and thin hands were all reddish and bruised at multiple sites due to the frequent trials of cannula insertion and intravenous injections.

Young Nimrod called his sister but she didn't respond as she was in a deep coma. She wasn't aware of him or anything, and the only thing she was aware of was darkness, suffering, and pain. *Young Nimrod* burst into tears. Profuse big tears came from his eyes, and the carpet beneath him became immersed in them. He closed his eyes and started to pray to ∞Illuhim∞, a prayer that he had never done so purely and humbly. He began begging to the higher being for his mercy and forgiveness. He prayed with all his heart. 'Please forgive me for my arrogance. How dare I compare myself with Your Majesty! I'm nothing but your humble servant. Please give me back my sister, please. I will become your biggest slave in the Garden of Eden, and I will serve you forever. I will bow to you forever. I will be the slave of your slaves and you can torture me, burn me, do anything you wish to do to me, but please give my sister's health back, please. I don't want anything but my sister's health back. Please give her health back, please ...'

That moment a human-like figure immersed in light appeared. He looked like a perfectly symmetric being with a halo of a strong energy around him as he approached him in the darkness. The closer it came the stronger the light became, and *Young Nimrod* continued repeating his prayer hoping that his prayer was being answered. He continued to devalue himself and beg for the light figure to save his sister, but after a moment, the perfectly symmetric lighted figure stopped approaching and began to turn away from him and from his sister as if the light figure changed his mind and no longer wanted to cure the little disabled child!

'Please come back! My sister needs you,' he begged. 'I will do anything you want me to do. Please come back, please, please, please. Why you don't forgive me?' He continued to cry with his eyes closed, then a warm hand touched his shoulder.

"He can't cure your sister," a voice behind him said.

Young Nimrod opened his eyes and saw his father's hand on his shoulder.

"But why?" he said.

The father came closer to him. "Because ∞Illuhim∞ doesn't exist. The only one who can do something for your sister is you."

"How?" *Young Nimrod* asked desperately.

"You can become a smart doctor and cure her," his father said.

"But there are no cures for her condition," he said.

"You can find one," his father said. "Your sister is not the only one suffering from this condition. There are many other kids like her, and it's nobody's fault. The world we live in is imperfect and it's the job of smart people like you to think and find a solution to relieve Nature's imperfections."

His father's words were very effective; they ignited the god inside *Young Nimrod* and gave him hope again. The next day, he went to school. His attention to his lessons improved and he was able to answer most of the questions again by himself. His confidence returned, and the smile gradually returned to his face. Even though his sister's condition didn't get better, *Young Nimrod* was hopeful that one day he would be the one who found a cure for his little sister and then apologize to her.

From that moment onwards, he started reading complex medical and neurological topics online and asked his father to buy for him medical textbooks. He was only nine years old by then so many of these books were clearly out of his league, but he was so determined that nothing at that stage seemed to stop him from his goals. He always kept on his desk a picture he took with his little sister when she was healthy, and the picture was fuel for him to keep studying and looking for a cure for her sister's condition. Day by day he was closer to understanding her illness and the available treatments which were all palliative and non-curative measures. The more he studied his sister's condition the more he understood the difficulty of saving her.

The main reason for his sister's paralyses was due to the extensive degeneration of her cortical neurons. These neurons were responsible for holding long term memory, implicit and explicit, conscious awareness and all the other information required to make the body function correctly. The promising thing was that children's brain were more plastic than adults which meant their neurons could regenerate, so with time, the partial paralyses could be alleviated by properly exercising the limbs. Also, stem cell and genetic engineering by that time was making promising leaps. The only problem with conditions similar to his sister's was that even if the cortical neurons are regenerated the information and the memory wouldn't be retrieved. In other words, it would be like having a damaged computer. Even if you could restore the corrupted hardware, there would be the chance that the corrupted or deleted files would not be able to be restored without a backup.

Young Nimrod thought that a large portion of his sister's memory and personality was already backed up in his own brain since he used to play and spend a lot of time with her. He remembered everything about her: her personality, her voice, and what made her happy or sad. He thought if science advanced enough it should be able to track his sister's data and information in his own brain and then it should be able to transfer it back to his sister's brain.

***

Young Nimrod began his scientific journey at a very early stage of his life spending most of his time reading lots of recent papers and books on his sister's condition. He emailed various labs around the world faking his age and representing himself as an interested PhD student through which he was able to share many of his ideas with them. He was hoping that some of his ideas would be taken seriously, and he himself was working on the details as he have already found some theoretical solutions for his sister's condition. He thought that by the end of the following year that he would have a complete model and design on how to fix and restore the permanent cortical brain damage. However, the technicality was still a major obstacle for him, he needed some time to arrange for the necessary tools and equipment to achieve the intended goal. Nevertheless, everything now appeared clear to him that within a short time he would be curing his sister and apologizing to her again.

That day he came back from the school skipping all the way home from happiness. As his mother opened the door for him she saw her smart young son with a wide smile on his face.

"Mother, I promise you will see my sister recover. I have found out how to cure her condition, so just wait for me!" he said to his mother eagerly.

"I'm proud of you, son, and I believe you can do it," she said.

In the night, *Young Nimrod* arranged the list of things he needed to collect to build his own lab and translate his theories into practice. He thought to himself, 'Everything is ready. Now, I can keep my promise to my mother and not only protect my sister but save her too.' He remembered his father's strong words which had ignited the god inside of him again. 'I'm now much stronger, much smarter. I have taken the challenge from Nature and I will win soon. I feel like I'm God,' he thought to himself.

That night he had a comfortable sleep for the first time since his sister's condition. When he woke up the next day, his eyes were still half opened but he could see his parents were confused, worried and in a hurry again! He saw his mother holding his little sister in her lap and rushing out. 'What is happening!' he thought to himself as he quickly jumped out from his bed without changing his pajamas and ran after them toward the car. He put himself into the back seat again before the car started to move. What he saw in the car was his worst nightmare. His little sister was gasping her last breaths. She was fighting death, and it seemed to be her last few minutes in life. Her eyes rolled upward and she was extremely pale. His mother was trying to sense her carotid pulse in her neck, and she was still able to feel the pulsation. She kept saying, "Please keep strong until we arrive, please." In a few minutes with father's speedy driving, they were able to arrive at the hospital. Their child was breathing hard but her pulse was getting weaker and weaker, so the doctors decided immediately to intubate her to assist her breathing. They didn't know yet what could be causing her condition to exacerbate so suddenly. Her brain stem was now in danger, and if the neurons in that part of her brain degenerated then the breathing and heartbeat would stop permanently and everything would go forever.

After taking her to the respiratory care unit, *Young Nimrod* and his parents were waiting outside cautiously hoping for any good news. For *Young Nimrod*, this was emotionally the most intensive moment in his life. 'I need her to stay alive at least for another month,' he thought to himself. He started to pray again to ∞Illuhim∞ in his heart. 'Please keep her alive, just for another month, or maybe another week. Please give me this chance. I know I was arrogant again, and I placed myself in your position. I admit I'm the scum among your creations, and I deserve your ultimate punishment, but please my sister has nothing to do with that, she is pure, innocent, and needs your help.' He kept reciting these words while his hands were shaking and his heartbeat started to increase. 'I can't lose her now after all I did in the last year to save her!'

One doctor came out from the intensive care unit and shook his head to his parents with a sad face, and his mother burst into tears while his father tried to calm her down. *Young Nimrod* was in a state of shock; he couldn't cry because he was yet to grasp what was happening and he was in complete denial. At that moment he heard his father tell the doctor that he would like to leave his daughter's dead body in the teaching hospital for scientific research in the hope that doctors and scientists would be able to understand conditions like hers and discover a cure for it to help others.

***

Back at home, *Young Nimrod* locked himself in his room as he eventually grasped the fact that his little sister was gone forever. He didn't come down for lunch nor for supper that day. His parents began to get worried about him as their frequent calls to him were not answered.

"Poor boy he studied very hard and he thought he was close to finding a cure, but now he is very disappointed," the mother said. "I think he was emotionally attached to his little sister and felt responsible for her health."

"We should give him some time. He will soon get over it," the father said.

"I don't think he will forget easily. I think we need to tell him that his sister is alive and now in heaven," she suggested.

"And how will that make a difference?" he said.

"It doesn't make a difference for her, but it might provide for our son a sense of emotional relief to believe that he can meet his sister again in another life," she said. "Please let me do that, as our son is not going through a normal situation and he is suffering now."

"Do what you think is right to do," the father said in a discouraging voice.

Young Nimrod recoiled himself under his desk for the entire day. He was thinking about his sister, and he remembered everything he read about death from his medical books. His sister's body was going through irreversible changes with her body cells decomposing back into elementary materials. Nothing now could be restored. 'I'm a huge failure. I failed everyone.' He remembered the day in the school when he said to his teacher that he wanted to become a god. 'How silly I was! I should have said: I want to become a failure, a waste, a piece of trash,' he said to himself. 'I'm nobody but a useless creature who can't save anyone.'

That moment he heard his mother was trying to open the door. "Where are you?" his mother said when she entered the room.

"Please leave me alone!" he shouted from under his desk.

His mother approached him and sat next to him under the bench

"Do you want to know where your sister is now?" she said.

"I know where she is. She is in the dissection room and soon her body will degenerate to nothingness again," he said in an angry voice.

"That is only her body, but her soul is in heaven. She is now a butterfly wandering among the flowers in paradise," the mother said in a soft warming voice.

"I know that is not true, there is no soul and you don't believe in it either," he said. "Please don't try to comfort me with such myths."

His mother realized that her plan would not work with her son. After all, he had grown up in an atheist family, so he would know that she was faking her belief in the afterlife no matter how much she tried to act realistically.

"Then, what are you planning to do? You can't stay under the desk and not eat anything forever," she said.

"I just want to die," he said.

The mother realized his son was in a deep depression, so she thought she needed to do something, otherwise, she couldn't afford to lose her remaining child. 'Think, please think,' she said to herself while she was trying to find another way to approach her son and relieve him of his depressive thoughts. She looked at her thumb and saw a faint scar of a recently healed wound.

"Look at this scar," she showed the scar to *Young Nimrod*. "I accidentally cut my left thumb yesterday. My entire body was in pain because of the wounded thumb. My legs took me to the bandage site, and my right hand took the bandage out and my eyes guided my other body parts to wrap the bandage around my thumb. All the parts of my body helped each other to fix my wounded thumb."

Young Nimrod listened tentatively to see his mother's point as she continued to explain, "The world we live in is like a body. When someone is in pain, others will feel the pain too, so they seek to find a solution to relieve it." She then continued, "You were in an emotional pain because of your sister's pain, and this has made you stronger and smarter. You almost found the cure for your sister's condition."

"But I failed and she is now gone forever," he said.

"No you didn't fail, you should use what you have found to cure other disabled children like your sister. They are suffering now and they need your help," she said.

"I only wanted to help my sister," he said.

"Don't say that! Nature has sacrificed your sister to find a cure for one of its problems, and now she has found the cure through you," she said.

"But why would Nature choose to sacrifice my poor little sister?" he said.

"Nature knew that you are smart, so she chose to sacrifice your sister hoping from a smart brother like you to find a cure," she said.

Young Nimrod shed a tear, "That is not fair. My sister wanted to grow up to be a young beautiful lady not to die and suffer," he said.

The mother exhaled a sigh and put some emphasis on her sentence, "You might not believe me, but it was your sister who accepted to sacrifice herself. She did that so that every kid with such a condition would benefit from your invention," she said.

"That is not true! You are just trying to relieve my pain. Nature blindly chose my sister," he said.

"But your sister was not blind, and she deliberately put you through emotional pain by making you fall in love with her then by leaving you early," she said.

Young Nimrod remembered his sister's last words when she said sorry to him before she fell into the coma; he wished his sister had never said that. It was like a deliberate set-up to increase his emotional pain even much.

"If you die now, it means your sister sacrificed herself for nothing," the mother said. "Nature will have to sacrifice many more children with your sister's condition until she finds another smart person like you who can find a cure, so don't let this cycle go on forever. You are already close to finding the cure, so try to save others. Try to save them in the name of your sister, and you can name your discoveries after your sister. She would be proud of her sacrifice and Mother Nature will list her sacrifice among the most valuable sacrifices. Your sister will be immortal!"

The mother then stood up to leave the room, but she turned to *Young Nimrod* to say her final words. "It's your choice. Die now and waste your sister's sacrifice or finish your invention and crown your sister's sacrifice."

Young Nimrod thought deeply about his mother's advice for a while, and then he looked at the picture of his sister on his desk. The picture had always reminded him of her and fueled him to strive to achieve the impossible. His sister was gone, maybe he needed to forget about her and move on with his life. His sister was one of many kids who were suffering, and he needed to throw away the picture. A picture that once stimulated him but now could hold him back. He took the picture down and found a lighter before igniting a flame at the corner of the picture. "Rest in peace my little sister," he said while watching his sister's picture burn in the hope that she would be erased from his memory.

Chapter 22

During one of his night shifts at the Rizgary teaching hospital, Sardar was doing his usual tour among the patients, and he came across a newly admitted one who had a recent trauma from a road traffic accident. His x-rays showed a fractured thigh, there was a traction set pulling on his broken leg. His condition and vital signs were already stabilized and he was on the operation list for the next day. During the history taking, Sardar asked him few questions to check his general condition.

"I have a severe pain in my thigh," the patient complained to Sardar. "Doctor, please give me a strong pain killer."

Sardar looked at his medical tests and history; the patient had a road traffic accident this afternoon, apart from a broken femur there were no any other serious findings, however, because the trauma was recent, there might be some torn organs in his abdomen or maybe a small latent bleeding in his skull that didn't show up yet in the medical images. In such cases, monitoring the vital signs was important, but what was more important was to look for any newly reported pain especially in the abdomen or any severe headache which could mean internal bleeding. The pain in this case was the best indicator because it usually appears before the deterioration of the vital signs which were recorded by the tools and devices connected to the patient.

Sardar couldn't easily decide whether to give the patient a strong painkiller to relieve him from his excruciating pain in his broken leg or not because a strong pain killer could potentially mask other pain sources which may appear later and indicate a serious new development. The decision to give or not to give a strong painkiller to a recent trauma case was not a sharply defined black and white situation in medicine. In his medical school, they taught him that doctors were essentially painkillers, after all, pain is the main reason that brings patients to the hospital in the first place. Relieving pain before diagnosing the situation firmly was not usually indicated because pain is the crowning achievement of Nature. Ever since neurons evolved to perceive pain, the survival rate in the animal kingdom had increased dramatically. For example, patients with Congenital Insensitivity to Pain with Anhidrosis 'CIPA' usually injure themselves without noticing and hence, their survival rate is much lower than those who feel the pain. Also, patients with diabetic neuropathy might usually pass away because of heart diseases without reporting or feeling any chest pain which is usually the initial symptom that brings the patient to the hospital to receive the necessary treatment and survive. Because pain was so important for the survival of our species, Sardar thought natural selection may push this trait even further to fine tune the perception of pain in the subsequent generations. In his current case he wanted to behave rationally and so prescribed a weak painkiller for the patient, a lightweight painkiller which could relieve the patient from some pain in his broken leg but would not mask other pain sources that could arise later due to serious internal bleeding.

    Later on that night he was lying on his hospital bed in the on call room hoping to rest and wished for no complications among the patients which could potentially disturb his night shift. He began to think about emotional pain, which was another type of pain and it was no less beneficial than the physical pain itself. The emotional pain that arose from the loss of a loved one or death of a close friend could be massive, although humans and elephants were probably the only creatures who mourn their dead. The afterlife promises could suppress this type of pain effectively but it could also mask potential problems in the world, problems that need proper understanding and diagnosis.

Science was still behind in curing death but the emotional pain arose from losing a loved one motivated many scientists to find a cure one day, hence, according to Sardar no faith should suppress the emotional pain with afterlife promises. Emotional pain might be the necessary sacrifice we have to pay to reach a bigger goal.

Sardar was immersed in his thoughts as he started to fall asleep, but suddenly his quiet night was interrupted by a phone call! The call was from a nurse informing him that one of the patients was in trouble, so Sardar quickly put on his white coat and rushed to the nurse's station. The nurse told him that the patient with the broken leg was still complaining from pain and couldn't sleep.

"Doctor, your painkiller didn't work. I still have pain and can't sleep," the patient said to Sardar.

"Is it the same pain from your broken leg or a new pain at another site?" he asked.

"No, it's the same pain, but your painkiller didn't relieve it," the patient said.

"Can't you endure the pain just for tonight? You had a recent trauma and I really don't want to mask other potential pain symptoms that may arise," Sardar said.

"One night without pain is better than a thousand nights with pain. Doctor please. I just want to sleep," the patient said.

The nurse came closer to Sardar. "Doctor, please let me inject him with a strong painkiller, otherwise, he will not let us sleep," she said.

Sardar finally agreed to his request but he found himself in a deep moral dilemma. On one hand, he blamed the religious clergies for giving afterlife promises to people, following their wishes, relieving them from the fear of death and masking the bigger problems of Nature. On the other hand, he himself, and many other doctors he knew, didn't usually act rationally and follow the patient's wishes!

The next morning, Sardar woke up from his sleep. He looked at the time and realized it was the time to do his morning tour among the patients before he could gave the shift to the next doctor. He started with the patient with the broken leg, "How do you feel now?" Sardar asked the patient.

"The second painkiller you gave me was great. I slept very well last night. Thank you," the patient replied.

Sardar looked at the vital signs and they all looked normal, and he felt lucky that the patient didn't develop any other serious problems that night. After all, his decision to give the strong painkiller was the right thing to do, he made the patient sleep comfortably without any pain, and he was able to sleep that night too without anyone waking him up during his sleep.

Chapter 23

Going back to the time when *Young Nimrod* was a teenager in the high school, he was an overachiever. In fact he was able to pass the exams from classes higher than his age, so the school decided that he can skip tenth grade and go directly to the eleventh grade where his age was only sixteen among a class of seventeen year olds. His eagerness and passion to read books that were out of his league was remarkable. His parents were very happy to see their son getting over the trauma of losing his little sister several years ago. He returned back to his usual life, stronger, smarter, and even more eager to invent something beneficial for humanity. "Our son will make us proud," the mother said.

"This is all the result of my wise upbringing," the father said.

"What! You barely talk to him!" she said. "It's all me who advises him and talks to him."

After a lengthy debate about who was to be credited the most for the child's upbringing, the father took out a book from a package he had recently bought for *Young Nimrod* at his request; the mother looked at the title of the bulky book.

"Is this a physics book?!" she asked with an eager voice.

"Yes it is," the father replied. "I find it a bit strange that he now asks me to buy books with advanced topics in physics. I don't know why he is no longer interested in reading medical books as before," he wondered.

"Maybe his real interest is physics. We shouldn't oblige him to become a doctor," she said.

"I see. His previous interest in medicine might have been due to his effort to find a cure for his little sister," he said. "I agree with you. We should now let our son to choose what he would like to be."

Later on that day *Young Nimrod* returned home from school, he found on his desk the book that he asked his father to buy for him. He immediately opened the hard covered book which was titled, *Time According to Relativity Theory and Quantum Mechanics* and he eagerly then navigated to chapter twelve which was titled 'Time Travel According to Relativity'. He began to read that chapter eagerly. This was not the first time he read such a topic, in fact, his online searches, and bookmarks were mostly articles about time travel. After he finished reading the chapter, he opened the drawer of his desk and took out the picture of his young little sister which was half-burned! Nevertheless, he was still able to see his little sister's smiling face in the picture. 'You are always in my heart; I will do anything to bring you back.'

He remembered the day when he forced himself to forget about his little sister and tried to get rid of her picture through burning it. He looked straight into her bright eyes which had survived the burn, and saw innocence, purity, love, and everything could have been seen through her eyes. The flashback of his sister's seizures, pain, and suffering all came back to his memory. 'I failed to save you despite considering myself a god, in fact I was responsible for your condition. My anger made you stress out and become vulnerable to the condition that took your life! I have been an arrogant person outside but nothing inside. I couldn't keep any of my promises. I had promised my mother to protect you but I failed. Above all that, I tried to burn your picture and dismiss you from my memories!' he thought to himself while tears and rage from his past behavior took over him. 'I swear that is not me. I'm not the kind of person who doesn't keep his promises. I'm not the kind of person who gives up easily, so just wait and see. I will bring you back even if I need to change the rules of physics!'

***

According to the theory of relativity, time is relative and it can be made to pass slower or faster depending on the speed of a reference frame, however, the change in time is barely detectable unless on frame velocities approaching the speed of light, and according to the theory, time would stop when the speed of a frame reaches the speed of light! Although Einstein's theory set the ultimate possible velocity to be the speed of light in a vacuum, some physicists suggested that in a hypothetical case if a frame passed the speed of light then time could be reversed.

The technicality of the procedure to make things move faster than light was impossible to be achieved anytime soon. *Young Nimrod* knew this, and he also was aware that the entire thing was out of his league. No matter how much he studied, or how smart he became, he would never ever be able to invent a time machine by himself. Luckily, that time in 2040, there was a respected science project called TNARK which had started ten years ago and all the scientific media were talking about it due to its ambitious futuristic goals.

The project's aim was to imitate Noah's ark, but not by taking a pair of every animal species into a ship and saving them, but by taking the best genetic characteristics from all the animal species and combining them into one body which would result in a super smart and a super powerful organism which could survive any environment.

Young Nimrod thought if TNARK project was successful in transcending humans into super-humans, their immortal bodies could survive the crushing forces of the black holes.

Hence, a super-human could safely pass through the wormhole, a bridge for space-time travel at the center of black-hole, without disintegrating inside it due to the immense gravitational force. 'If I have the immortal super-body, I could travel back in time using a wormhole bridge at the center of one of the black holes to save my sister in the past,' he thought to himself.

Young Nimrod's attention diverted toward the TNARK project. All his plans since then were how to get closer to that project and participate within it. He felt lucky that he lived in a time where such a trans-humanic project did exist. However, one thing puzzled him: if time travel was possible, then why he hadn't he seen any super-humans coming back yet? Was it because time travel was impossible or that the future super-humans deliberately chose not come back? He kept thinking about this puzzle until one day he saw a TV interview with the renowned astrophysicist, Neil Baron. The interviewer asked him some questions about the time travel.

"Do you think time travel is possible?" the interviewer asked Neil.

"There is no question about that. Einstein's theory of relativity clearly says that 'time' is a relative concept. It can be slowed down, sped up, or even reversed depending on the relative movement of one frame to another frame," he answered.

"Then why hasn't anyone come back from the future at least to say 'Hi' to us?" the interviewer asked.

"To be able to say 'Hi' to your past or to the people in your past, you would need to go back in time as an independent observer," Neil answered. "I don't really know how someone could do that, but my guess would be that even if you could do that, you couldn't change your past because your present depends on it."

"Even saying 'Hi' to your past can change it?" the interviewer asked eagerly.

"Even saying 'Hi'," Neil confirmed. "It's like the butterfly effect. Think of it as a movie with a coherent story. Each event in the movie leads to the upcoming event, you can't simply edit any specific event in such movie without changing the outcome." He continued, "Let me put it simply, if someone went back in time and killed your great-grandfather, then you would not exist, and if you don't exist many other things that depend on your existence would not exist too, so the chain would go on forever."

"So you are saying the super-humans of the future will never choose to travel back in time?" interviewer said.

"And why should they? They are now in their perfect form, immortal, and living happily. Why would they choose to disturb their existence?" he said.

Young Nimrod bit his tongue from rage while watching the interview. 'How can the future super-humans be so cruel? Seeing a past of pain and suffering but yet deliberately choosing not to come back?' he asked himself. The content of the TV interview was very disturbing for him because it meant he couldn't go back to save his sister without making a series of changes to many other interconnected events which could ultimately affect the entire reality. 'If TNARK is able to produce the super-body in my lifetime, then I will definitely choose to travel back in time to save those who were suffering in the past,' he thought. 'I will never accept to live in any attractive future without saving my sister and all the other people who have been sacrificed in the past. The fact that no one has come back from the future to save my sister means that TNARK was not able to produce the super-body in my lifetime and its future outcome is a heartless super-human who doesn't think like me!'

Young Nimrod began to realize the horror of the reality he lived in with the terrible, unfair Mother Nature which everyone loved! Evolution itself was entirely based on sacrificing poor creatures who couldn't survive through Nature's harsh environments. The survival of the fittest was necessary to filter out faulty genes, and given enough time, evolution would be able to produce a perfect creature which could perfectly pass Nature's ultimate challenge. A super-human who would become the crowning achievement of evolution, a perfect form that could accommodate and survive any environment. If it came back to its past, it could see the past imperfections, and it would see the sacrifices made for it, but it couldn't intervene or save those who were suffering in the past because saving them would mean the extinction of the super-human itself. The entire thing was like a one direction path where there is only one winner at the end, and everybody else is just a mere sacrifice for the winner!' The realization of this unfair reality rendered *Young Nimrod* completely powerless.

He looked at the burnt picture of his sister. 'Every time I think there is hope, the impossible strikes again and all the doors are closed on me!' he said to himself in a frustrated voice while shedding tears of sorrow. 'But does a future super-human have a heart? Emotion? Mercy or any good quality? How could it simply live on the pile of sacrifices and sufferings made for it and yet be happy?' For *Young Nimrod*, this was morally unacceptable. This was the first time he wished that ∞Illuhim∞ of the Abrahamic faith was real. 'At least there is some hope in that reality,' he thought to himself.

Then he remembered the figure of light he saw during his prayers for his little sister. 'Was that ∞Illuhim∞ himself?' he wondered. 'Could ∞Illuhim∞ himself be a super-human from the future? Could he be the future product of TNARK or something similar?' he kept thinking then he looked up and shouted in an angry voice, the voice of someone who felt betrayed, "∞Illuhim∞ I know you are up there in your perfect form, living in the Garden of Eden with many angels and looking down upon us! How could you see my little sister suffering but not save her? I just can't understand that. Is it because you can't sacrifice your current perfect state for the past?" He followed "A real god would give up his kingdom and choose to sacrifice himself for everyone"

***

That night *Young Nimrod* fall into sleep on his desk, but his sleep was full of nightmares. A hopeless dark reality was immersed in broken symmetries as the gods of the future fed upon the sacrifices of their pasts! How unlucky to be born into such a reality! What was our purpose in this universe? Are we here to find the cure for Nature's imperfections? Are we here to prepare a fertile ground for evolution and merciless Nature so that a god will emerge from our sacrifices? Are we here to serve his existence? Will he appreciate the sacrifices made for him? Will he ever decide to come back in time to end our endless suffering?' *Young Nimrod* was immersed deeply in a sleep where these thoughts came back to him repeatedly until the next morning when a ray of light came through the window next to his bench and hit his face. He opened his eyes and lifted his head trying to expose his face fully to the light to escape from the dark nightmares which were still haunting him even with eyes half-opened!

Suddenly, he saw another door of hope opening to him 'If super-humans own our future, we own their past,' he thought. 'I can change their future by changing their past. I can change the mind of a future super-human by trying to understand how a mind works and how to control it, then I can intervene in TNARK project with a plan to control their future outcome and make it behave like I want.' He had the crude thought, although he didn't know the details of his plan, but the idea was an enough fuel to get him going.

He decided to study more about the human mind to understand it better. By the age of 28 he had already made a fortune, so he began to close himself from many of the world's big laboratories by either funding their projects or contributing to them directly especially TNARK project since it was the leading trans-humanic project at that time.

Many years later, TNARK held its annual private meeting among its high profile scientists and funders, and in the meeting the latest findings and technologies that science had reached which could help to make the super-human possible were presented.

A group of scientists presented their latest achievement in genetic engineering. They showed a model of a body that looked like a human but the underlying structure was a hybrid from many species. They also exhibited organic skin that looked like human skin but was tough, resistant to burns, cuts, and stretching. The internal body was a highly configured system of energy production. It didn't have stomach, kidney and intestine, because after all the super-body didn't need food to get energy since it derived its energy directly from nuclear fusion inside him.

For many scientists, it looked like within years TNARK's dream would become a reality but their final obstacle was the brain. How could they transfer human consciousness into the super-body?

There was another problem that came up at the meeting. Some of the elementary materials that were necessary to produce the proposed super-body were extremely scarce! The question which presented itself was: how could they produce a super-body for everyone living on the planet, nine billion super-bodies?!

According to the group, given the availability of some of the rare but necessary elements such as promethium and yttrium for their project, they could only build few super-bodies! This brought back Catherin's warnings about using scarce materials in the project. Nevertheless, scientists decided to take advantage of any possible idea that could be successfully implemented in practice without caring much about which elementary materials were being used.

It was obvious if that proposal was successful, then because of the limited number of super-bodies, only a subset of humanity might be able to take advantage of the trans-humanic projects! This was simply not acceptable among the scientists and everyone insisted that if such project ever became reality then its services should be available to everyone.

The limited number of the super-bodies which TNARK could produce and the inability to transfer consciousness to these super-bodies became the project's major enigma. From that moment on, the attention and the effort of all its scientists and contributors was directed toward solving these two remaining issues.

***

In 2050 during the annual private meeting of TNARK, one of the neuroscience laboratories claimed that they came up with a solution for the two riddles at least in theory. They claimed that TNARK didn't need to make so many copies of the body since the body was immortal and resistant to the threats posed by the universe's deadly forces, hence, reproduction and gender defining parts were not necessary. For the brain part, they came up with a design that could potentially combine the memories and the conscious awareness of many people into one single super-brain. They called the process 'Collective Consciousness'.

The super-brain would be able to hold the memory, personality, opinion, and the conscious awareness of all nine billion people alive together. The Collective Consciousness proposal presented itself in the meeting as the most practical design and the least costly since it required only one super-body, so the committee decided to give huge funds to that solution.

According to the Collective Consciousness proposal, since all the necessary information that defined human identity and the sense of self-aware are embedded within the configurations of the heavily interconnected neurons inside the brain, then the proposed interconnections between the neurons of the super-brain should be proportional to that of population. There were a lot of differences among people in the way they used their brains to think and remember, but there was a high degree of similarity which was supported by many brain imaging studies.

For Collective Consciousness to work, the super-brain should be able to fairly represent the entire brain population of all the nine billion brains composing it. Hence, the 'democracy' concept came into play, and this involved the ancient idea of combining many brain efforts together through voting. If 90% of people were against 'something' then the super-brain should be against that 'something' with 90% probability. To achieve that, 90% of the inter-neuronal connections within the super-brain should be arranged in a similar way to the 90% of the brains who voted against that 'something' and only 10% of the inter-neuronal connections within the super brain should be arraigned to yield an opposite decision.

The committee was not 100% happy with the proposal, but it was the most plausible and practical one in their hands at that moment because the neuroimaging technologies for reading inter-neuronal connections were already available, and the large 3D bio-printing companies were already close to be able to bio-print all human organ tissues including the brain tissues.

There was another non-science related problem associated with the Collective Consciousness proposal and it was discussed intensively during TNARK's private meeting: What if some people refused to be a part of the Collective Consciousness or opposed it? Some argued that people should have the freedom whether to participate or not and be a part of the super-brain or stay in their current form, similar to evolution where some cells in the past decided to stay as free living amoebas while others combined to form multi-cellular organisms. After all, the purpose of evolution was to maximize the variability among its species so that it increases their chance of survival from unexpected threats which may lead to the extinction of one variety but not another.

Finally, the committee agreed that the discussion about how many people should participate or not was a political one and it was not of their concern at the moment, but as scientists they should be able to find new ways to save life on earth, otherwise, life would face extinction sooner or later because of various threats such as the Doomsday Meteor.

***

When *Young Nimrod* received the detailed report from the last private TNARK meeting, the proposal of Collective Consciousness irritated him a lot. 'They are misunderstanding democracy' was his initial feeling. 'How did they agree on this plan?' he asked himself. The problem of democracy for *Young*

Nimrod was evident. With democracy, common ideas would dominate, rare ideas would be dumped, the process wouldn't recognize the quality of a specific idea, and all it would assess would be quantity! The Collective Consciousness presented the same problem for *Young Nimrod*. 'I have the best idea. The best plan to save this world is embedded in my brain, and I'm the only one who possesses a high quality moral ideology that cares about everything. If TNARK made its super-brain to be based on the collective knowledge of nine billion people, then TNARK will be the grave of my ideas. Silly, selfish, common ideas which are shared by the majority of people would excel and dominate over the super-brain! On the other hand, rare but high quality ideals such as mine would be dumped forever and, hence, the ideas of common illiterate and ignorant people would control the most sophisticated super organism in the universe!'

He realized that this could be one of the reasons why probably nobody had come back from the future yet. 'If ∞Illuhim∞ is the product of such collective knowledge then no wonder why it is not coming back to save us from our horrors,' he thought to himself. 'I need to make some changes. TNRAK has already decided to play by democracy. If they insist on that, I will need to play their game too by making the majority of people to think like me before TNARK is able to build its super-brain. I need to make everyone on this planet think like me, and even if I die, the future generation should think like me. I own the past and I'm currently living it, so I can do something to make future humans think about coming back to save us from this cruel Nature no matter what the odds are.'

From that day onwards, *Young Nimrod* began seriously to set a plan, an effective plan that could achieve the spread of his presumed high ideals. He remembered a thrilling technology for brain control that he had come across during his studies. It was called optogenetics, and although it has been around for 50 years, it didn't have any practical application so far. Its use was mainly restricted to scientific research, but for *Young Nimrod* this technology could have the potential to control people's minds directly, however, the process was intensive because it involved direct stimulation of the genetically modified neurons by pulses of blue light which required opening the skull and exposing the brain tissue directly to achieve the stimulation.

He created a detailed plan with its execution spanning over several years. His master plan was to make as many people as he could on earth think like him, share his ideals, and to think about everyone's suffering not only in the present but in the past too. 'What is gone is not gone. What is gone has to be fixed.' This was the new motto people should believe in, according to *Young Nimrod*. 'We should not submit to Nature. Nature has to submit to us. We are not bound by the rules of physics. The rules of physics are bound by our beliefs.' These were the new ideals *Young Nimrod* kept thinking about and how to impose them upon everyone. 'If I make more people think like that then TNARK's super-brain would not rest unless it found a solution for the poor souls and the sufferings in the past.'

He remembered his mother's words about Nature's sacrifices to progress herself toward perfection. 'No mother, you were wrong. Nature made her biggest mistake when she tortured and sacrificed a poor soul in front of me! If this is what Nature has to do to progress, then I'm anti-Nature. If that is the law of the universe, then I'm the lawless,' he said to himself in a confident voice.

Young Nimrod also found a loophole in the Collective Consciousness proposal. If an idea was shared by many people, it would dominate over the other solitary ideas. What was more, because the ideas were embedded within heavily interconnected neurons, they were also connected to other separate networks that may hold other ideas which could dominate too even if they were less commonly shared ideas! This problem existed in the Collective Consciousness design because it was inherent within the 'democracy' system itself. For instance, the majority of voters may have a strong opinion about some controversial topics such as same-gender marriage or immigration, hence, they might vote for a candidate who strongly shares these views with them on a narrow domain of issues without knowing or caring about whether the same candidate shared with them many other ideas such as the candidate's views on the health system, economy or taxes. Thus, the candidate's views on these topics could survive the election and could be imposed upon the public even if they were not shared by the majority of the voters.

Young Nimrod found that the Collective Consciousness proposal, since it was based on democracy, was strongly liable to the same issues, but these could play to his advantage now that he didn't need to copy all his ideas to the people. If he made the majority of people follow even a narrow domain of his ideas strongly, then his entire personality could dominate over the TNARK's super-brain. 'The future god would be me, or at least thinks and behaves like me,' he thought to himself.

***

In 2055, *Young Nimrod* had determined his long-term plan which involved several steps:

First, he needed to genetically modify the neurons in the human brain, since a genetically modified virus could do that, all he needed was to work with some biochemical laboratories to build a harmless airborne virus so that it could infect as many as people as were on the planet with it. He also wanted the lifespan of the virus inside the human body to be short and the immunity of the human system to be able to fight and remove the virus from the body, as this would make the evidence disappear and ensure the harmless nature of the virus.

Second, since the blue light couldn't pass through the human skull, the virus needed to be able to modify the brain neurons to be stimulated by higher frequency lights such as ultraviolet or x-ray as these frequencies had better penetration and could reach deep brain parts such as the amygdala and hippocampus without opening the skull. These brain parts were important for emotion and memory formation, but unlike the cortex, they were situated deep in the brain.

Third, he needed to have access to the brains of a large number of people. Luckily, this was quite possible at his time because of large companies that were using a helmet to interface with their users through reading their emotions and their brain signals like the gaming company Virtual-world™ and the social web page zanzor.com. At that time, it was estimated that 70% of young children and teenagers were already using the helmet for interacting with their games and social media, and that age group was preferable for *Young Nimrod* because of their fresh and adaptable brains.

Fourth, he needed to build and promote for some specifically designed games and online posts that promoted his ideals during the stimulation of the brain parts that were associated with memory and emotion. This would reshape and consolidate the brain of the recipient to be similar to that of *Young Nimrod's*, and they would gradually dream about similar things and share similar ideals to *Young Nimrod*.

Finally, he began to fund various labs to make his plan possible, but he still needed some new technologies to be invented before he could be able to execute the plan, nevertheless, he was so sure about his plan, that he didn't even shed a tear when his parents passed away because he was certain that he would find the cure for everything! All he needed was to make sure that the future super-human thought like him and had his morals.

***

By 2058 *Young Nimrod* has already spent millions of his own fortune to achieve the plan. He expected to get a reply from the many laboratories he funded and urged them to make the necessary changes in the optogenetics field, but years later, none of the laboratories were able to send him the good news he waited for! He had received emails and reports from several labs detailing their failures in making neurons excitable to ultraviolet or x-rays, and few weeks later he received another report from another laboratory he funded to make a harmless airborne virus for the optogenetics. Again, the report yielded all negative results!

This made *Young Nimrod* very angry because he had to take on a lot of risk to keep the project secretive. He spent a huge amount of money to keep the mouths of lab members shut and to continue working on something so controversial, and he even needed to pay for a professional assassin to execute one of the lab members when he found evidence that he was intending to inform the media about the project.

Young Nimrod was the kind of person who never used swear words, but the failure reports he received that day after all the years and effort made him shout and swear. "Stupid neuroscience!" he shouted while hitting his desk. "Every science field advances exponentially except neuroscience. This field advances like a f*cking turtle!"

That day he wandered around thinking about what to do next, after all, many years had passed since his initial plan. He thought he would be able to start copying his brain into the minds of many people by now through the specially designed new helmet, but he was still at step zero! What made his day worse was the fact that the Collective Consciousness staff had already reported to TNARK's committee that they were successful to bio-print the brain tissues of two insects into another insect's brain, and the resulting insect behaved similarly to what they expected from their design. They promised that within the next three to four years, the Collective Consciousness project would be a reality for human brains too.

That was not good news for *Young Nimrod* because he still hadn't spread his thoughts and ideas to the people. 'I'm still nobody in this big world, and the majority of people don't share my high ideals!' he thought. 'If I do not do something within a couple of years, TNARK will produce a heartless selfish super-human who will never look back into the past sufferings! I need to do something soon. I can't entrust my plans on un-invented technologies related to the brain and neuroscience because these two science fields are very unpredictable and advance too slowly.'

While he was wandering around his office thinking deeply about his next step, at that moment, he peeked through a set of books on his bookshelf. There was a copy of the holy§cript! Surprisingly among so many books he had read, the holy§cript was the only famous book that he has never read from cover to cover! In fact, he didn't even remember when and where he got the book. 'Oh, probably Media Rozhgar brought it here,' he thought to himself.

From desperation, *Young Nimrod* took the holy§cript down from the shelf and began to read page after page, chapter after chapter. He realized that many stories and phrases in the book were already shared by the minds of so many people around the globe. *Young Nimrod* felt he was peeking directly at the contents of the brain of the majority of people without using any brain imaging technique, and all of this by just by reading a book!

After reading more than half of the holy§cript, he suddenly paused as if he saw a light, an idea that could save him from failure. He immediately realized that he was looking at the details of his next plan! 'How did I overlook this book for so many years?' he asked himself. 'According to the clergies, this is the only book you need, yet I deliberately ignored reading it!'

Young Nimrod was now convinced that with some luck and determination he could achieve this new plan within a couple of years because the technologies required for this new plan were already invented. They just required some modifications. But first of all he needed to educate people more about the end days and its signs as described literally in the holy§cript, so he wrote a movie script about '*the rise of the Antichrist*' and sent the script to a famous movie director in Holywood with a large amount of money to fund its production by himself and make it a blockbuster hit within a couple years.

Chapter 24

Lee Shark the 45 year old Chinese billionaire was the CEO of the biggest and most revolutionary 3D printing company by 2060. He had three degrees in various academic and business topics including marketing, technology, and psychology. In his later life, he went on to become a successful merchant and entrepreneur, and his academic knowledge about marketing and psychology made him read customers' mind. He knew what made people buy products, so he first invested in what he thought could be a hit product for the next century, the general purpose 3D printer!

Through his many successful investments he had made a great fortune, but his crowning investment was in 3D printers, and his company gradually became one of the biggest 3D printer suppliers around the world. The company he owned re-invented the 3D printer. Now they could print everything from small household objects to living tissues just with the click of a button. Large 3D printers also made easy-to-build, cost effective bridges, houses and buildings.

With his large fortune, Lee Shark was among the big funders of TNARK project. When Neil Baron proposed his idea about changing planetary rotations for some planets in the solar system, making them suitable for human life, Lee promised to build a large number of houses or even cities using his 3D printing facilities if science was ever able to make any planet in the solar system habitable for human life.

Many people considered him an idol and inspiration, and his TED talk was very popular and inspirational. Here was a man from a moderate income family going through a lot of life troubles to finish college, earn three subsequent academic degrees then become one the richest men on the planet!

Lee's contributions to alleviate pain and poverty on the planet were immense, and using his 3D printers he built many houses to shelter refugees for free. He built artificial rivers using a specially developed 3D printer that dug burrows in the ground through reading a digital map illustrating the paths and the branches of the river course, and this technology changed many desert lands to green and productive fields.

In his latest TV interview, he said that he was currently working on a big project which would solve many of the world's problems, and he promised to do what he could to have a positive impact on life on earth. "We need to think of ourselves as gods. If we do so, our self-confidence will increase immensely and then we can achieve the impossible," he used to often say during international conferences and TV interviews.

Chapter 25

Ericson was driving his black Toyota in London when he noticed in his wing mirror a white Land Rover following him! 'How did they know I'm in London!' he wondered. 'Stupid Interpol must be aware that I know they are following me!' He was very irritated with Interpol as they had increasingly stalked him recently. 'I need to do something; I need to get a lawyer soon,' he thought. That moment he saw the traffic light at the next intersection turn yellow, and he thought if he could get through the light before it turns red, he could leave Interpol's car behind and disappear from their sight. He pushed the gas pedal forcefully and sped up as far as he could to pass the traffic.

The next day Mark heard the unexpected news from Agent Roger as they met in his ICPI office again. "Ericson was killed in a road traffic accident!" he said to Mark.

"How?!" Mark said showing his surprise.

"He went through a red light and was hit by another car," Roger answered.

"Was he aware of you following him?" Mark asked.

"Unfortunately yes. I think he was trying to leave us behind when he went through the red light," Roger suggested.

Mark thought for a while as he did not know whether to be happy or not for such news. Deep in his heart he was afraid that his main suspect might not be the one he was looking for, nevertheless, he was confident that Ericson was hiding something relevant to their investigation. "Can we get a permit to investigate his office? I need to get access to all his classified documents as soon as possible."

Mark urged Interpol to move quickly since the recent investigations after the accident with Ericson's secretary had led to the conclusion that Ericson had illegally sold and shared classified laboratory research data with someone outside his TNARK project. Recently, police were able to find documents revealing those parties which Ericson had shared TNARK's latest inventions with them in return for money and among those, someone with a fake ID called *Young Nimrod!*

That was terrible news for Mark because it meant that Ericson was not *Young Nimrod* himself. He was just another scientist used by him! 'I need to act soon,' Mark thought as he found himself coming back to the start again. He was clueless again about the mastermind's identity, *Young Nimrod*. The only clue Mark had was that his main suspect acted according to the prophecies of Abrahamic faith! He tried to read the holy§cript by himself to see if he could uncover another link but he found it difficult to decipher the holy§cript in the way Hast usually simplified the prophecies to him.

Soon he gave up reading the holy§cript by himself and decided to meet Hast again to ask him more questions about the end-days prophecies. He hoped that he could catch another clue, after all, Hast was the theologian and he was an expert in the end-days prophecies. Mark picked up his cellphone and called Hast again.

***

Two days later Mark met Hast again at the Sheraton hotel in Erbil. He revealed to Hast that his main suspect for *Young Nimrod* was Prof. Sanders but now he was dead and that the investigations found that he had sold many of the classified brain reading technologies to *Young Nimrod* through the span of several years, "If *Young Nimrod* is the false prophet, what would he need the brain reading technologies for?" Mark asked Hast.

"I think before you can 'write' you need to be able to 'read'," Hast suggested. "I think he needs the brain reading technologies to understand how the mind works and this would help him to use the optogenetics properly."

"Hmm," Mark thought. "So they are all part of the mind control prophecy!"

"I wonder if Padsha Mali, the faith-healer, is the *Young Nimrod* we are looking for?" Hast suddenly suggested.

"That was what I actually came here to ask you," Mark said. "You told me that Padsha Mali looks like the Antichrist, but who is the false prophet then if Padsha Mali is *Young Nimrod* too?"

"As I said, I think the false prophet could be the AI-revolution owned by Padsha Mali," Hast said.

"That can't be true. I investigated the life of Padsha Mali; he was nobody until very recently when we started our investigation," Mark said.

"Who knows? The Antichrist is the king of mind control, and he has probably made everyone believe that he was a normal guy until recently," Hast claimed.

"I don't see a reason why he would do that, and besides, all the data I have indicates that *Young Nimrod* and Padsha Mali are two separate people. *Young Nimrod* is the mastermind," Mark insisted.

"What if the AI-robot is self-conscious and is now helping the Antichrist?"

"You mean an AI-robot acts on it is own and promotes for Padsha Mali online?" Mark asked.

"Yes."

"That is unlikely because many of the online posts and videos against Padsha Mali are promoted by someone with fake IDs and accounts links back to *Young Nimrod*, too," Mark said.

"Really?" Hast was surprised. "Why would *Young Nimrod* promote against Padsha Mali?"

"That is what I want to understand," Mark said. "Why would the false prophet promote against the Antichrist?"

"I wonder if we misunderstood the prophecies," Hast said.

"Do you remember any more prophecies about the false prophet and the Antichrist in your theological studies?" Mark asked.

Hast felt he was back to the zero point and started to think deeply again about who *Young Nimrod* might be. 'He should be a person with high influence, maybe someone rich who has access to information with governmental and scientific institutions. He should also has the ability to fake IDs and track Interpol's investigation since that would make it harder for the police to uncover him,' Hast thought to himself.

"Can you urge Interpol to arrest Padsha Mali for interrogation?" Hast said.

"I'm afraid I can't without evidence. He has a lot of followers by now and owning a special kind of water with healing power is not a crime," Mark said.

"You have a bigger case here," Hast said. "That man is trying to instigate an apocalypse!"

"But how can I convince Interpol that he is the Antichrist and trying to turn the earth upside-down? Do you think anyone would believe me without any palpable evidence?" Mark asked.

"I understand and Neil Baron himself thought it was impossible to bring the sun from the west unless building hugely insane thrusting engines all over the earth," Hast said.

"If someone is currently trying to build these thrusting engines then he can't hide them and everyone would know about it," Mark said. "The entire process requires lots of time and lots of workers."

Hast thought about that point for a while then he suddenly paused! "What if he was using large 3D printers which can build anything without too many workers in a very short time?" he asked.

When Mark heard the word 3D printers he suddenly realized the plausibility of the idea. "That could be possible because I have heard that the new generation 3D printers can print anything imaginable, no matter how large, provided you put enough amount of the necessary elements into their tanks," Mark said. "I wonder if Lee Shark, the CEO of the biggest 3D printing company, is involved?" he suggested.

"Actually, Lee Shark could have been a perfect candidate for the Antichrist himself," Hast said.

"Why do you think so?" Mark asked.

"Well, he is rich, smart, and he is able to control minds with his convincing speeches. That is why he is usually invited to TED and other important international conferences." Hast continued, "What is more is that he doesn't hide his ambition to be like a god and also encourages others to think like they were gods!"

"But you said the Antichrist is blind and he is not" Mark said.

"He is blind to the truth," Hast replied.

"What truth?"

"The truth that there is only one god, ∞Illuhim∞, and no one can become like him," Hast said.

"Then, what holds you from saying that he is the Antichrist?" Mark asked.

"As I said, according to the prophecies, the Antichrist comes from Babylon," he replied.

"Maybe one of his ancestors descended from Babylon, or maybe he is the false prophet who helps the Antichrist?" Mark suggested.

"Maybe," Hast replied as he began to think about other famous and powerful people who were rich and could have access to both TNARK and 3D printing technologies.

"Kogar Shervan was also …," Hast started saying but before he finished Mark eagerly interrupted.

"Could you repeat the name?"

"Kogar Shervan, the previous governor of Shinar Land," Hast repeated. "He was also very obsessed with 3D printers and he used it for many projects in the region during his rule."

That moment Mark sensed a thrill going through his body, as if he had found the last piece of a puzzle, but at the same time felt furious as he remembered what Hast told him about the Antichrist's mind controlling abilities. From that moment on, Mark couldn't un-think the possibility of Kogar being the *Young Nimrod* himself. 'But why would he hire me to investigate the identity of *Young Nimrod* if he is *Young Nimrod* himself?' he asked himself. 'Did he want to see what an Interpol investigation lead to through me?' Mark remembered the emails he was receiving from Kogar throughout his investigation asking for more updates about *Young Nimrod*. 'I was so silly trusting him blindly and updating him about my investigation progress! If he is *Young Nimrod*, then he now knows how far Interpol is from his suspicious activities through me!' Mark concluded.

"Do you think Kogar comes from Babylon?" Mark asked Hast suddenly.

"That is quite possible," Hast said. "He comes from Shinar Land, and Shinar is geographically very close to the ancient Babylon."

"So do you think he could be the Antichrist?" Mark asked.

Hast was surprised by Mark's question but also found it intriguing. "That is an interesting conclusion, but I wouldn't like to think of Kogar as the Antichrist," Hast replied.

"Why?" Mark asked.

"He was a very good governor, and people loved him. He was also very honest and after his wife died, he promised not to marry again and to my knowledge, he has kept his promise so far. It's been ten years since," Hast said.

"Mind control," Mark reminded Hast.

"Sorry, what do you mean?" Hast asked Mark to clarify more.

"We have been controlled by him," Mark said.

"What makes you jump to this conclusion?" Hast asked curiously.

Mark turned to Hast to reveal the truth, "He was the one who instigated this investigation"

"Did Kogar employ you to investigate *Young Nimrod?*" Hast said.

"Yes," Mark replied.

"And now you think he is the *Young Nimrod* himself?" he asked.

"Yes unfortunately. I think he was tracking Interpol through me!" Mark said.

Hast thought for a moment then turned to Mark as if he had found another clue leading to Kogar, "He is also the founder of zanzor.com, the social media which uses a helmet to read users' emotions. If you are right, that will answer why he needed the brain reading technologies from Prof. Sanders."

As Mark navigated back through the electronic correspondence with Kogar, his suspicions grew more intense.

He turned to Hast, "I'm sorry to involve you in this, but I think for your safety you should opt out from the investigation from now on."

"Are you kidding!" Hast protested. "If Kogar is *Young Nimrod*, then he already knows about me, and there would be no point for me to back down now, besides I'm interested in uncovering the truth even more than you are."

Mark knew he would get this answer. Hast was a man motivated by his religion to act selflessly and who believed in a higher aim which was to save people from the Antichrist!

"OK then," Mark said. "I think we need to act before Kogar knows that we know."

Chapter 26

Young Nimrod was in his underground operation room thinking about his next major step. A couple of months ago, he provided Padsha Mali with a private TV satellite station, so that he could broadcast his preaching and faith-healing to the entire world. He looked at the trends and noticed that the viewers of the TV channel had increased dramatically since the last month, but he needed to promote the channel even further.

The private satellites broadcasting Padsha Mali's preaching had thrust engines attached to them to change their speed and direction around the earth so that their signal transmission to their receiving points on the ground would stay fixed during the great event. 'Every eye will be on you, Padsha Mali, when the day comes,' *Young Nimrod* thought to himself. 'This TV station will be the only one working during the apocalypse, so people need to know about it and watch it desperately when that day comes.'

At that moment he saw a message on his screen from someone he hired a while ago. He opened the message to reveal its content:

Dear Kogar
Our current investigation indicates that Lee Shark could be Young Nimrod*! I will update you when I find more information.*
Yours, Mark

'That is good. Interpol still doesn't have a clue about my true identity,' *Young Nimrod* thought. Moments ago, he was a bit worried that new clues may lead to him after Prof. Sander's accidental death, but after seeing the email, he was reassured. He did find Mark's email a bit strange since it revealed the suspected identity to him so quickly after Ericson's death! Nevertheless, the email was a relief as it showed that so far no one from those he had hired had reached any essential clues about his identity and his plan!

Because of his influence as a former governor, Kogar was able to reach the police's classified documents and investigations, however, large international security organizations had private networks which were hard to hack or get information from, so one way to overcome that was by hiring private investigators from within those organizations. Those private investigators would have access to the internal workings and in case they found any clues, he would know about it! Luckily, so far, none of the investigators he hired from the FBI, Scotland Yard, Interpol, and Asayish had found any important evidence that could lead to him.

That moment he looked around for Media Rozhgar in his underground operation rooms, but he didn't see her anywhere and neither did she answer his calls! Since she hadn't stuck to her usual routine, it left Kogar wondering where she was.

Chapter 27

Media Rozhgar's cousin, Zaniar, was a previous friend of Mark's at Interpol. He had left Interpol to work as a private security manager for one of Kogar's Tek-Brain branches in Erbil after his cousin, who was in close relation with Kogar, encouraged him to do so in return for a good annual salary from Kogar. And Zaniar was the one who suggested Mark's name when Media told him about Kogar's desire to hire a private investigator from Interpol & ICPI.

Zaniar had a four year old child who his cousin, Media, loved, and she came to see and play with the child twice a week usually in the evenings for a few hours. Other than that, nobody knew where she was going the rest of the time. Zaniar knew his cousin had close relations with the previous governor, Kogar, and helped him with his important duties, but that was all he knew about their relationship because his cousin was very secretive about it.

Since Kogar had disappeared from the public, many of his communications and deals were done through Media Rozhgar. People didn't know the reason of his hiding for such a long time. Before, they used to see him frequently on TV interviews and shows, but after his resignation from the position of governor, he gradually faded away from the public eye. Nobody had heard about him since then, and Mark had only met him once several months ago in regard to his query into the blue light emitters. Their communication since then had only been through email messages which he used to update him about his investigations into *Young Nimrod*'s identity.

***

Last night after Mark and Hast's lengthy quest into the identity of *Young Nimrod*, Mark decided to meet his old Interpol friend, Zaniar. Since they were close friends, Mark trusted Zaniar implicitly and he was sure that Zaniar would not involve himself with Kogar in any suspicious activity. However, he suspected Zaniar's cousin, Media Rozhgar, was involved as she was Kogar's business administrator.

Since Mark didn't have any direct contact with Kogar except through email, he thought Zaniar's cousin might help to uncover Kogar's plan. He decided to meet Zaniar that day so that he could find out more about Media. Once Mark had contacted Zaniar telling him that he was in Erbil with a colleague, Zaniar immediately invited them both to his house that evening. "Do you know if we could meet with your cousin, Media Rozhgar, in person?" Mark asked Zaniar while still on the phone.

"She might visit us tonight," Zaniar answered "Come to my house and you might be lucky to meet her."

"That will be great," Mark said. "We will visit you later."

Later that evening both Hast and Mark were welcomed at Zaniar's house. Mark began the conversation by talking about their past at Interpol and Hast asked Zaniar why he had left the organization. One hour later, the doorbell rang. "This could be her," Zaniar said while going to open the door. He was followed by his four year old child who looked eager to meet the comer.

Once the door opened, Media immediately showed her smile to the child and picked her up and the child was so happy. It was though she was meeting her second mother!

Media Rozhgar had always wanted to have a child, but since her current lover didn't want to have children nor could marry her because of the public promise he had made during his time in political office, she understood that she wouldn't have a normal family life if she chose to stay with Kogar, but she was still in love with him and didn't want to leave him. She regarded Zaniar's child as her own and she visited Zaniar frequently to spend time with her cousin's small daughter.

Unlike other days, her cousin had two guests tonight. One of them looked familiar and she remembered him as the Interpol agent who Zaniar recommended for her when Kogar needed to investigate some issues with Virtual-world™. After the introduction and sitting for a while drinking tea, Mark started to ask her questions.

"Sorry to bother you," Mark said, "but I really would like to meet Kogar again in regard to something very important. Do you think it would be possible to arrange a meeting?"

"I'm sorry, but Kogar is very busy at the moment, and he doesn't want any meetings, but you have his email, don't you?" Media said.

"Indeed, but what I need to tell him can't be discussed over email," he said.

"I can take your message to him if you'd like," she said.

"Don't worry. If you think there is no way to meet him, then we should forget about our meeting here. I will just stick to emailing him," Mark said.

During the entire discussion, Media felt that Hast was trying to tell her something but didn't have the courage to say anything! Nevertheless, Media was able to read messages from people's eyes and what she felt was that Hast was trying to give her a warning! At that moment, Media felt that time was passing fast, and she needed to go back to Kogar soon. She took leave of them but before she left, she turned back to the two guests and had final eye contact with Hast while trying to close the door behind her.

"Please take care," Hast whispered to her before she left.

Later on, when Hast and Mark left Zaniar's house, Mark told Hast that he had put a GPS tracker in Media's pocket, and he would be able to find Kogar's location soon.

"Why did you do that? You will be putting her in danger," Hast said.

"I'm sorry but the world is in danger; I need to do something soon," Mark said.

***

On her way back, Media looked carefully around to make sure nobody was following her before driving back to Kogar's residence. She was usually very careful about being tracked. During her meeting with Mark she had noticed that he had put something in her coat pocket in a very sneaky way, but she pretended she hadn't noticed in front of Mark, but she knew it was a GPS tracker. She decided to throw the tracker somewhere so that Mark would not be able to find her location. 'They are really looking for Kogar, but why is the Interpol agent trying to locate him?' she asked herself. 'Kogar trusts me and I should never fail him.' She thought about a way to misdirect Mark, and decided not to go back to Kogar's that night but instead stay in a random hotel and hide the GPS tracker under a hotel bed.

That night she kept thinking about Hast's last words. 'He urged me to take care and he looked worried the entire meeting, but why? I'm not in danger. I'm working with someone trying to save the entire world,' she thought to herself while lying down on the hotel bed. She knew that Kogar was up to something big recently but she never questioned it. She always trusted Kogar and helped him. 'Kogar is the one who understands all the suffering in this world. He looks at it and connects with it every day through his visual eyeglasses, and I have no reason to fear his plan, in fact I need to stand by him until the end. I'm sure he is planning for good,' she thought.

Because Media was attracted to people who showed sincere concerns about others and had a sense of responsibility and leadership, her frequent thoughts about Hast and his words made her dream that night. In her dream she saw chaos, destruction, and dead bodies all around. The ground beneath her had started to split and she couldn't jump to either side and instead fell into the ground before the earth split completely open underneath her. She was able to catch herself on a prominent rock on one side of the split, and she tried hard to pull herself up, but she couldn't. On the top, Kogar was standing and sending his hand to help her. When she looked up she saw the man she had loved all her adult life was sending his hand down to save her, she tried to release her hand on the rocky ledge to catch Kogar's hand. At that moment, on the other side of earth split, Hast shouted loudly to her not to trust Kogar. "He wants to use you for his plans; he doesn't want to save you," Hast yelled to her.

Still in her dream, she thought this couldn't be true. 'I need to trust him. Our relationship is based on trust, and he wants to save me and everyone else.' She extended her right hand to Kogar and when he caught it, she released her left hand. Now it was all on her lover to save her. Kogar tried to lift her up to safety but he couldn't. He tried again but his hand got tired and he was about to fall himself. Media urged him to release her so that he could save himself at least.

"I can't save you," Kogar said.

"Please release my hand and save yourself," she urged him.

"I'm sorry, I'm not God ... yet," he said to her in a regretful voice.

"I trust you, so let me be your sacrifice," she said.

Hast was still shouting on the other side of the earth split, "Please don't sacrifice yourself for him! He is a false God."

"I promise I will come back to save you when I become a god," Kogar said while releasing Media's hand and she fell deep into the darkness.

That moment Media woke up and saw that was 3:00 a.m. She thought this would be a good time to leave the hotel, and leaving the GPS tracker there, she carefully looked around when she left the hotel and drove to her next destination, another random hotel!

Chapter 28

Kogar was worried that Media Rozhgar hadn't come back yet. When he called her again, finally she answered and told him that she had to stay at her cousin's house. This was the first time she had done that, but Kogar didn't ask her the reason because their relationship was built on trust. He only asked her whether she was OK or needed any help or reassurance, but something in his mind told him that she was hiding something from him.

He looked at the screen and everything for his plan was ready. All the progress bars from the 3D printers he was using to print the tools of his plan were showing 100% completion. 'I need to start sometime within the next month,' he said to himself, 'and everything should be fine. I have planned carefully for everything.'

At that moment the indicator showed another new message from the Interpol agent, Mark. This was the third message from him in just two days! He opened the email to read its contents:

Dear Kogar,
We found some new evidence that proves Lee Shark's link with Young Nimrod.
Yours, Mark

Kogar found it strange that Mark was emailing more frequently! 'Did he feel ashamed of his previous failure and now wants to prove himself? And what evidence has he found to link Lee Shark with *Young Nimrod*!'

Kogar thought Mark's behavior was not normal, so he started to analyze his behavior comparing the agent's email sending behavior before and after what happened to Ericson.

The AI-robot was able to analyze the timing between each email sent and also how much time was spent on each email by calculating the time from the opening of an email to the sending of it. The analysis showed dramatic change in the behavior. Before Ericson's death, emails were sent to him with long spaces of time in between, a week or more, or usually as a reply to his own requests, and the duration his client was spending to write each email was short around one minute on average for each email, but after Ericson's death the frequency of the messages he received increased dramatically. He received three messages in just two days and the duration his client was spending to write each email according to the AI-robot was increased to 10 minutes on average per-email!

'It looks like he has thought very carefully about the content he needs to send to me, even though his messages are as short as before, but there is indication that he deletes and re-writes the words again and again! He is clearly hiding something from me,' Kogar thought to himself, then to be sure he put the report by the AI-robot into a psychology software for behavioral analysis to analyze Mark's email changing behavior. The software showed the probable causes for the change in behavior and the confidence rate for each cause as below:

1. The sender has fallen in love with the receiver and is now trying to propose --- 25%
2. The sender is a teenage girl who has suddenly got pregnant and now trying to tell her mother (the receiver) --- 20%
3. The sender has suddenly become paranoid about the receiver --- 18%
4. The sender has got new information and is trying to hide it from the receiver --- 10%

5. Undefined other behavioral changes --- 20%
6. Normal behavioral variation --- 5%

Kogar got worried. He realized that his client was definitely hiding something and not telling him the truth. 'He is definitely not in love with me nor is he pregnant!' he thought to himself. 'I'm sure he still doesn't know about my plan, but I need to eliminate him before he finds out more.' He took out his mobile and dialed one of his favorite assassins informing him about his next target.

Chapter 29

When Media came back to Kogar's operation basement, she apologized for her absence the previous evening.

"Don't worry," he said to Media. "I was just worried about you when you didn't answer my calls."

That night Media was very compelled to ask about Kogar's plan, not only because of her meeting with Hast and Mark, but also because Kogar's behavior had changed a lot recently. He looked worried all the time, and he had spent all of the last two months in this underground operation basement looking at the blue progress bars on the screen. He hadn't shaved his beard for about three months, and neither he did cut his hair. His long brown hair and beard made him look like a different person, and since he had disappeared from the public for a while, if he reappeared now people would not recognize him immediately!

That night she had more nightmares. She saw more destruction in the world in her dreams. It was like Doomsday and everyone was running and the earth was splitting everywhere. When she woke up again later that night, Kogar wasn't in the bed beside her. Even though it was after midnight, he was still awake in the operation basement in front of the big screens moving around and thinking hard as if he was at the final stage of his grand plan, the plan he promised to fix everything in the world.

'What is he really up to?' she asked herself as she was thinking about the destruction she saw in her nightmares. 'How can he be so sure that his plan will bring good, and what if his plan fails? I need to ask him. I have the right to do so.' She collected her courage and walked toward Kogar.

"What are you up to?" she asked him suddenly.

Kogar sensed her question was asked in weird tone as if she was interrogating him. "I'm trying to save the world. You know that, don't you?" he asked her back.

As Media kept seeing flashbacks of the destruction she saw in the dream, she couldn't help but come forward boldly with her suspicion, "Do you plan to destroy the world before saving it?" she asked showing her worries about the safety of the plan.

"I wouldn't call it destruction, and you should trust me," he said to her trying to reassure her.

"Then why is Interpol looking for you?" she asked.

That moment Kogar remembered the reason she had given for her absence last night and the suspicious emails he was getting recently from his Interpol agent. He suddenly felt he was being betrayed by the person he trusted the most, and he was filled with anger and rage. He couldn't hold himself back from attacking Media by forcefully grabbing her neck and threatening to choke her.

"Did you say anything about me to Interpol?" he shouted at her. "How could you betray my trust!"

Media was terrified by Kogar's aggressive and unexpected behavior. It was as if he was a completely different person! She could hardly breathe as he forced his hands into her throat. "I didn't betray you!" she whispered as she was trying with her hands to release Kogar's grip around her, but his grip was powerful and she couldn't overcome it, so she pushed her hand against Kogar's face and her long fingernails stuck into his left eye. Kogar sensing the severe pain released her neck.

Media Rozhgar ran toward the corner after she was released. She was crying hard. "After all these years, how can you still not trust me!" she said while tears streamed down from her eyes.

"I'm sorry. I lost control," he said as he realized he had overreacted, and he remembered his childhood rage toward another innocent life! Then he began to notice that his left eyelid was bleeding. He pushed his palm against the injury to stop the bleeding. "I really need to make the plan succeed. It's the only path to our salvation and I can't afford losing it," he continued.

"I saw you destroy everything in my vision," she said.

"To save this world from its miseries, some sacrifices need to be made," he said. "People will not understand that but I thought you understood me. I need you to be on my side until the end."

Upon hearing him admitting that he was ready to make sacrifices for his goals to come true, Media started to see the truth! Many years ago when she fell in love with him, they started to go out together. She thought she had finally found someone she loved and loved her back until he invested in a social website called zanzor.com where he asked her to put the head cap on to measure her true feelings! Media refused to subject herself to the human made tools telling Kogar that love is not measurable with such tools. This reaction made Kogar paranoid, lost interest in her and eventually breaks up with her. Soon Kogar found someone else to love through the website that supposedly measured true feelings. Kogar's relationship with the other woman developed into marriage, but then later on, his wife was murdered during an assassination attempt targeted toward him.

When Kogar made a promise to stay faithful to his wife and not to marry again, Media's feeling toward him grew again. She couldn't leave him alone when he contacted her again, and she went back to him and they started a secret relationship. She accepted that she would need to sacrifice her wishes for a normal life for Kogar, and she willingly sacrificed everything to stay with him and to help him with his plans, but now she was starting to understand everything!

"Did you sacrifice your wife to boost people's emotions toward you during the elections?" she asked boldly.

Kogar realized that Media was no longer on his side and he could no longer hide the truth from her. "I didn't choose to sacrifice her, Nature did," he said. "Nature wanted me to rise up."

"Do you plan to make me your next sacrifice?" she wondered.

"No, can't you see! Sacrifices are not for me. They are for a higher goal, and you have already sacrificed a lot by giving up your wishes and staying with me helping me to achieve it," he said.

Then Kogar went to a corner and opened a long box. He took out an expensive looking sword. "Do you know whose sword this is?" he continued. "This is King David's sword, and I have spent millions to get this sword. By this blade, half of the ancient world has been conquered, and many sacrifices have been made by this sword, but it still needs one more sacrifice," he followed. "A valuable sacrifice, a sacrifice that will change the world, a sacrifice that will change the mind of ∞Illuhim∞."

Media realized that Kogar would do anything to achieve his goals, even if he needed to destroy half of the world. He saw everything as a mere sacrifice for his goals, and she thought she needed to do something to prevent him. Perhaps today was the last day of her life, but she needed to act soon to save the world from this evil, her true love!

Chapter 30

Mark realized that Media Rozhgar had deceived him as he found his GPS tracker in a random hotel room. This only meant one thing for Mark. 'She knew about the tracker and she is helping Kogar with his plans!' He also realized that he and Hast could be in a real danger from now on, so he called Hast and informed him to take care. Hast quickly took his family to Sardar's house temporarily to distance them from himself as a safety precaution. Then he met Mark again in the Sheraton Hotel to discuss their next steps now that they were certain that Kogar was *Young Nimrod*. They still needed to obtain his location and strong evidence to convince the local police to arrest him since he was a very high profile person.

At the hotel, they put a large map of Shinar Land on the table with a list of possible places for Kogar's current location.

"Where do you think is the most probable hideout for Kogar?" Mark said pointing to the map and the list of possible locations.

"I think it's impossible to find out this way because Kogar has countless company branches and institutions working under him. His operational base could be anyplace on this list," Hast said.

"If Media visits her cousin frequently here in Erbil then Kogar must be close," Mark said.

"Well, with all the fast transportation means in 2060, she could be working with Kogar anywhere!" Hast suggested.

"You are right, but I still think Kogar's current location is no more than 100 miles from here," Mark suggested.

That moment the local TV channel in their hotel room was presenting an interview with a well-known preacher of Abrahamic faith, and during the interview he was urging people and governments to take Padsha Mali down because he thought that the faith-healer would soon be getting evil power and would become the Antichrist, and if nobody did anything to stop him he would eventually destroy the world!

When the interviewer asked the preacher what his evidence was for his claim, the preacher started to talk about the signs of Antichrist. "The triple 6s in Hebrew are clearly evident in the wrinkles on his forehead, his left eye is blind, he has a reddish face, croaky voice, and eyebrows which turn down! The evidence is clear, so what more do you want?!" The preacher said, "∞Illuhim∞ made the signs clear so that faithful people would recognize him."

"But the Antichrist asks people to worship him instead of God, and Padsha Mali doesn't do that. He is even healing people in the name of Abrahamic God, ∞Illuhim∞," the interviewer said.

"He only follows Abrahamic faith and heals people now to attract them to himself and make people emotionally attached to him, but once the end-days come, I'm sure his true face will be revealed. I urge people not to fall for him. The true healer is ∞Illuhim∞," the preacher kept repeating in addition to his warnings during the interview.

Mark was watching the interview every now and then while discussing with Hast the possible locations for Kogar's base.

"How can they let a preacher spread such hate against this man on a national TV?" Mark wondered.

"I agree this will only polarize the world further," Hast said. "Many other social media outlets are now increasingly preaching for hate!"

At that moment Mark received a call from Zaniar, Media's cousin. He told Mark that he was worried about Media because since the last meeting she hadn't visited nor did she answer any of Zaniar's phone calls. Mark told Zaniar on the phone to come to their hotel to discuss what they thought about Kogar with him.

"How could you tell him our address?" Hast protested to Mark. "He might be involved with Kogar, too."

"I don't think so. I trust him a lot, and he is a very close friend," Mark answered.

Several minutes later, Mark stood up and went near the window to grab a glass of water. Hast saw a red laser point on Mark's forehead, so he immediately jumped to push Mark away right before a bullet shattered the window. They both ran to hide underneath a bench away from the window. Mark realized a sniper was on the opposite building. He looked at Hast to make sure he was not in the sniper's sight, and he saw Hast holding his arm to stop some bleeding.

"Are you OK?" Mark asked Hast.

"I'm OK. It is just a superficial scratch," he answered.

At that moment Mark saw a black towel at his hand's reach, so he took it and folded it around a ruler he found under the bench to build something to look like a human head then he lifted the folded towel up to see whether the sniper was still aiming at them. It was just a fraction of a second later that another bullet passed through the folded towel! Mark immediately realized that they were now trapped under the bench because of the room's large window they couldn't safely reach the door on the other side. Hast took his phone and called the local police security, the Asayish. Then, he peeked at the TV screen which was still running the interview with the preacher, and his attention was immediately drawn to the urgent news highlight on the bottom bar which read:

BREAKING NEWS: *Big explosion at Nimrud town*

The urgent news at the bottom bar shocked Hast, and he immediately realized the importance of that location to *Young Nimrod*.

"I think I know where Kogar is! Look at the TV," Hast said to Mark.

Mark moved his head to get a peek at the TV and he saw the news. "We need to go there quickly. If the police get here, we won't have time to reach there quickly enough," Mark said.

"It's only a small step to the door," Hast said to Mark while hinting to him to push the bench together until they got to the other side of the room.

A masked sniper on the other side of the building looked carefully through the zoom for any movement under the bench, but he realized the entire bench was moving! He shot a few bullets toward it but without effect. Soon the bench would be out of his sight, so he needed to act quickly, otherwise, his target would run away. He took out his old Russian weapon, the RBG7, and ran down the building quickly to block his target's way before they could step far away from the hotel.

Hast and Mark got close to the room's exit then they quickly came out under the bench and made a run toward the door. Escaping, they ran down the stairs to the outside garage where Hast had parked his car. Mark and Hast entered the car feeling a bit of a relief as they were about to escape unharmed, but then as their car turned around to enter the main street, through the side window Mark saw a figure of a masked man sitting on his knees holding what it looked like an old RBG7 weapon over his shoulder! Mark quickly shouted to Hast to jump away from the car, and it was only a brief moment later that Mark found himself thrown onto the ground from the force of the explosion. Mark's view became dark for a brief moment as recovered but he saw Hast holding his leg. 'Maybe a piece of shell harmed his leg!' he thought, although on first look it appeared that no major harm was done. But the nightmare didn't end there. Mark realized the masked man was standing over his head holding a gun toward his face. Mark thought this was the last moment of his life, so he closed his eye to accept his doomed fate. That moment he heard a loud gunshot and a heavy object fell over him. When he opened his eyes he saw the 'object' was the masked man who was now soaking in blood over him! He looked forward to see who shot the masked man; it was Media's cousin, Zaniar, who had saved his life! Hast realized the masked man was not Media's cousin as he initially thought. He stood up and his leg injury gave him severe pain, but it wasn't a big deal for him. All he thought about at that moment was to get to the Nimrud town as soon as possible.

"Your cousin is in danger. We need to get to Nimrud town quickly," Hast urged Mark and Zaniar.

Mark took out a cellphone from the masked man's pocket, and he quickly peeked through the man's recent messages. There were a series of text messages between the assassin and an unidentified phone number. Mark immediately realized what they were messaging about, so he pressed the reply button on the masked man's cellphone and sent the message: 'mission accomplished'.

Zaniar directed Hast and Mark toward his car, and they all got in the car. "Can you drive to the airport? Our private jet is there," Mark said to Zaniar.

"There are endless security checks at the airport, especially now that an explosion has happened and we shot someone!" Zaniar said.

"Nimrud town is only 60 miles from here, so we might get there more quickly if we drive fast," Hast suggested.

***

Nimrud town was a historical town located by the Tigris River 20 miles south of Nineveh. It was the place where Nimrod was thought to have ruled the entire ancient world. The town was destroyed and rebuilt multiple times. When Kogar became the governor, the place became a military site with a huge wall surrounding it and it had multiple security checks. For Hast, this looked like a perfect place for Kogar's operational base; it also had historical importance so no wonder *Younger Nimrod had* decided to choose it. After 40 minutes of driving they reached the site. The police and Asayish were all over the place, and faint smoke was still visible in the sky indicating a strong, recent explosion. Zaniar was a security chief himself, so he was able to show his badge to the police and inquire about the details. According to the police, four of the guards in the building were severely injured due to the impact of the huge explosion.

Also, the investigation indicated that the epicenter of the explosion was a secretive operation in the basement where the police had found several burnt human body parts along with damaged computers and hardware, but the police still hadn't identified the identity of the burnt body parts nor the reason for the explosion, but they had already sent samples for DNA testing, and they were still waiting for the results.

According to one guard's testimony, he had received a call from Kogar before the explosion telling him that he was sorry for everything. The explosion happened immediately after, but the guard had a minor injury because he was far away from the main building entrance at the time.

Upon hearing these words, Zaniar began to cry while Hast and Mark reassured him by patting his shoulder. "Let's wait for the DNA results. We don't know yet if she was with Kogar or not at the time of the explosion," Mark said.

"But why didn't she come back to the house?" Zaniar said then he started to swear at Kogar. "That bastard, how could he do this?"

Mark signaled to Hast to follow him to a quiet spot to have a private conversation. Meanwhile, Zaniar calmed down a bit to wait until the DNA results came back.

"Do you think Kogar committed suicide?" Mark asked Hast. "His phone call to his guard indicated he was up to something suicidal!"

"But why he would commit a suicide?" Hast asked.

"Maybe he was confronted by Media, or our last meeting with her caused a dispute between them," Mark suggested.

"So you think the dead body parts belong to them?" Hast guessed. He felt a bit of relief thinking that the true apocalypse might still be far away.

"I still don't know what *Young Nimrod* was planning!" Mark wondered. "Why he was helping Padsha Mali and at the same time promoting against him?"

Hast found Mark's question intriguing and began asking himself, 'If *Young Nimrod* was Kogar himself, then what was his motive? And why would he give up so easily?' Hast went back and forth thinking about the prophecies and what they had uncovered so far, 'What was Kogar planning by trying to demonize Padsha Mali and showing him as the Antichrist?' he thought deeply while touching his forehead with his index finger with eyes closed. As he began replaying everything he knew from the holy§cript, suddenly he saw the darkness! The darkness he feared all this time, and everything became clear to him,

'Doomsday is coming! It's close, not within a year, not within a month, not even within a week, it's happening now!' he concluded.

"PLEASE CALL INTERPOL NOW!" Hast shouted to Mark. He told him that he had figured out the Antichrist's plan and that the third world war would happen anytime from now. They also would need to travel back to New Delhi as soon as possible!

Mark found Hast in a state of anxiety and worry, "If he is trying to control people's mind through a helmet, what will he gain from instigating a world war?" Mark asked.

"The blue light emitters were just a decoy to misdirect us! The Antichrist doesn't need optogenetics to control our minds," Hast said. "I will explain on the way but we need to act now!"

"Should we wait for the DNA results to come back?" Mark asked.

"I'm sure poor Media is gone, and we will only waste time if we wait!" Hast said confidently.

"Then let's go back to the airport and then take the private jet to New Delhi," Mark said as he now had no option but to believe that Hast knew the truth.

Hast told Mark that there was no time to explain what he had figured to Zaniar or to tell him anything at that moment because he was emotionally unstable awaiting the DNA results which would not be good news for him. They decided to sneak in into his car and they drove quickly out of Nimrud town back to the Erbil International Airport where the private jet was.

Mark took out his cellphone while Hast was driving, and he called Interpol and urged them to warn the US government of a possible nuclear explosion very soon. He also urged them to warn the offshore cities of huge upcoming tsunamis. Mark was shouting through the cellphone asking Interpol to take his warnings very seriously, and he also urged them to send some special forces to Padsha Mali's town south of New Delhi as soon as possible.

"I need to visit my family first," Hast said while driving the car.

"I thought you said the entire world is in danger if we don't get to New Delhi soon?" Mark asked to protest against Hast's proposal to visit his family, but soon he regretted his stance as he thought a father's feeling toward his son would be immense.

"You are right. I shouldn't visit my family, after all my family is not more than any other families who are in danger," Hast replied. "But I need to tell the truth to my wife. We do have very similar views, and she will understand very quickly," he continued. "I think this will be my last trip, and I need my wife to take on the mission and save people from the Antichrist when I'm gone," Hast said.

Chapter 31

October 23, 2060 was a sunny day in New York and for Tom it was an exhausting day at work. During his lunch break he found himself a spot on a bench in Central Park to enjoy the hamburger he had bought from McBurger Queen. On his first bite he was quiet satisfied with the taste, so he brought up his hand up to take a look at the contents of the hamburger, but as he extended his hand up and away to enjoy looking at the layers of salad and beef while he chewed, he also saw the vast green field of New York's famous park. People were laying around, children were playing, and further away there was the compelling view of Manhattan's famous skyline. The entire view was beautiful.

That moment he remembered his lengthy discussion with his colleagues at work today about the faith-healer, Padsha Mali, and whether he was the Antichrist or just a good guy. One of his colleagues went even further saying that if US government didn't do something about Padsha Mali, he would soon become the Antichrist and bring destruction to the entire world.

'What a waste of time,' Tom thought to himself. 'Why is everybody nowadays talking about the Antichrist and the signs of end-days? They are more eager to see an apocalypse than the Doomsday Meteor itself! Why shouldn't we all just enjoy a peaceful life without talking about the end-days?' he asked himself. 'Tomorrow, I'll warn them that if they ever bring up this topic again at work, I will complain to the boss.'

Then he turned around and saw a beautiful lady sitting next to him, and she was looking at him! Tom wasn't sure whether the lady was making eye contact with him or just looking at his hamburger. He brought his eye back to the hamburger, but he couldn't see the hamburger anymore, but neither could he see his hand, or anything! Everything in front of him was engulfed in a very bright light, and he instantly had a strange feeling that his entire body no longer existed. He felt that his head was floating in the emptiness! 'What the hell is happening?!'

This was the first question that came to Tom's mind as a group of neurons in his brain processed the new information they had received from Tom's visual center. His logic neurons concluded, 'If suddenly nothing is visible, then something terrible must have happened. Tom should immediately run away from the danger.' Once the logic neurons began to process the sensory information so that they could choose which direction Tom should run to, they realized the dilemma. 'Wait! If everywhere around Tom is now invisible, then where should he run to? And how can he run without a body?'

The intensive signaling forward and backward among the interconnections of different logic neurons had now reached the next solution, 'We need to make Tom scream, and if we do that, someone will come to help him.' The logic neurons started to send pulses downward voting 'yes' to stimulate the executive neurons, however, before reaching the target, their message was outweighed and inhibited by a group of very conservative logic neurons called dignity neurons voting 'no' for screaming.

Conservative logic neurons were a group of neurons whose job was to vote 'no' for any new idea that defied a pre-stored protocol in the human's superego, a list of optimal voting decisions that were filtered with natural selection through millions of years of life and death of members within a species. Since screaming was not completely a new idea, after all, shouting for help was one among the extremely important traits for survival, this decision was not against the standard protocol, however, the voting 'no' to screaming came from another group of neurons called dignity neurons, and these were extremely conservative neurons. Their job was to vote 'no' against any proposed idea that could affect Tom's image as a tough and respected gentleman.

Dignity neurons were the reason why Tom existed in the first place. Tom's mother was attracted to Tom's father solely because he was a tough guy with a sense of pride. The dignity neurons insisted on voting 'no' for screaming because looking tough increased the survival chance of Tom's genes according to their previous experience in the environment Tom's ancestral tree came from.

Although the logic neurons tried to look for other solutions but they couldn't find any because Tom's current situation was unprecedented. The logic neurons were having a big dilemma; on one hand they were experiencing a very weird condition which looked very serious, a floating head without a body! On the other hand, dignity neurons wouldn't let their only solution pass. This was Nature's democratic system where the brain was the parliament, and the neurons were parliament members. Their main goal was to vote for optimal decisions that lead to Tom's survival or at least the survival of his genes.

Tom was lucky because he had the best parliament members. The decisions coming out from these members made him survive through all difficult life situations thus far, but not all humans were lucky enough to have such clever parliament members. In Tom's case their votes were fine tuned and hierarchies upon hierarchies of different neurons, diverse opinions, and lots of 'yes' and 'no' voting lead to one outcome, an outcome that either determined Tom's survival for another day or lead to his final extinction.

Hence, the basic logic neurons began to send some impulses to the advanced logic neurons. These neurons were higher in the hierarchy and their processing of information required more time, but if they decided to vote 'yes' for screaming, then the dignity neurons couldn't override their decision because advanced logic neurons ranked higher than dignity neurons.

The advanced logic neurons concluded, 'If everything looks white and invisible around Tom, then there is nobody around so Tom can scream without degrading his image in front of anybody...but wait! If nobody is around to help, then what is the use of screaming in the first place?' The advanced logic neurons stuck into a loop without being able to decide 'yes' or 'no'!

That moment memory neurons at hippocampus came to help as they sent information to the advanced logic neurons reminding them that Tom was at Central Park and was surrounded by many people who could potentially come to help. That moment the loop broke and the advanced logic neurons were about to vote 'yes' for screaming, but just before that happened, more specific memory information came from the hippocampus reminding the advanced logic neurons that there was also a beautiful lady making eye contact with Tom! The advanced logic neurons began to re-think. 'The beautiful lady making the eye contact with Tom could be into tough guys, hence, she had the potential to become a future mother for Tom's children!' At that moment, the advanced logic neurons switched their vote to 'no' for screaming siding with the dignity neurons.

One billion years ago when the first logic neurons appeared in the first host, they were able to survive and pass themselves to the off-spring hosts recreating different copies of themselves in different hosts, with some luck and some wise decisions they kept spreading and copying themselves with their main responsibility being to maximize their survival by learning from their host's life experience and their surrounding environment. With time as their host needed to adapt and change while facing new challenges and new environments, the logic neurons diversified into different subgroups like: memory neurons, feeling neurons, basic logic neurons, liberal and conservative neurons, dignity neurons, etc.

Some of the very highly ranked neurons became 'pain neurons' and their job was to make their host uncomfortable when he/she was in danger so that their host would either run away from the source of the danger or at least scream for help, but to assess whether a situation was dangerous or safe, another group of neurons acquired analytical abilities and became the basic logic neurons. These neurons further diversified into conservative logic neurons and liberal logic neurons.

The conservative logic neurons acquired a 'good past experience' saving ability. This was their logic for assessing what was dangerous and what was not and it was very simple: since their host survived so far, that meant what their host was doing so far was good for survival, so let us keep repeating that and avoid doing new unexplored things.

However, this logic was severely counteracted by the liberal logic neurons, and their logic was more complex: if we keep staying in the same environment and repeating the same things, then we will not have the chance to discover many new things in this reality which could later prove to be useful for survival so let's explore and try new things. Unfortunately, this logic came at a big price for the short term which was risking the life of many hosts and sacrificing them for the possible greater good in the long term.

Among these two groups, neurons diversified into more extreme subgroups such as 'dignity neurons' which were set to vote 'no' for anything new without compromise, and 'far-liberal neurons' which were set to embrace or try anything new without thinking too much about the consequences. The proportion of these two subgroups varied a lot among the hosts living on earth depending on the environment each host grew in.

As for Tom, the supporters for dignity neurons were far outnumbering their opponents, hence, things got extremely tough for the basic logic neurons to pass on their only proposed solution for Tom's current situation. 'We need to do something. We can't simply give up now after so many years of successful decisions. We don't want to fail now!' The basic logic neurons reached the conclusion that Tom's condition was so serious that there was no room for dignity here, and democracy would not help at this stage because the dignity neurons would not listen and their supporters in this current host were too many! Hence, they decided to ask for emergency laws to be applied to inhibit the dignity neurons temporarily.

The basic logic neurons began to send impulses to the ABC-survival neurons. The ABC-survival neurons were at a lower hierarchy than the logic neurons but they had direct communication with the highest cognitive brain centers including the highly ranked pain neurons. The basic logic neurons sent their complaints to these neurons reporting the situation as extremely dangerous. The ABC-survival neurons immediately sent extreme warnings to the pain and conscious centers at the highest level neurons in the hierarchy to apply the emergency law and strip the dignity neurons from their voting rights.

Once the highly ranked pain neurons received the warning from ABC-survival neurons, they began the process of generating an uncomfortable feeling that would make Tom experience a very severe pain consciously; a pain that would urge him to forget his own name, a pain so severe that would make him scream like a one year old child!

So far only 900 milliseconds had passed since all these back and forth votes were happening in the subconscious of Tom's brain. Now the conscious feeling of the situation and the pain started to emerge for Tom, however, the conscious processes required much more time and effort. Before Tom began to feel actual pain, everything became dark and he disappeared into a void. He had been sitting only 100 meters from a detonated nuclear bomb!

Chapter 32

Hast and Mark were now at the airport heading toward their private jet to fly to Padsha Mali's town near New Delhi again. Moments ago, Hast met his wife and little son to say farewell to them, and he revealed Antichrist's horrific plan to them. It was too late, and they wouldn't be able to do anything to prevent the upcoming catastrophe. Regardless, Mark and Hast decided to go to New Delhi where the Antichrist's destination was. Mark looked at the news from his mobile and realized that the beginning of the horror had already started.

"Oh, God! The news says a nuclear explosion happened at the center of Manhattan just now," Mark said in shock.

"The Antichrist is going to ignite a nuclear war between the world's big powers to make them busy while worse is planned," Hast said.

Mark called Interpol again to warn them about possible global earthquakes and tsunamis, and he told them the name of the main suspect responsible for all of these and he urged Interpol to send extra forces to New Delhi where they would be able to arrest the suspect, but before he could finish saying everything to Interpol, his cellphone connection was interrupted.

"Stupid Interpol," Mark said once he realized the connection interrupted. "They didn't take my previous warnings seriously enough."

"I don't blame them. It's hard to convince anyone with this story, but I hope they act quickly now," Hast said.

"I wasn't able to tell them everything before the connection was lost," Mark said in a frustrating voice.

***

Meanwhile in Russia, the head of the Russia, President Dimitri Pavlov, along with his own ministers were in an urgent meeting in a deep underground secret basement near the city of Orenburg. They were all sitting around a long table while a big screen showed live views from Moscow and other major cities in Russia.

The ministers were involved in an intensive discussion about what should they do or expect after hearing the horrible news of the nuclear detonation in New York. All their satellite based communications with the world had been disrupted for an unknown reason! The Russian authorities tried hard to condemn the act and to say they were innocent, but because of the worldwide sudden disruption in communications, their message was not widely spread or heard everywhere properly. Now they were afraid of an inappropriate reaction from the other side.

"We should act now before they destroy all our cities," one minister said.

"But why will they blame us? We have nothing to do with what has happened," the president replied.

"The US government will not believe us; they were accusing us from the beginning of planning against them when one of our nuclear bags went missing," the minister of foreign affairs said.

"Do you think the US hacked our satellite system so that we would not be able to do anything while they are preparing to attack us?" Dimitri said to the defense minister.

"We still have our wired and non-satellite based communications intact with our nuclear weapon bases, so we can still attack them on your orders!" the minister of defense replied.

The discussions went on for a while whether or how they should they act if the US attacked them, and how should they defend themselves if what they feared happened.

At that moment, one of the ministers who was sitting near the big screen shouted with a thrilled voice, "I HAVE AN IDEA! This idea could save us all and prevent the third world war," he said eagerly.

Everybody in the room turned toward him, but soon blood left their faces as what they saw on screen brought shock and fear!

"My idea is ...," he continued.

"The third world war has already started," someone interrupted him. "Look behind you!"

He turned to the screen to see that his brilliant idea to stop the third world war had already vanished! It was too late to prevent it. The live view screen was showing a huge and scary mushroom cloud over their beloved capital Moscow!

"How dare they attack our capital without even waiting for a day?!" the president said angrily.

"We don't know if it's them. It could be the same terrorists who stole our nuclear bag," the foreign affair minister said.

"I'm sure it's the US government. The mushroom cloud is huge, and they are the only one who have the power to hack into our satellite system and own such a massively destructive hydrogen bomb," the minister of defense said. "Now please let us answer them appropriately before they annihilate us."

President Dimitri thought there was no other option at this stage. Their only communication and messaging with USA will now have to be through nuclear heads, so he brought his secret national security bag onto the table. The bag had several red buttons on it, and it was connected to all their nuclear base powers through different modes of communication systems: earthly wired, wireless, and satellite. These were all to make sure that at least one of them would work in case of a hack or any unexplained malfunctions in the system.

The screen on the bag showed multiple lines and spaces for several passwords, and each password was known and kept by a minister. The final password was only known to the president himself who would have the final say to initiate the process. They had enough nuclear weapons to destroy all the major American cities. Everyone in the room entered their passwords and finally the president pushed the red button which would send the message to all the military commanders around the country to act on their own and gives them the green light to start hitting the predefined targets in the US and its allies in the west.

Chapter 33

Far away in an unpopulated land at the border of China and Siberia where a few months ago big generators which had the revolutionary technology to provide cheap electricity to many Chinese and Russian town cities were installed, Mr. Chee, an independent old farmer who was working in a nearby region, felt subtle but persistent vibrations in the ground beneath him. In the distance, he saw a huge amount of smoke coming out from thousands of huge thrusting engines as they expelled large amounts of fire and smoke visible behind the mountains. 'Is this how the new technology works to generate electricity?' he asked himself. 'This is very noisy and looks very bad for the environment. I need to file a complaint against this project,' he said to himself as he took out his mobile and took a picture of part of the thrusting engines which looked like huge space rockets tilted to the south and which belched a huge tail of fuel to the north. When the farmer tried to share the picture on social media, he noticed there was no internet connection!

***

On the other side of the planet in the middle of Atlantic Ocean, Admiral Brown, the head of US submarine number-234 had received some emergency orders to stay ready for a nuclear war, but after that, suddenly he lost his connection with his command center. He no longer knew what to do, and he realized he had lost the satellite connection with the entire world. Then he ordered the submarine staff to take the submarine to the surface again, and from the zoom of the periscope he noticed something strange was happening on some of the isolated Atlantic islands. There were over a hundred huge thrusting engines expelling their powerful thrusts toward the south. 'What the hell is this?' he asked himself. 'Just two months ago there was nothing on these islands. Are we in a wrong location or has someone created an entire industry on these isolated islands within such a short period?'

***

The head of Interpol, Sir Farad, was very worried and angry after he received a sudden harsh warning of a near apocalypse from one of his agents, and now that the nuclear war had started between the world's major powers, many cities reported earthquakes and tsunamis especially on in southern European cities. 'Is all this chaos due to the nuclear war or is it the apocalyptic end that many religious clerics predicted in the last few months?' he thought. 'How was it possible that Interpol's intelligence system couldn't predict this sudden eruption of chaos?' He tried again to contact his agent, Mark, but all of Interpol's major communication systems were corrupted! They could no longer use their satellite system, and every electronic device was suddenly down due to an unrecognized computer virus which had globally infected all computers.

Interpol called some of their most intelligent IT members to fix the problem and get rid of the virus. Sir Farad also ordered two of their airplanes to head to Padsha Mali's town in response to Mark's request, but now he had lost connection with them too! Farad thought he needed to contact with Mark again at any cost because it seemed that he was the only one holding essential information! He remembered Mark's last words before the connections failed telling him the name of the main culprit!

"When will you be able to fix the satellite system?" he asked the IT staff furiously. "Who could build such unfixable virus; don't we have the best hackers and computer scientists in the world?!"

"We already got rid of the hacking virus, but we still don't know why it's not working yet!" the staff member said while scratching his head.

After few hours of hard and tedious work, one IT staff member concluded, "I guess there is another problem. The virus was just a decoy to misdirect us from the real problem!" He claimed, "Our GPS system can no longer locate any of our satellites!!!"

"How can they all disappear from our system at once?" Farad asked.

"Oh, I've found one," one of the team members said. "I think our satellite locations have changed in space, but they are still there."

"Who could change the location of all our space satellites?" he asked. "Can't we fix that soon? I really need to communicate with our agent, Mark, ASAP."

"I'm afraid not, sir. It looks like our satellite positions in the space are continuously changing, and they look like they are moving!" the IT man said.

"That is so strange. Who is controlling their movement?" he asked.

"If you give us some time to monitor their speed and direction then we can redirect our receivers on the ground accordingly. We can then fix the communications, but I'm afraid we will need some time to do that," the IT man suggested.

Farad recalled that they were not the only ones having problems with their satellite and communications system, but all the TV stations and communication systems around the world seemed to have stopped! 'How can someone control the movement of all the satellites at once!' he thought. 'Could it be the earth itself is changing direction? This could explain the earthquakes and tsunamis!'

Chapter 34

October 25, 2060 was a remarkable date in human history. After many decades humans had kept relative peace, and there had been no major world wars after World War II. This war was not like any war before, and humans had reached their peak destructive power with nuclear weapons which could wipe out cities in a blink of an eye. A huge number of casualties, not within years but within hours, could happen, and people were displaced all around from fear, earthquakes and tsunamis. People were too scared to go back to their homes, so some of them decided to stay in the streets while others decided to camp in the holy☼houses praying for God.

Everyone looked for answers for what was happening, but nobody was able to give a convincing answer. All of a sudden TV stations and the social media all stopped working! People couldn't communicate through their mobile phones. Everybody started to ask whether it was Doomsday.

Despite all the chaos and destruction, Padsha Mali's TV was the only working TV station! At that moment, its screen was only showing a countdown, and the countdown was showing five hours and was ticking down! 'What does that mean?' people asked themselves as everyone started to tune their TV to that station when they realized it was the only working channel. All of the big screens in the streets and city centers were now tuned toward that TV channel, so that the people who were staying in the streets could watch! People were asking themselves, 'Why is Padsha Mali's TV station still working? Is he the one responsible for all the calamities happening now? Is he the one who started the nuclear war, and why has he done that? Is he really the Antichrist?'

That moment Kate Gould was in Cambridge among a large group of people gathering to look at one of the big screens in Midsummer common showing the countdown on Padsha Mali's TV, and then she remembered Mark and his colleague's visit to her place in Trinity college a few months ago asking about Newton's prediction for the date of Doomsday. At that time she didn't take what the two men were investigating seriously, but after their visit, she started to see and hear weird things on social media: missing nuclear heads, appearance of a faith-healer with miraculous powers, then all the social media's hailing about the Antichrist and the apocalypse. And now, she was witnessing a total chaos. 'What is really happening?' she asked herself. 'Mark might know something about this.' She took out her cellphone to call Mark only to remember that there was no communication signal!

Chapter 35

Hast and Mark were now in their private jet heading to New Delhi, and they would reach their destination in less than an hour but the pilot realized it was becoming increasingly more difficult to navigate through the air using the available navigation system inside the jet. He couldn't depend on the landmarks below him either as they were changing independent of the jet's movement! The radar system and AI-computer inside the plane showed extreme difficulty in calculating the target destination accurately.

"The navigation on bigger planes will be impossible," Mark claimed. "I don't think the back up from Interpol will be able to reach us."

"Will we be able to fly over Padsha Mali's place peacefully when we arrive?" Hast asked.

"I think we should land somewhere close before reaching New Delhi. I'm sure we will be taken down by force if we go further," Mark said to the pilot.

"I think so too. Someone who goes this far will not let airplanes fly off easily," Hast said.

"OK," the jet pilot said. "There are no nearby airports, so I will land on any empty field near the town directly beneath us, but the landing might be a bit difficult, so hold on!" he said while bringing the airplane's nose down. As the jet crashed into some hard bumps during the landing, Hast felt again the pain of his recent injuries in his arm and leg, but fortunately the landing was safe.

"Are you guys OK?" the pilot asked when the landing was complete.

"I guess so," Hast answered.

"I don't think I can take off from here," the pilot said. "There is some damage to its tires, but I will try to stay in the plane awaiting any signal from Interpol headquarters."

Hast and Mark left the pilot and the jet walking toward the center of the nearby small town. Even though it was late at night, Hast and Mark could see huge crowds of people on the streets and roads wandering around and talking to each other. Many seemed to be afraid to enter or go near large buildings. Hast remembered his nightmare where he saw the feared crowd marching toward their Judgement.

He began to pray in his heart for the people. While he was looking around, he noticed many people gathered around a huge screen at the center of their town looking and waiting for a countdown which was four hours to zero at that moment. He asked someone in the crowd, "What is this?"

"It's Padsha Mali's TV station, and it's the only TV channel working," someone answered in the crowd.

"So what do you think Padsha Mali is?" Hast asked someone in the crowd to see what the general public was thinking about him at that moment.

"What! You haven't figured it out yet?" someone in the crowd replied. "He is the Antichrist; he is the one responsible for the world war and everything."

"And how do you know he is the responsible one?" Hast asked.

"Look, why is his the only TV station that is working and all the other TV stations are disrupted! Also, haven't you seen his face? All the signs of Antichrist are there, or maybe you haven't read the holy§cript at all?" he asked Hast.

Hast stayed there for a while asking several other people in the crowd to get their general opinion. He realized that the situation was very complex to explain to people, and nobody would believe him anyway. They were all preoccupied with what they saw as the truth! He needed to do something soon before the countdown reached the zero hour. The darkness of the night started to fade, and it was going to become morning soon!

"I think we need to go to the Padsha Mali's town as soon as possible," Hast said to Mark.

"We need to get a car then," Mark said.

At that moment the dark sky suddenly got brighter, and a ray of light appeared though sky on the horizon. Some people were shocked in their places, and one shouted in surprise, "Hey look at the sun!"

"It is rising from the west!!" another one shouted loud in the crowd.

Mass hysteria started upon seeing the sun rising from the west! This was the final major sign before the Antichrist arrived! Someone in the crowd warned other people, "I think the best thing to do now is to run away as far as we can from Padsha Mali. He is the Antichrist, and when the hour zero comes, he will reveal his true face and he is going to kill and torture anyone who doesn't submit to him and recognize him as God!"

Some people began running toward the holy☼house building nearby the town center while others gathered attentively around the TV screens.

"Why don't you wait for a scientific explanation for this?" Mark asked someone from the crowd who was urging people to run away from this town.

"Science! Pfff," he answered. "They filled our heads with global warming and hitting meteors, but who predicted today? Ha! Was it science or the holy§cript?"

Hast looked at the far side of the town to a main road. "I'm going to Padsha Mali's town," he said while starting to run toward that road.

"OK, hold on! I will come with you," Mark said as he started to follow him. Once they reached the main road, they raised their hands to stop the coming cars hoping that one would stop for them. After trying several cars, finally one car stopped. A guy in his late 30s was driving it.

"What can I do for you?" the driver said.

"Could you please take us to Padsha Mali's town on your way?" Hast asked.

"You are lucky. I'm going there myself so get in," the driver said.

"Thank you a lot," Hast said while opening the back door to enter the car.

"By the way, my name is Bakir," the driver said.

"I'm Hast and this is my colleague Mark," he said. "Nice to meet you."

As the car drove, a curious conversation started about each one's motive to go to Padsha Mali's town.

"Can I ask why are you going to Padsha Mali at this time?" Bakir started.

Hast realized it was complicated to explain the situation since they don't even know the mindset of their driver or his preoccupations, but Mark came up with the answer. "Once I had cancer and he cured me."

"Oh, interesting. He also cured my mother from her advanced breast cancer," Bakir said.

Hast realized Mark's answer was a good starter for conversation. Now they knew Bakir's mindset. He was someone who felt he owed Padsha Mali, so he trusted him and wanted to visit him despite all the recent horror stories and accusations about him! Bakir wanted to get answers himself.

"I saw a lot of cars on the other side of the road driving away from Padsha Mali's town, so we were lucky to find you," Hast said.

"These people are crazy. Padsha Mali is a good person," Bakir said. "God has blessed his hands with healing power, and he himself doesn't ask people for anything. From the day he cured my mother I have watched most of his preaching, and he always asks people to worship the true God, ∞Illuhim∞. He has never asked anyone to do otherwise." Bakir continued, "Only because of some silly physical resemblance, people are accusing him unfairly of being the Antichrist, and that is so rude! He's only a guy who wants to help us."

Hast sensed Bakir's feelings and his thirst for the truth, so he patted Bakir's shoulder to reassure him. "Don't worry; Padsha Mali is not the Antichrist."

Chapter 36

After two hours of driving, Hast, Mark and Bakir arrived at the center of the town where Padsha Mali's preaching hall was based. They saw huge crowds of people around the hall, and there was also a big TV screen outside showing the countdown which was now 20 minutes until zero.

"He still has a lot of supporters," Mark said.

"I think they are those who have had a loved one cured by him. They still trust him and want to show support," Bakir said.

Hast saw fear in the eyes of most of the people who were waiting there. They were looking for answers from him. "I think people all around the world are now looking at his TV station," he said. "We need to go inside the hall."

They pushed through the huge crowd until they reached the main gate where several guards with guns were standing by the gate. "Please could you let us inside?" Hast asked one of the guards.

"I'm sorry, but the hall is full and we can't let any more in," one guard replied.

Hast and Mark spent several minutes convincing the guards to let them in and finally the guard agreed, but first they were asked to put away all their mobiles, cameras, and electronic devices. Then one guard checked their pockets after they put away their stuff, and he also had with him a special detector to check for any metals.

After the security guard checked Hast, Mark and Bakir, he let them in. As the three entered the hall they saw that the huge crowd inside all were standing and looking up. High on the second floor's front wall was a small door opening with a forward protrusion coming out from it, and a microphone was fixed to a stand on a Podium. This was the place where Padsha Mali usually preached for his TV station. According to the crowd, Padsha Mali was expected to show up at time zero and give an important speech. Time zero was now just few minutes away, so all eyes in the hall were up to that protrusion from the wall. All eyes around the globe were now pointing toward the big screens on the roads and streets, as they closely watched the countdown which was now only a minute to zero and was ticking down 59, 58, 57…!

Mark took out his cellphone from his pocket secretly to look if he had any connection back with Interpol. "Damn it, still no connection," he said.

Hast was shocked when he noticed the cellphone in Mark's hand, "How could you get that past the security check?" he asked.

"That is what I'm trained for. I sneaked my phone into the guard's pocket when he was checking me then took it out again from his pocket once he finished," Mark said.

"That was so irresponsible! If the guard had found out, he wouldn't have let us in!" Hast said.

"Sh…!" someone from the crowd urged them.

That moment everyone in the hall became silent; it was the hour zero. Everybody was now looking up to the protrusion in the hall's front wall, as a figure came out from the small door situated high in the beginning of the protrusion. People all around the world were looking attentively at their TV screens which were now showing someone walking over toward the microphone to give a speech. As the figure closed in more and more toward the recording cameras, it became clear who it was.

Padsha Mali was now standing in front of a big crowd; all the eyes around the globe were looking at him in front of big screens waiting cautiously for his speech.

Chapter 37

It was the moment of truth. The sun came from the west and all the prophecies in the holy§cript had come true. People from all around the world, on the streets of Paris, London, Berlin, New Delhi, etc. were now looking up at the big screens waiting to hear the truth. The man who had supernatural power, the power to heal diseases, the power to heal cancer, and the power to control the media was now standing in front of a microphone! 'Is he the Antichrist himself, the next major prophecy of the holy§cript?' people asked themselves. 'What should they do if he was?'

Despite all the fears, people who were inside the hall had only one wish: they wanted to see their beloved faith-healer deny all the allegations and re-assure them that he was still the faithful servant of ∞Illuhim∞. Bakir and the others inside the hall were eager and afraid at the same time to hear Padsha Mali's first words. There was increased tension as he was now about to open his mouth to say his first words.

"If…," Padsha Mali started. "If you want to be saved …," he continued as people around the screens everywhere listened attentively. "If you want to be saved …," he repeated again with a little pause. "BOW TO ME NOW!" he shouted to the crowd beneath him. "I'M YOUR GOD, YOUR ONLY SAVIOR!"

The crowd beneath started to stare at each other in shock. They had just heard what they feared the most, and they didn't know how to respond or act.

"EVERYBODY BOW TO ME NOW, OR YOU WILL DIE!" he said more firmly and aggressively.

These words produced great fear inside everyone, and nobody in the hall was prepared for them, yet these words were not unexpected by the many people watching the event faraway through the big screens in the streets, 'A suspicious healer who looks like the Antichrist, appears after major prophecies come true, dominates the media, and threatens everyone asking them to bow to him! Who could he be other than the Antichrist himself,' people thought. 'Only an ignorant fool who hasn't a clue about Abrahamic faith would not know who the Antichrist was by now!'

Bakir felt deeply betrayed in his heart, 'Why I was so blind? Everybody around me knew that he was the Antichrist, but I didn't believe them! I took my mother to him and extolled his virtues to many others, but he must have controlled my feelings by healing my mother! He controlled everyone's feeling through his healing powers. I should have only asked ∞Illuhim∞ for help. Padsha Mali took advantage of us by preaching for Abrahamic faith, but now he is showing his true face. This was a test for us but we failed,' Bakir thought to himself regretfully. 'I will not fall for the evil again never, ever.'

"I WILL NEVER BOW TO YOU, ANTICHRIST," Bakir shouted loudly responding to Padsha Mali in a bold voice.

It was only a moment after Bakir's shouting that a death ray, like a powerful thunderbolt came down from the hall's ceiling directly toward Bakir! It only took a fraction of second for his body to evaporate, and he vanished in front of Hast and Mark! People around him saw nothing remaining from him except the smell and the smoke of a burnt meat!

Panic spread among the people inside the hall. Many tried to run out, but all the doors were shut and the tall windows were out of their reach. They were all trapped now, and their only way to be saved from certain death was to bow to their master, Padsha Mali. People who were watching the event on the big screens in the street were shocked upon seeing the horror unfold.

Their immediate thought was, 'Are we safe from this Beast?' They remembered all the catastrophes and earthquakes they went through during the previous night, and they realized that they were not safe or out of the Beast's reach. He soon would trap them and torture them unless they denounced their faith and worshipped him instead of the true god, ∞Illuhim∞. Fear and panic rapidly spread among the people across the globe!

"BOW TO ME NOW!" Padsha Mali shouted again to the crowd.

Some people in the front of the hall started to sit on their knees to bow, but someone from behind warned them, "Are you going to denounce your faith because of a man's threat?!" he asked them. "How will you answer yourself in front of ∞Illuhim∞ after this life?"

"If you bow to him, you will be saved in this mortal life!" another one shouted. "If you don't, you will be saved in the other immortal life."

At that moment two thunderbolt beams came down from the ceiling directly to hit both questioning men and evaporate them immediately!

"BOW TO ME OR YOU WILL ALL DIE!" Padsha Mali repeated again.

One of those who was about to sit and bow for him stood up again refusing to bow. "You can take our bodies, but you can never take our minds," he said proudly before another thunderbolt hit him and he vanished.

More people inside the hall were now encouraged by all these brave sacrifices, so they gave up trying to get out of the hall and instead turned back toward the front wall facing Padsha Mali. They were ready to embrace death rather than submitting to him. The death ray started hitting them one-by-one starting with those people shouting anti-Antichrist slogans. Others, who were outside the hall in front of the big screen, ran away while others stayed to show their solidarity.

Shortly everyone around the world simultaneously started praying asking the lord, ∞Illuhim∞, for his mercy and help. The preachers among the crowds everywhere reminded people that there was another prophecy: 'God will send someone to save the world from the Beast.' They preached, 'God has promised us that he will not leave us alone when the evil one rises, and he will come back for us, and he will send us his beloved Savior, the Messiah.' This brought back hope among the scared people who had witnessed the horrible events.

People around the globe were inspired by the bravery shown by the people inside the hall who courageously faced the Antichrist and refused to submit to him. As they saw the horror continue on the big screens, they spontaneously started to sit on their knees facing the sky and praying for ∞Illuhim∞ to ask for help. They implored him to send his promised Savior, the Messiah!

"∞Illuhim∞ you have promised us, so please send the Messiah," someone from the crowd prayed with a loud voice.

"AMEN," everyone from the crowd said together.

Shortly this act spread to everywhere simultaneously as if it was programmed in the subconscious of people's brains. This is what they needed to do when the Antichrist appeared. The Messiah was the only one who could beat the beast, and hence everybody needed to pray to God to send him soon before the Antichrist caused more damage.

Our Lord, as you promised us
Send your Messiah to save us

People all around the globe started reciting these prayers sincerely and deeply in their hearts. It was the first time a prayer, in such a huge scale with sincere feelings and simultaneously all around the world, asked the Lord for his help. Someone could have heard the waves and the vibrations in the air coming in all directions from the surrounding nearby towns as everybody prayed in synchronicity.

Among the crowd Howard Nerd now realized that his theory was under a big test! 'Everybody is now wishing and believing that something will happen. Their beliefs and wishes are directed toward one thing,' he thought to himself. 'According to my theory, Nature should fulfill their wishes because everybody around the world is now praying for something to happen sincerely, and if their wishes don't come true now, it means Nature has wasted a lot of mind quanta energy for nothing. Even if the Messiah doesn't exist, Nature needs to create one to preserve the balance!' Howard thought to himself while patiently waiting to see if the predictions of his theory would come true.

Chapter 38

Padsha Mali was the only boy and the oldest child of a poor family of eight siblings. He developed primary congenital glaucoma in his left eye which had rendered him blind in that eye for life. His mother was a housewife and his father was a preacher of Abrahamic faith. His father knew the entire holy§cript by heart, and to financially support his big family, he practiced faith-healing in return for a small charge. He was well known among the local people in his town, and the family's real income was primarily based on gifts and donations by people Padsha Mali's father had cured in their town.

When he was young, Padsha Mali attended many of his father's faith-healing sessions and he learned many skills from him. He observed that there were two types of patients: those who had a physical illness, and those who were possessed by a bad spirit. His father told him that the holy§cript could heal all the diseases but it could heal the 'possessed' patients even quicker because the bad spirits couldn't stand the word of truth, the word of God.

As a faith-healer his father's life was not easy. Doctors in his town hated him, and they frequently accused him of fraud and mistreating patients especially ones with psychiatric disorders. Because of the doctors' beliefs, the ministry of health forced Padsha Mali's father to put a billboard in front of his house to discourage patients from visiting him which read:

There is no such thing as 'possession'. If someone you knew accused of being 'possessed', he or she must likely have a conversion disorder and needs to be seen by a psychiatrist.

Despite the sign, patients still came to see him to ask for help and treatment. One day, the police came in and arrested his father because of one patient's complaint. He had treated him as being possessed but later on it turned out he had in reality suffered a stroke that affected his brain, and when the patient passed away, forensic doctors blamed his death on the faith-healer's malpractice. The police decided to arrest Padsha Mali's father and he was jailed for a year, and it was a hard time for the entire family and for Padsha Mali, as his father was the main bread winner in the family.

As the oldest kid in the family, despite his young age, Padsha Mali needed to take care of the big family. He decided to travel to New Delhi every morning to polish rich people's shoes and come back each evening to hand over the money he earned to his mother. In turn, she was barely able to buy the necessary food and clothes for the entire family. Fortunately, nice people from their town still visited and brought them donations. The hard year passed and his father was finally released, but he signed a declaration letter in the police department declaring not to practice faith-healing any more.

Unfortunately, their happiness didn't last long. Padsha Mali's father fell unconscious soon after his release, and when they took him to the hospital, he was diagnosed with brain cancer. Padsha Mali saw the look on the doctor's face who diagnosed his father. It was the happy face of someone who had finally got their revenge and said, 'Now that you've got cancer where are your faith-healing powers? Why have you come to medical doctors for help? Isn't the holy§cript enough for you?'

The doctor was surrounded by his medical school students and he was explaining Padsha Mali's father's condition to them in English. Although Padsha Mali didn't understand what they were saying, he clearly felt they were mocking his father and his faith-healing practices.

When his father woke up from his coma in the hospital, he urged the family to take him home. This was in spite of doctor's orders. They had recommended that he receive chemotherapy but the father's pride was strong, and he refused to get conventional medical treatment. He was even angry that he had been taken to the hospital while he was unconscious. "I only need the holy§cript. It is my treat," he said to the doctors and nurses.

Padsha Mali felt happy with this decision because he couldn't stand the humiliation of his father staying in the hospital seen by all the doctors who mocked faith-healing. 'They don't understand possession and exorcism, and they are hiding the truth from people to keep them away from the truth. I have seen my father healing the mute, the deaf, and the unconscious. I have seen them healed with only a few verses from the holy§cript. Their medicine can do nothing, and my father is not a fraud. He didn't charge people, and he only wanted to help them to get rid of bad spirits,' Padsha Mali thought to himself.

A few years later, his father died from the cancer despite reading the holy§cript daily, but this has made Padsha Mali's faith in God even stronger. He always knew that God was the only one who decided who was to be healed and who was not. He believed that his father's incurable cancer was a test from his god to see if he stayed faithful to his majesty despite all the troubles, and he now needed to show ∞Illuhim∞ that his faith was unshakable more than ever.

Years passed and he started to take over his father's old job, the faith-healing. He learned the entire holy§cript by heart and like his father he didn't charge anything from those he was healing. He started to work day and night with only four hours of sleep. People started to love him for his honesty and his sincere willingness to help. His practice made him able to distinguish those with physical illness from those who he called 'possessed'. To avoid the problem his father got into, he advised his patients to visit their doctors too and should only come to him as a second opinion. He gradually became well-known in the surrounding towns and people started to visit him more and more bringing him gifts and donations. He always told his patients that he didn't do this for money, and all he wanted was to help people to get rid of bad spirits and show the healing power of the holy§cript and God's words to everyone. He wanted to increase people's faith in ∞Illuhim∞.

Many years passed and he got married then had two beautiful children. His life was moving on fine until one day someone calling himself *Mr. Young* came to visit him. The man held a bottle of water.

"You have blessed hands, so you can treat the possessed," he said.

"No, it's not me. It's the god of the holy§cript who treats them," Padsha Mali said.

"But the holy§cript needs the right person, a truly faithful person with a pure heart to recite it, and that is why everybody is not a faith-healer," he said.

"I think ∞Illuhim∞ loves me, and that is why he wants to introduce his message through me," Padsha Mali said.

Mr. Young put the bottle in front of him. "Do you know what you could do with a holy water that has descended to us directly from the Eden Gardens by a fallen meteor?" he asked while Padsha Mali listened. "You can cure cancer," he followed. "Unfortunately, we don't have too much of this water and it needs your prayers and your blessed hands for the miracle to work."

Padsha Mali didn't believe him at first, but once he tried the water on some hopeless cancer patients, he saw the miracle. A few weeks later people came back to him expressing their immense gratitude for his extraordinary healing powers. When he met *Mr. Young* again, he was promised more of the holy water on the condition that he used it considerately and not to tell anyone about it. After all, *Mr. Young* reminded Padsha Mali that it was ∞Illuhim∞ who cured people with the holy§cript through his blessed hands with the help of the holy water. The holy water alone was nothing. Padsha Mali soon became famous. People started to talk about his ability to cure cancer, and articles and international TV reports were made about him. He was soon visited by everybody around the world. High profile political figures, famous people, football players, and even some of the doctors who blamed his father for malpractice now visited him for help when they or their loved ones got cancer.

Family and relatives urged Padsha Mali to take this opportunity to become rich by curing wealthy people and charging them with a lot of money, but he refused. He was eager to help and cure poor people before the rich. All he was asking for from the people was to stay faithful to ∞Illuhim∞.

Nevertheless, Padsha Mali soon realized that because of his blindness some people were accusing him of being a latent Antichrist who was waiting for the right moment to show his true face! After all, the majority of people didn't have cancer or they chose not to visit him for help, so he disregarded the painful accusations. His eagerness to help people made him sleep only for one hour a night and he spent most of his time preaching and healing people. Now he had his own TV station, thanks to *Mr. Young* again, he would spend every minute in his life spreading God's word. He also treated people live on TV showing the miracle to everyone.

One day, he looked in the mirror after hearing another famous preacher talk about his resemblance to the Antichrist and who had discouraged people from listening to him. He looked at his face closely asking himself, 'Am I really the Antichrist? Why don't people look into my heart? They don't know about me, my life and my beliefs?' He asked God why he had made him this way. 'People would have trusted me much more if I wasn't created blind in my left eye,' once he prayed these words to God but then he remembered that according to the teachings of the holy§cript, people should trust God and thank him for what he gave and what he took so he immediately begged ∞Illuhim∞ to forgive him. 'I was so arrogant for complaining about the eye you took from me. You have given me one eye to see, an amazing wife and two beautiful children. You have given me the power of healing and high status among the people. You have given me everything and yet I'm still asking why you took one eye from me! Please forgive me for my arrogance. I will stay faithful, and I will spread your message with all my power.'

A few weeks later, Padsha Mali met *Mr. Young* again, but this time he didn't look normal. There were multiple scratches and cuts on his face, and he was barely recognizable and looked like a different person! He asked Padsha to tell all the people who were queuing in front of his preaching hall, which had recently been built for him by *Mr. Young*, to leave and come back the next day! It was very difficult for Padsha Mali to do that because no matter how tired he was, he never asked the people who needed his treatment to leave his hall. He always put people's health before his own rest, but this initial request would turn out to be very easy compared to *Mr. Young's* next request!

"Tomorrow I need you to pretend that you are the Antichrist and ask people to bow to you," he said to Padsha Mali.

"WHY?" Padsha Mali protested in shock.

"Don't worry it's just a test. We want to see how many people will follow the Antichrist if he comes," he said. "Wouldn't you like to test their faith?"

Padsha Mali suddenly realized something. "Is that why you chose me in the first place? Did you choose me for this test because I resemble the Antichrist slightly?"

"Slightly?!" he repeated after him.

"I thought you wanted me to help people and spread Abrahamic faith," Padsha Mali said in disappointment.

"That is what exactly I wanted to do!" he said. "This is why I want to put their faith into a real test."

"But I have healed many of those people, so if I ask them anything they will feel obliged to do so even if I ask them to bow to me. I don't want to put them in a difficult position," Padsha Mali protested.

"No, that is exactly why you need to do that. If they feel obliged to bow to you because you healed their loved ones, then they should be ashamed for doing that. This test will be a good lesson for them not to repeat that in case the real Antichrist appears," he said.

"In all my preaching and during my faith-healing, I have always reminded people that it's ∞Illuhim∞ who is the true healer and not me. I have told them that I'm only a medium between them and God and nothing more," Padsha Mali said.

"So now it's a good time to test to see if your preaching has worked. Let's test their faith," he said.

Padsha Mali thought deeply for a while then he shook his head to reject the proposition. "Even if it is just for a test, I still can't put myself in God's place and ask people to worship me instead of him."

Mr. Young was now convinced it was too difficult to persuade Padsha Mali peacefully, so he took out his mobile and showed him a recorded video of his family! In the video they were all tied up and shouting for help! Padsha Mali was so enraged at seeing the images that he tried to attack *Mr. Young*, but one guard grabbed him from behind. Sensing even more trouble, Padsha Mali shouted for the guard outside to come help him.

"Your guards are my guards, you fool!" he said to Padsha Mali.

"Please, don't harm my family. What do you want from me?" Padsha Mali asked in frustration.

"It's simple. Just do the stupid test and your family will be safe," he said.

Padsha Mali didn't have a choice so he finally agreed to do what *Mr. Young* told him to do. The rules were simple and he was told to spend the night in his room with all the doors and windows locked. He would be isolated from the world, and then in the next morning, he had a simple line to tell the people who would be waiting for him in the hall. *Mr. Young* told him that anything he would see happening next was just a scenario to test people's faith! He might see people dying in front of him, but it would all be part of the test, so he wouldn't need to worry about them.

***

It was a long night for Padsha Mali, and he couldn't sleep. He was thinking about his family all that night, and the next morning when the door was unlocked for him by a guard, he went to his usual preaching place. He was surprised to see a huge crowd waiting for him inside the hall. The people's faces looked tired and fearful as they were attentively waiting for his speech. At first Padsha Mali hesitated to shout to them asking them to bow to him. 'I prefer to throw myself off this podium and die instead of putting myself in the Lord's place,' he thought to himself but then he remembered his family's doomed fate if he decided to do that. 'It's just a test. I don't mean it in my heart, so God please forgive me. I'm always your faithful servant, and I will only do this as test, but I don't mean my word.'

He then started to shout at the crowd asking them to bow to him. He was afraid that the crowd would respond to his request and bow to him immediately, but then he saw someone from the crowd rejecting his request boldly and a death ray hit him. At first Padsha Mali was terrified but then he remembered *Mr. Young's* words, 'Everything is just a scenario to make the test look real.'

He shouted at them again asking them to bow. He was now relieved to see that his followers were fixed on their faith and didn't bow for a human even if their lives were threatened. He was very heartened by their reaction and their appropriate response. 'This is all due to my preaching,' he thought to himself. 'I taught them not to bow to anyone but ∞Illuhim∞.'

He repeated the same lines again and again, each time saying it louder and bolder just to make sure that the test was successfully passed by his followers.

Moments later, he started to hear a loud voice that seemed to come from a large crowd behind the hall. 'Is there another crowd outside? What they are shouting for?' he asked himself. Then the voices get louder and louder, he started to hear them more clearly. They were praying to God asking him to send the Messiah!

The crowd inside the hall also began to call and pray for the return of Messiah! Padsha Mali didn't know what to do at this stage, as the test was a clear success according to him, and no one was deceived by him, but why hadn't he received any signal to announce the end of the test. 'Maybe *Mr. Young* still wants me to continue,' he thought. When he said his final bow to me command, it was only a second later that he realized the entire world was now wishing him dead! 'Everyone is now watching me and thinking that I'm the Antichrist and praying for the return of Messiah to save them!'

Suddenly, a bright light shined down from the ceiling dome to the floor. A ray of the light hit Padsha Mali's eyes, and it was only a fraction of a second later that he saw the figure of an angel in front of him. He had a pair of white bright wings and the armor of an ancient knight with shining beads. He held an expensive looking sword, a sword of a king, and as he looked into the face of the angel which was half covered with the armor, his long brown beard and hair seemed familiar to him but he couldn't recognize the face because it was partially covered with the armor.

Padsha Mali tried to say something, but it was too late; the sword has already passed through his chest to his heart. He felt extreme pain. 'This can't be a part of the test!' The world in front of him began to fade away, and he saw the relief on the crowd's faces beneath him. They were so happy as if they were saved from a tyrant! He was the most hated man on the planet, and at that moment, Padsha Mali himself wasn't sure if he was indeed the real Antichrist! He fell onto the ground while everything was fading into darkness, the last image he saw was his children's faces before everything in front of him disappeared. '∞Illuhim∞ please forgive me for putting myself in your position. I'm nothing but your humble servant.' That was his last prayer before falling to the ground below covered with blood.

Chapter 39

"People of the earth, it's now officially the end of your story, your amazing long story. You are the survivors. You went through many difficult times, hunger, thirst, horror, and sadness but you have finally made it. We have been watching you all the time.

"You may be wondering why we left you all this time to suffer! We were always wishing to come and save you, but the key to unlocking your suffering was in your hands all the time. Today you proved yourselves, you unlocked the path by yourselves, and ∞Illuhim∞ is proud of you. You were once his favorite creation, he created you in his form, in a perfect shape. Among all his creations, you were his masterpiece, and he made you rulers of the Eden Garden. Angels and demons were your servants ... but then ... you fell into the devil's trap. You broke the trust that ∞Illuhim∞ had in you, and from that moment, it was your duty to prove yourself again.

"The evil was disguised among you for all these years, and his plan was to deviate you further from ∞Illuhim∞. He ignited the war among you, and he was planning for your total destruction. He came to you in the form of the Antichrist and set himself in God's place! Despite his dominion, his power, and the horror he set into your hearts, today you proved yourself again. You refused to submit to his wishes, you united together, you asked ∞Illuhim∞ for help, and you did that all with one heart. Your determination against evil has re-established the lost trust again between you and your creator.

Although you made a large step today towards your salvation, the evil is still here. He implanted hate against you, humans, among other of God's creations in the Garden of Eden. The past sins that you and the people before you have committed are immense, so you will need to fix the past before being able to return to the Garden of Eden! But don't worry, I'm the Messiah, and I have been given the responsibility to show you the path of your salvation. All you need is to follow my word, and I will illuminate the path for you, and soon you will become kings again in the heavens."

That was the part of 'the Messiah's' speech after he took on the 'Antichrist'. The presumed Messiah stood up, with his shiny armor, his long brown hair and beard, and his partially covered face. In the eyes of people, he was the Godsend who had just fallen from the sky to be the savior of their dreams. People in the hall began to bow for their Messiah to show their respect and submission to God's beloved savior.

***

Hast's biggest fear had come true, the literal interpretation of the holy§cript! He stood there among the crowd in shock; his religion had been hacked by evil! 'Abraham didn't free us from the tyrant, Nimrod, only to become slaves again!' he thought to himself. 'Abraham's message was all about freedom, and we all miss-understood his message and his revolution toward a free society with independent thinking. There are nine billion minds in the world; it's like nine billion parliaments, every one with a different life experience and a different wisdom. If we all think for ourselves, the path to the truth will be revealed but evil doesn't want that. He wants to control all our minds through one portal, the Antichrist. We paved the path for evil to control us through preaching hate, distrust, and demonization. The evil grew by feeding from the terror we envisioned for ourselves, and now he is much smarter and more powerful than ever. He will enslave us in the name of God,' Hast concluded. 'I need to do something...I need to save people from the new slavery. If he is the *Young Nimrod*, then I need to be the *Young Abraham*!' At that moment Hast turned to Mark.

"Mark, could you record me with your mobile? I will try to reveal the truth to the world!" he said.

"But I don't have a connection," Mark said while looking at his mobile. "Oh! Never mind, start..."

That moment TV screens all over the world suddenly went blank! The world stood speechless after what they had just seen, they had witnessed what they could have never imagined a year ago. They saw all the prophecies come true. They saw Doomsday, and they saw the rise of the Antichrist, and now they had just witnessed the return of Messiah. It was like the truth had finally revealed itself to everyone; even the most aggressive skeptic of the Abrahamic faith was now seeking forgiveness from the Messiah.

Despite people's concerns at that moment, Howard 'Nerd' was thrilled! Finally, he was able to witness the ultimate proof of his underrated, wonderful theory. He began to jump around from the joy as it was his Eureka moment. He wandered around telling everyone he was meeting about his ultimate theory of everything: The Mind Quanta-Soup.

Chapter 40

When the morning alarm went off, Raimon was in a deep sleep. Yesterday morning when he saw the first news reports of the nuclear bomb detonation in Manhattan and the threat of possible worldwide war, he immediately thought he should keep himself from the trouble of looking at the horror stories on TV and social media, so he took his sleeping pill and decided to sleep for a while. This was his habit, to run away from the headache of caring about the crazy things happening in the world, but this time he had taken two pills of Valium.

Now his eyes were half-opened and he still hadn't realized that it has been more than 20 hours since he had gone to sleep. He wanted to ignore the alarm and stay in bed for another few hours, but then he suddenly remembered yesterday's horrible news. 'Oh, I'm still alive,' he thought to himself. 'Dublin was not hit by a nuclear weapon!' He stood up from the bed and switched on the TV to see the latest updates from the last 24 hours, but he couldn't tune in to any working TV station. 'Did they hit every TV station!' He opened his laptop and there was no Wi-Fi signal. He looked at his cellphone and again there was no signal. 'Large damage might have happened everywhere,' he thought to himself.

He looked at the window which was facing west in his room and saw sunlight shining into the room from it! 'It must be the sunset,' he thought to himself as he moved his head near the window to have a clearer look at the sun disk. 'Did I sleep for 30 hours!' he looked again at the digital clock on the wall, but it was clearly indicating 8:20 AM! He thought that the clock might be broken, so he found his watch and it was 8:20 AM. again. That moment he remembered a sponsored post he had seen on the news feed of his social page which prophesied that on the end-days people would see the sun coming from the west. 'This can't be!' he thought to himself.

Raimon was in his late twenties, and he had never had a religious experience or went to the holy☼house except for once ten years ago when he attended his mother's funeral. He still remembered his mother's last words urging him to stay faithful to ∞Illuhim∞. "Promise me to keep your faith. I want to see you again in heaven," she said to him before her last breath in the hospital.

"I promise," Raimon answered but deep his heart he was pledging not to go near the holy☼house for life. From that time on, Raimon kept himself away from religion. He drank heavily and partied most nights and every weekend. He kept on with his wild lifestyle until he realized that while he was in his current job, he wouldn't be able to save a penny for his future nor for a family. Nevertheless, at that moment of realization, he decided not have kids. 'Why should I save money for other people?' he asked himself. He kept living his life by the motto of YOLO (you only live once).

Meanwhile, five months ago a new neighbor moved into the house next to his flat, and the new neighbor seemed very religious, as he was going to the holy☼house twice a week. During one of the holy days he invited Raimon to join him at the holy☼house to praise and thank the Lord for his virtues.

"Why should I praise and thank a God who took the life of my mother early despite she prayed to him every day," Raimon said to the neighbor as he remembered the last moments of his loving mother's life.

"No, you misunderstood ∞Illuhim∞. He doesn't take lives. He just transfers them from one place to another, and I'm sure ∞Illuhim∞ loved your mother and that is why he took her to a better place. If you come to the holy☼house once and opened your heart, you would realize how much he loves you, too," the neighbor said.

"I'm sorry pal, but I can't believe in ∞Illuhim∞. There is no evidence of his existence, and I'm a man who wants evidence," Raimon said.

"There is a lot of evidence, but you haven't seen it yet," he said.

"Then, I will stay atheist until I see some," Raimon replied.

"You will see. I was like you, an unbeliever, but then God showed me the truth. I will pray for God to show you the truth," the neighbor said before leaving Raimon.

A couple of days later, Raimon saw a post on the news feed of his social page showing a faith-healer healing cancer through prayer and the holy§cript. When Raimon looked further onto the name of the faith-healer, he realized the story was reported in many professional media outlets. 'This can't be true; the man is clearly a fraud,' he thought to himself. 'How can people be so naïve.'

That wasn't everything for Raimon, and as the days passed, he kept seeing posts and videos online about the faith-healer and the Antichrist warnings! He kept reporting the videos or labeling them as 'not interested', but they kept coming back to his news feed page in an increasing frequency because many of them were sponsored posts! 'Why the hell I keep seeing these posts? I'm almost about to become a theologian!' Then he remembered his neighbor's words saying that he'll pray for him to see the truth! 'I need to ask my neighbor to stop praying for me!' he thought to himself mockingly.

Now, after Raimon woke up from his lengthy sleep, he remembered all those prophesies he had been warned of in the last month through the social media: the last world war, the rise of Antichrist, the return of Messiah, and the sun coming from the west. 'What the hell has happened since yesterday?' he asked himself. That moment he heard someone knocking on his door, and he quickly went to open the door. He was eager to meet someone to ask him questions and to confirm that he was not dreaming. When he opened the door, he saw that it was his neighbor.

"Hi, my friend. Everyone is going to the holy☼house to recite the Messiah's words. Would you like to join me now?" he asked.

"What happened?" Raimon asked.

"You don't know!" he said.

"I have been asleep for the last 24 hours or even more."

"Are you kidding me? The world was on fire and you were sleeping!" he said in amazement. "I thought you were now praying on your knees asking for forgiveness from the Lord!"

"Why should I have done that? Could you please tell me what has happened?" Raimon asked eagerly.

"I can't tell you everything now. I'm in a hurry to join the others," he said as he was trying to leave Raimon.

"For God's sake tell me what happened!" Raimon demanded fiercely as he was desperate to get an answer.

The neighbor turned to Raimon again, "You really need to soften your heart. To know what happened, come with me to the holy☼house and find out yourself."

"But I don't know how to pray," Raimon said.

"It's OK. We are going there to recite the Messiah's words and learn them by heart," he said while he started to walk. Raimon decided to join him as he quickly put on his shoes and grabbed his coat.

"Did the nuclear war between countries happen?" Raimon asked while they walked.

"Yesterday, Padsha Mali, who turned out to be the Antichrist as everyone had expected, ignited the world war. All the TV stations and social media went down except the one he was controlling," he said.

"You mean the faith-healer's TV station was working?" Raimon asked.

"Yes, before the Messiah returned, Padsha Mali appeared on the TV asking all of his followers and everyone watching to worship him instead of ∞Illuhim∞," he said. "Most of his followers revolted against him at that moment, but we saw on the big screens he was killing them mercilessly."

"How could he kill them? The faith-healer was just an old man?"

"Do you still not believe that he was the Antichrist? You should have stayed awake and watched it yourself! He was controlling lightening and used the bolts to hit everyone standing against him or refusing to bow to him."

"What happened then?" Raimon asked.

"That moment we all started praying asking the Lord to save us from the Beast. I suspect everybody did the same thing all around the world, and shortly after our prayers, we saw the Messiah falling from sky through the ceiling of the hall, and he took the Antichrist down with his blessed sword. He then revealed God's message to everyone. I couldn't remember all his words, but now we are heading to the holy☼house to help each other learn and remember all the words together, and you should do it too if you want to be saved."

"How do you know what happened on the screen was real?" Raimon asked.

"You are still in denial!" the neighbor said to Raimon in a frustrated voice. "When we first met, you said you only needed one piece of evidence!"

"I'm sorry. I believe your words but I just need to make sure about the authenticity of the show you saw on the TV."

The neighbor then pointed toward the sun. "Look at the sun coming from the west this morning. Does that look like something Photoshopped to you? What would you say to God when you meet him? Would you say there was no evidence?"

"You are right, but I just need more time to think and comprehend everything," Raimon said in a submissive voice as the truth he had built for himself in the past years was now shattering quickly!

"We are living the end-days. There is no time for thinking, and you need to decide soon," the neighbor said to him. "I'm sorry to say this but if you don't believe in Messiah after the truth has clearly revealed itself, your punishment will be doubled."

Raimon thought deeply about his mother's last words. May be these were a message from God and that does God loves him that is why he was seeing all these things. That moment they were getting closer to the holy☼house, and a huge crowd of people was gathered around it.

"What should I do to be saved?" Raimon asked finally revealing his will to convert.

"It's easy," the neighbor answered. "All we need to do at this time is to surrender to the Messiah, memorize everything he says and follow his teachings unconditionally. He has God's message and he knows the path to our salvation better than anyone else."

Chapter 41

One week had passed since Nergz had last seen Hast before his flight to New Delhi. She was still at Sardar's house with her child and was waiting for any news or communication from Hast. 'We are probably the only ones who know the truth,' she thought. 'I can't reveal the truth yet because the entire world is now biased toward the evil one believing that he is their savior.'

Nergz remembered the intense last discussion she had with Hast and Mark before they set off for New Delhi. When Hast had described Kogar's plan to her and to Sardar, Mark had intervened. "I still don't understand why Kogar has gone through all the trouble of igniting an apocalypse just to impersonate the Messiah," he said.

"He wants people to submit to his plans without questioning him," Hast answered.

"But he is a massively rich man, and he could make many people to submit just by paying them money," he replied.

"With money you can buy people's bodies but you can't buy their minds," Hast answered. "What you propose is what companies usually do; they hire employees to do what they want them to do in return for money."

At that moment Sardar intervened, "With religion you can hire followers who will do what you want them to do for free, for their entire life and it all will continue for generations."

"But Kogar invented a cure for cancer. He could have bought people's hearts with that alone," Mark said still trying to get a satisfactory answer.

"Remember that scientists have invented antibiotics and vaccines and saved millions of lives, but still they are not remembered by many," Sardar said.

"Kogar's ultimate aim is to impersonate ∞Illuhim∞, but since he doesn't have the power yet, he is going to impersonate the figure of the Messiah first," Hast said.

"But how can he impersonate ∞Illuhim∞? He doesn't have any supernatural powers," Mark said.

"I don't know, but he may use TNARK's technology to gain more power when he takes control of the world," Hast said.

"What more does he gain by impersonating ∞Illuhim∞?" Mark asked.

Sardar intervened again, "Through natural selection and rules of apostasy during the ancient times, only our grand ancestors who chose to submit to the higher authority survived. So regardless of whether ∞Illuhim∞ himself exists or not, we the survivors do exist because of him. Hence, it is natural for us humans to see ∞Illuhim∞ as the most feared and the most loved superpower at the same time."

"That is really terrifying!" Mark said. "If Kogar is planning to impersonate ∞Illuhim∞ then he might make up a fake hell and a fake paradise!"

"It's all our fault," Hast said. "We failed to introduce the true god to people, and instead we introduced the Antichrist to them!"

"What do you mean?" Nergz asked Hast.

"All this time our focus has been about the Antichrist, the apocalypse and terrifying people with the Lord's punishment! The evil one took advantage from the hate we preached. Now we have the responsibility to correct our mistakes. We need to introduce the true god to the people, the God who is all loving and all merciful, and living within us, the true ∞Illuhim∞."

That was the last time Nergz saw Hast and Mark before they set off, but before Hast left, Nergz saw him turning his head again to say his last words to her, "Remember, we can't fight hate with hate. Evil will always take advantage from the hate we preach."

Chapter 42

One week after the Messiah's dramatic return, Kogar was in his new operation room in Padsha Mali's town looking at the trends on his new screens. Many cities had survived the nuclear war because the change in the earth's axis and the shutdown of satellite system had made the targets less visible and harder to be hit. Nevertheless, the destruction was evident in many places, the radiation levels increased and with it the risk of getting cancer increased, too. Kogar knew this was going to happen and he was prepared for that, after all, he already had the cure and he was 'the Messiah'. People expected him to heal, not to say that he wasn't already a savior in the eyes of public. He was the one who had taken down the Antichrist and had saved people from his destruction, and he was the hero that the prophecies had predicted. And those who were not aware of the holy§cript would read it and would soon realize the truth, the truth that only existed in this reality, the new reality imposed upon people, parallel with their beliefs. 'It's too late for the world to realize the other reality. Nobody will think of that or have an interest in looking for it. It's the end-days, everyone's biggest concern would now be salvation and God's satisfaction and their only path for that is through me, the Messiah,' Kogar thought to himself.

'No one will be able to tell my real identity' he thought to himself as he looked at the mirror, and saw the effect of the mask and the chemical injections to his face were already giving good results and making him look like the figure of 'Messiah', the one described in the holy§cript. Kogar thought he would take off his armor in his next speech, and he would reveal his face to the public, the face they expected to see from the Messiah.

He also made sure to place small working light bulbs into his coat when he appeared to give his speeches to the crowd.

'This is what people expect from the Messiah, the perception of enlightenment,' he thought. 'People of the earth will soon rise again, but they will do that under my rules and my guidance. They will take everything I say to heart, and my speeches will be imprinted in their brains. My mind will be their logic neurons, and their minds will be the memory and executive neurons for my logic. My books will be recited by them on every occasion, and my advice will be their guidance. Legends will be told about me, books will be written on me, countless amounts of research and studies will be made on my advice and my speeches. As time passes, everybody will think like me, behave like me, and I will be their idol. I will be in every mind for generation after generation, and humans will be naturally selected according to the rules set by me. My ideas will gradually start to be imprinted in their genes, as this happens, my views will become their common sense, my personality will be transferred to everyone.' He concluded.

Chapter 43

One month later, Nergz still hadn't heard any news of Hast and Mark. Day by day she had become increasingly worried because telephone communications and the internet was restored and many TV stations had now started broadcasting again. The majority of the online articles and TV programs were about 'the Messiah' and his speeches, and any word that came from the man was taken for granted to be the most valuable and would be discussed endlessly on TV shows and online posts.

Nergz knew the truth, but she couldn't do anything about it. Nobody would believe her anyway at this stage. She was looking for a way to spread the truth to people; this would be her responsibility alone if Hast didn't come back to her soon.

She had stayed at Sardar's house for the month after Hast left for New Delhi, but yesterday she had decided to take the risk and go back to her own house. She left her little son, Abraham, under Sardar's care until she could make sure that her house was safe again. When she got back home, she realized somebody was monitoring it. She looked through the window at a man who stood on the opposite side of the street. The man didn't look like he was armed and didn't seem dangerous, but the second time she peeked through the window, the man saw her and signaled to her to come out. Nergz decided to go out to confront him; she took a kitchen knife just in case.

"What do you want from me?" she said when she cautiously got closer to the man outside her house.

"I have been waiting for you for over a week. I can't talk about everything here, but please would you come with me? It's very important," he said.

"Why should I trust you?" she said.

"Please, you need to trust me at this stage. I have important information about your husband," he said. "You need to come with me to Interpol's new headquarters. It's not very far away from here."

When Nergz heard about Interpol, her intuition told her to follow and trust the man; he didn't seem like a foe to her. She followed him to his car before they drove together to a private jet, and then they set off. After one hour, the plane landed in a very small village and she accompanied the man to a small and derelict house in the village. 'How can this be Interpol's headquarters?' she thought to herself.

"A group of us who know the truth are hiding out here waiting for a plan to get the message out," the man said to Nergz while she entered the house.

"Is this Interpol's headquarters?"

"I know it looks small, but we have deliberately spread ourselves into small groups all around the globe."

Nergz looked at the many computers and hard drives all around the living room. She thought around 30 people seemed to inhabit the house, and one of them identified himself as the current head of Interpol, Sir Farad.

"It's an honor to meet you my lady," Farad said. "Your husband was a hero; because of him and one of our agents, we know the truth."

"Do you know where my husband is?" she asked eagerly.

Sir Farad asked someone to play a video for Nergz. She looked at the video which had been recorded on a cellphone. It showed inside Padsha Mali's hall during the time when the 'Messiah' was presenting his first speech right after killing the 'Antichrist'. The video showed Hast challenging 'the Messiah' to uncover his partially seen face, and then an intensive argument between Hast and Kogar, the presumed Messiah, grew just like the ancient argument between Abraham and Nimrod. Kogar seemed to be losing the argument against the evidence presented by Hast to the crowd. The crowd started to grow suspicious of Kogar because they were still wishing for their favorite faith-healer to be innocent, so the conspiracy theory presented by Hast seemed plausible to them. Suddenly, the sound of an explosion and multiple shootings could be heard in the video. After that, the video abruptly ended.

"Unfortunately, we think everyone in the hall was massacred," Sir Farad said.

Nergz started to cry. "Why didn't we see this on the TV screens?"

"We think that the live-feed from the hall lagged behind the real events by around one minute or so. Kogar was clever as he did that to avoid televising any unexpected events, but now he doesn't know that we have this video of him," he said. "Mark was lucky because we were able to fix our connection back with the satellite exactly at the start of his recording and were able to broadcast the video back to our satellite! We now know why the TV screens blanked out suddenly after Kogar's speech, and why he was wearing armor that hid half of his face to only reveal it in the following days. We think that if he had revealed his identity at that moment, his looks were still very similar to Kogar's apart from the long brown hair and beard, so he was obliged to change his facial features with plastic surgery a few days later before revealing his face completely to the world," Sir Farad explained.

"I wonder why he didn't change his face earlier?" someone asked.

Then Nergz realized the probable reason, "I think he wasn't planning to execute his plan that day, but Hast and Mark were very close to catching him or at least causing trouble for him, so he was obliged to set his plans off earlier," she said.

"I see," Sir Farad replied.

"Also, I wonder whether you found any evidence in Nimrud town, Hast told me Kogar's operations were based there?" she asked.

"You are right," Farad said, "Before the world war started, an explosion happened there and our agent, Mark, was already there and he informed us that there were some unknown burnt body parts in the site,"

"Did you find out who those body parts belonged to?" she asked.

"Unfortunately not, because the world war started briefly after our agent left the place and then the location was hit by a nuclear head, destroying everything within three miles around that place, but we think it belonged to one of his assistances or his guards." Farad answered.

"It's obvious that he wanted to destroy all the evidence there," someone suggested.

"I wonder why you haven't shown this video to the world yet?" she asked.

"Kogar is now controlling everything. If we do that, the video will be removed before it could become viral and he will be able to locate us and annihilate us before we could upload it again," Sir Farad said. "Now, our current plan is to spread the truth to the most trusted people around the world first, and once more people know the truth, then he won't be able to eliminate the truth even if he could eliminate us."

"We should tell the people that he is the real Antichrist," Nergz said.

"But how can we convince people? He is not blind in his left eye," someone responded.

"He is blind to the truth and that is what the prophecies meant," she said.

"But he doesn't ask people to worship him," another one said.

"He will do that soon," she answered. "He is currently trying to override Abrahamic faith with a set of his own rules, but once he gains more confidence, he will ask for more obedience from us."

"If we do that, I'm afraid the cycle of the Antichrist and Messiah will go on forever," Sir Farad said.

"No, this one is the last one," she said confidently. "We need to demonize him, make people hate him and warn them from following him."

"How can we stand against him? He is so powerful now," Sir Farad said.

"∞Illuhim∞ is the most powerful and he is on our side," she said.

At that moment she remembered Hast's last words to her. 'I'm sorry Hast. I know you said we can't fight hate with hate, but this one is the real Antichrist himself, and he deserves nothing but hate and hell. I will not let such scum override the rules set by the holy§cript, the rules that transcended us to humans and set us apart from other animal species,' she thought to herself.

She walked toward an empty space in the room and turned to the small crowd in the room as if she was the next leader of the opposition. "We need to ask our preachers to promise hell for him and for everyone following him."

Chapter 44

One year later, the world was polarized between two groups, those who called themselves the Followers of the Messiah and those who called themselves the Opposers of the Antichrist. Kogar was sitting in his divine hall curing the diseased with his blessed hands, and a huge crowd of people queued outside. An old man was let in by the guards, and he came in and bowed in front of Kogar bringing his head forward to him waiting to be touched. At that moment, Kogar was having some deep and unsettling thoughts about a recent video, promoted on a private media out of his control. It featured a clergyman warning Kogar's followers with eternal torture in hell. Kogar brought his hand close to the old man's head when suddenly the old man grabbed Kogar's hand and looked up at him!

"Do you remember me?" the old man asked.

Kogar had a strange feeling when he looked at the man's face. He did look somewhat familiar to him, but where had he seen him? His dreams?

"Have we met before?" Kogar asked.

"We met a very long time ago. I see you came back to finally defeat Abraham," the old man said.

The words struck Kogar hard, and the man seemed to resonate and reflect his thoughts. 'Is he from my imagination?' he asked himself.

"Who are you?" Kogar asked the old man.

"No wonder you don't remember!" The old man stood up and announced, "I'm the Son of the Morning."

Kogar had a look of fear and surprise at the same time. 'How can my imagination look so real to me?' he thought.

"I have met with your grand ancestor Nimrod thousands of years ago," the old man said. "He was humiliated by Abraham after he failed to make the sun rise in the west. People lost trust in him as a god and he was ultimately defeated." The old man continued, "Before he died, he made a strong promise to make the sun rise from the west, and his promise was so strong it seems that it has passed through generations. It took you, after so many generations, to come back and satisfy his promise."

"What is your point?" Kogar asked.

"You are God now," the old man said. "No new Abraham can stand against you. Go out and tell people to recognize you as you deserve."

"Am I God?!" Kogar wondered.

"Yes, even by Abraham's account you are God," the old man said. "Abraham said that his God would bring the sun from the west on the Judgment Day and you have already done that. Go out and tell this to people! It's in their holy§cript, so they will believe you and they will worship you directly."

"But more people will call me the Antichrist and preachers will warn my followers with eternal hell and torture," Kogar said thinking about the clergy on the video.

"They built a fictional hell for your afterlife. You built a real hell for their current life," the old man said. "Let them enjoy the symmetry. After all, isn't it your job to bring symmetry back to this broken world?"

After saying these words, the old man stepped back, and he became much larger. A pair of asymmetrical red wings appeared on his back, and one of the wings seemed to have been burned or damaged!

"You need to follow the other gods from the other stars," he said.

"Follow them to where?" Kogar asked eagerly.

"To the center of the galaxy where largest black hole in this universe resides," he said.

"Why to a black hole" Kogar asked.

"There, the highest level of evolution is happening among the gods from all the other stars. The new god of this universe will be born soon," he said. "You need to follow the other gods soon."

As Kogar heard these words, a strong thrill passed through his blood, and then he realized the figure of the weird looking archangel was starting to fade away from his imagination. Kogar was no longer sure whether what he had heard was real or it was just his internal imagination. He looked in front of him, the angel was about to disappear completely. Kogar threw his final question to him hoping that the fading archangel was still able to respond, "What should I do to become an immortal God?"

"You need to make everyone on earth believe in you as God," the archangel said then disappeared completely.

These words were so strong that Kogar's body felt numb. He felt he was already transcending. All he was thinking about was how to become God and join the other gods from all the other stars at the center of the galaxy. 'From now on there will be two types of people: those who accept to submit to me and those who will be burned in my hell,' he thought to himself.

Epilogue

5 years later, Nergz woke up from a deep silence, she was lying on her back and everything was blinding dark around her, as she stretched her hands around herself, she realized that she was trapped in a narrow groove, 'Where am I?' was her first thought. The last thing she could remember was her being captured by Kogar's army, and then was taken to an execution room where her arm was injected with something, after which she fell unconscious.

The night before her capture she met with some of her devout followers in a small house along with some others who were trying to join her side seeking for the truth. It was part of her job to convince them and reassure them that who they thought was the 'Messiah' was no more than the heartless Antichrist.

After preaching to the group for a half hour, Kogar's army found their location and surrounded the house! Nergz knew she will be captured one day but there was no other choice for her. She needed to spread the truth to everyone, she knew that no matter how careful is she, one day a traitor will infiltrate to her preaching session and uncover her location to Kogar.

It has been more than five years since she became one of the main leaders of the opposition, and the most wanted person by Kogar's army, with her strong and confident message the opposition followers were increasing day by day, more rebellious groups began to emerge everywhere as the time passed. Kogar was no longer able to keep his image as a loving 'Messiah'; he began to persecute the opposers, either by punishing them publicly or spreading the fear. He made a big army from his devout followers who were seeing him as their God and were ready to sacrifice themselves for him unconditionally. It was the strongest and largest army at that time and was very committed to follow the commands of their leader, the 'Messiah', word by word. Kogar's army was led by Haran, a heartless person, and the right hand minister for Kogar in the last two years.

The rebel groups on the other side were powerless, dispersed groups without a well-defined center. They were keeping their life either hidden or disguised among the followers of 'Messiah'. Haran was seeking for the life of these rebels aggressively, rewarding anyone who gave information to uncover their locations and punishing anyone who hid them. It was a big victory for him when he finally arrested the opposition's main leader, Nergz.

Nergz was now finding herself inside a coffin buried deep. 'Did they bury me alive?' she asked herself. She tried to push the cover away from herself, some dust fall inside the coffin, nevertheless, after some struggle she was able to come out and what she saw next left her shocked!. She was in a graveyard and it was dark in the night yet she could still see the bloody colored sun disk in the dark sky! The sky view had a reddish tint. She saw people coming out from their graves; some were like zombies others were just bones infested with ground insects but briefly after coming out from the graves their flesh grew on them again! 'Is this life after death?' she asked herself. Then she saw everybody began to march toward a large holy☼house building far away on a large hill. It was the only visible building in the dark that has shiny walls and gates. Stairs were going up to it from all the sides.

As she advanced with the people toward the building, then she saw people crossing over a long narrow woody bridge built directly over a deep valley which was filled with lakes of fire and lava. She heard the screams of people underneath. Nergz immediately remembered the passages from the holy§cript which described this bridge and promised the faithful an easy passage to the other side while the unbelievers would have to suffer the horror of crossing it hoping they could pass over the terror beneath them, but a dragon which was guarding the bridge underneath would never let the unbelievers to pass. Once they reached the other end of the bridge feeling the relief and hope, they would be dragged back again to the beginning of the bridge, and they have to pass through it again and again running from the scary dragon. With each escape trial, it would become harder for them to cross the bridge and run away from the dragon so they would finally give up and fell into the hell beneath them.

Nergz knew she should be able to pass the bridge easily because she was a faithful believer in ∞Illuhim∞ and she should soon meet all those she loved. She would be able to meet with ∞Illuhim∞ face to face soon she crosses the bridge and then she would reunite with her son and her husband again in the heaven. Without any fear or hesitation she started to walk over the woody fragile bridge, as she looked beneath, all she saw was a lake of lava and hot flames engulfing the countless bodies of so many unbelievers, they were in a state of persistent pain and bitterness with no hope shouting for mercy and forgiveness.

As Nergz heard the screaming below the bridge, she began to feel for them, but she closed her eyes and ran toward the other side of the bridge. As she expected, it was an easy cross for her. Now all she had to do was to reach the holy☼house where she expected to meet with ∞Illuhim∞ for her Judgement. Once she reached the gate, she saw an angelic guard greeting her and welcoming her to the Lord's house. As she entered the gate, she found herself in a large marvelous hall. An archangel with asymmetric red wings stood by a curtain which seemed to be a layer between her and someone else behind it. 'Could it be ∞Illuhim∞?' she asked herself.

"Wellcome to the Lord's kingdom, today there are no King but him" the archangel said. "As a faithful follower, it is an honor to see you here and now the Lord himself will meet you in person and promises you an immortal life in his paradise"

At that moment, Nergz bow on her knees to the curtain eagerly watching and waiting to see his majesty. As the curtain faded away, it revealed something that shocked Nergz and rendered her speechless. Antichrist himself was the one behind the curtain sitting on a golden throne! Nergz immediately stood up and backed off. "This is not possible, you are not the God," she said.

"He is the God," a voice came behind the archangel.

When Nergz turned she saw Hast holding his baby in his lap. She began to shed tears upon seeing her husband and her son, and she immediately ran toward them to have a hug with them but before she could reach them she collided with a transparent barrier which was separating Hast from her.

"You can't reunite with your family until you declare your submission to the Lord," The archangel said to Nergz.

"He is right," Hast said behind the barrier "You need to believe in him as your God. He is the true ∞Illuhim∞!"

Nergz was shocked upon hearing Hast saying that. "He is the Antichrist and you know that! He deceived everyone!" she protested to Hast.

"We were wrong," Hast said.

"Then why are we not in hell already?" she asked.

"Because we were faithful to ∞Illuhim∞ throughout our life" Hast said. "We mistook his identity before our death but he was merciful, he knew I was confused and forgave me. He will do the same for you if you renew your faith and declare him as your God now."

Nergz backed off a bit and tried to think hard. Things looked very strange; she no longer knew what the truth was and what the lie was. 'Have I mistaken the God all my life,' she thought to herself.

"I saw people suffering in hell," she said. "Who are they and why they are not forgiven?" she asked turning toward the Antichrist and the archangel.

"These were the unbelievers," the archangel said. "You knew that would be their fate, didn't you?"

"I knew, but I also knew that the true God is all loving and all merciful," she said.

"What do you mean?" the Antichrist replied in an angry voice "Wasn't I merciful enough to forgive you after you denounced me for the last five years and preached against me?"

"I'm sorry I was confused," she said. "I appreciate your mercy, but can I ask you for another favor?"

"What is that?" The Antichrist asked.

"Would you please forgive everybody else, and give them another chance just like you have given me?" she asked the Antichrist.

"But these were the unbelievers, and you know according to the rules they should be burned forever," he replied.

"I know but I also know that your mercy is unlimited," she said.

She waited tentatively for a while to hear back from the Antichrist as he was thinking, then the Antichrist turned to the archangel. "I command you to release everyone in hell and gave them an eternal life in our paradise."

Then he turned to Nergz "Now you saw my mercy, would you still go against me after you saw the truth?"

"He is right," Hast said. "Nergz, give up already and submit to him now,"

Nergz thought for a bit, "I was so close to choose the wrong but now I know the truth," She saw some relief in Hast's eyes when she said that. "Don't worry Hast. I will meet you soon," She said to him.

"I see you realized the truth finally," the archangel said.

"Yes, the truth is now much clearer to me," she replied.

The Antichrist turned to her, "Now declare me as your savior and your Lord,"

"I think you misunderstood me," she said to him, "When I said the truth is now clearer, I meant now I'm certain that you are the Antichrist more than any time ever!"

The Antichrist was filled with anger upon hearing her response, "I will send you to hell forever if you don't regret what you have just said immediately,"

"He is right" Hast shouted to her behind the transparent barrier. "Please don't be insane, we can meet together again,"

"Yes, we will meet together," she said. "But after I pass the Antichrist, who is facing me now," she said to Hast with a smiling and confident face.

"Why are you denying the truth?" The Antichrist asked her "Haven't you seen me raising the dead from the graves and bringing the sun from the west. Haven't you seen all my power and all my mercy?!"

"It's not the power that makes ∞Illuhim∞ a God," she said.

"Then what makes him a God?" The Antichrist asked.

"You will never understand why you can't become like ∞Illuhim∞," she said.

"How can you be so sure, what have you seen in ∞Illuhim∞ haven't seen in me?" he asked.

"You broke your rule," She said.

"I was showing my mercy, I made the rules and I can change them," he said.

"God doesn't break his promise," she said.

At that time the Antichrist turned to the archangel, "She chose hell, I command you to give her what she chose"

The ground beneath Nergz split and she fell into a lake of fire and lava, that moment she screamed from agony and pain, and after a moment, everything became dark and silent again as she woke up into another reality.

***

Nergz now found herself restrained in a chair, she couldn't move her hands neither her feet. She was not able to see anything, as her head was covered with a helmet; the head cap was firmly covering her head and her eyes. She soon remembered the brain controlling technique Hast told her five years ago when he was investigating the Antichrist, 'Are they using that technique to control my dreams?' she asked herself. She tried to free herself several times but she failed.

She listened carefully to hear what was going on in the room and she was able to hear an intense discussion between two guys in the same room, she tried to lift up her head so that she could peek through the slit under the helmet, she was barely able to see but she recognized them immediately. Kogar, 'the Antichrist', and his minister, Haran, were in an intense discussion!

"Why don't we eliminate all the opposers," Haran asked Kogar.

"I can't eliminate every one of them," Kogar replied, "They are already mastering their hideout. Even those who follow me, I can't fully trust everybody. Some are pretending to follow me and hiding their true beliefs."

"Why don't we use this optogenetics technique to convince someone else, another leader?" Haran suggested.

"I need to convince her. Most of my opposers trust her. If she believes in me, then most of the opposers would do the same after her," He said.

Nergz was able to see the faint figure of Kogar through the slit; he looked very angry and desperate to find a way to convince her, as he was punching the wall and Haran was trying to calm him down, "If I don't do something soon, the Meteor will be hitting us in two years and everything will be gone, I need to reach the center of the galaxy soon," Kogar said.

"I think she was very close to submit," Haran said. "If you hadn't broken the rule, she would have believed in you."

"Nothing will work with her," Kogar said in a frustrating voice. "I have already tried not to break the rule in my previous attempt, in that case, she said that her God is a merciful loving one and I'm not."

"That is absurd, I wonder if she really believes in a well-defined coherent God!" Haran said.

"She is just an obstacle Nature put before me," Kogar said. "People like her are determined to rebel against me no matter what I do for them!"

"I think if we try with her several other times she will submit at the end," Haran said.

"That is what I'm going to do, she doesn't know me. I will never give up, I'm the God and how can a God give up!"

That moment Nergz realized that her submission to Kogar's will might be inevitable. She couldn't remember any of the previous trials that Kogar was talking about! the only thing she could remember was that in her dream she was very close to be deceived. 'If Kogar controls me, he then can control all the other opposers through me. I can't let myself be a tool for his evil plans. The truth should stay. I need to sacrifice myself for the truth,' she thought. That moment she decided to commit suicide but there was no way to do so as she was restrained tightly to a chair. She began to hold her breath forcefully, as time passed, she increasingly felt suffocated, but that was her only choice even though she knew that her act of suicide is punishable! 'God, please forgive me for committing the suicide,' she thought, 'If the Antichrist controls me then many people will be deceived and will be punished by you because of my failure. I have no choice only to sacrifice myself for the greater good, please do help them after me, please send them your true savior, the true Messiah,' that was her last thoughts before she fell unconscious.

Cast of characters

∞Illuhim∞: The God of the universe in this book.

Hast: The theologian and the leading character.

Nergz: The second leading character, Hast's wife, and a historian.

Mark: The Interpol agent and a private investigator.

Sardar: The doctor and Hast's brother.

Kogar Shervan: Previous governor, owner of Tek-brains and zanzor.

Padsha Mali: The famous faith healer.

Media Rozhgar: Kogar's business administrator and his secret lover.

Zaniar: Media's cousin and a security manager for Tek-Brain.

Lee Shark: The CEO of the largest 3D printing company in 2060.

Dr. Bernhard Johnson: The head of TNARK in 2060.

Sir Farad: The head of Interpol in 2060.

Prof. Ericson Sanders: The leading neuroscientist in TNARK.

Prof. Neil Baron: The famous astrophysicist working for TNARK.

Prof. Catherin Smith: An influential genetic scientist.

Bakir: Unfortunate son of a loving mother with breast cancer.

Kate Gould: Mark's ex-partner and researcher.

Howard Nick: The founder of "the Mind Quanta-Soup" theory.

John Badu: The manager of Virtual world™.

Roger: An Interpol agent and Mark's assistant.

Aabha: A brilliant biochemist and a friend of Mark.

Tom: A tough guy with a high superego but with a bad luck.

Raimon: A confused post-apocalyptic person (who could be anyone)

Abraham: The founder of Abrahamic faith.

Zoroaster: The founder of Zoroastrian faith.

Nimrod: The King of ancient Babylon and the nemesis of Abraham.

Haran (4000 BC): Nimrod's right hand minister.

Haran (post 2060): The Antichrist's right hand minister.

Son of the morning: Lucifer, the archangel with asymmetric red wings.

Dear reader,

Thanks a lot for purchasing this book; I hope you enjoyed reading it as much as I enjoyed writing it. The purpose of this work was not to devalue or promote for any system of belief or thinking. It was just a collection of thoughts trapped in my mind for a long time, here I translated some of it into words and tried to share it with you. Hopefully, you liked it! I would love to see your feedback. Your honest review on Amazon or goodreads will be deeply appreciated and it will be encouraging for me to share more of my thoughts and learning experience through these fictional characters.

H.A. Ormziar

Join us on:

brokensymmetries.com

facebook.com/brokensymmetries

twitter.com/haormziar

goodreads.com/ormziar

Printed in Great Britain
by Amazon.co.uk, Ltd.,
Marston Gate.